'Small-Minded G[...] [...] each short, action-packed [...] on [...] ideal for teen readers ... McGann's direct, gritty style of writing certainly packs a punch. He describes the future world with exacting detail, and some of his inventions are almost Asimovian in their originality and execution ... A talent to be reckoned with' *Irish Independent*

'A gripping dystopian thriller, with echoes of *A Clockwork Orange*, [it] has plenty of action to thrill teenage readers' Nikki Gamble, *The Bookseller*

'A fugitive-style thriller ... an extraordinary novel. McGann's vision is by turns clever, quirky and chillingly Orwellian ... Dark, witty and violent, *Small-Minded Giants* is a truly thrilling and brilliantly imagined book' *School Librarian*

'Highly visual and exciting ... dystopian vision that is expertly crafted' Becky Stradwick, Borders, *Publishing News*

'Futuristic, gripping thriller' *The Book Magazine*

'McGann – as one might expect with his previous credentials – draws us into a complex argument about the effects of capitalism and competition on a closed society that is utterly interdependent' *farah-sf.blogspot.com*

'McGann's effective dystopic vision is backed by [...] storytelling' John Newman, *Publishing News*

One of the most original and thought-provoking books I've reviewed in ages. It is stylishly and skilfully written' *Books for Keeps*

'...a compelling, compulsive, atmospheric story' *Irish Times*

'... fights, flights and regular plot twists' *TES*

Also available by Oisín McGann

ANCIENT APPETITES

www.oisinmcgann.com

SMALL-MINDED GIANTS

Oisín McGann

CORGI BOOKS

SMALL-MINDED GIANTS
A CORGI BOOK 978 0 552 55473 2

First published in Great Britain by Doubleday,
an imprint of Random House Children's Books

Doubleday edition published 2006
Corgi edition published 2007

1 3 5 7 9 10 8 6 4 2

Set in Bembo

Corgi Books are published by Random House Children's Books,
61–63 Uxbridge Road, London W5 5SA

www.randomhouse.co.uk

Addresses for companies within The Random House Group Limited
can be found at: www.randomhouse.co.uk/offices.htm

Mixed Sources
Product group from well-managed
forests and other controlled sources
www.fsc.org Cert no. TT-COC-2139
© 1996 Forest Stewardship Council
FSC

THE RANDOM HOUSE GROUP Limited Reg. No. 954009

A CIP catalogue record for this book is available from the British Library.

Printed in the UK by
CPI Bookmarque, Croydon, CR0 4TD

For my giant little brother,
Darius ~ a mind apart

Acknowledgements

Writing is a solitary business, but no one creates a book on their own. As ever, I must thank my family for their ongoing enthusiasm and support – they are responsible for my best qualities. My thanks also to my agent, Sophie Hicks, for doing what she does so well, and for her tact and reassurance throughout the process.

Whatever concerns I might have had about working with a great big 'corporate' publisher like Random House were allayed almost immediately by the easygoing, conscientious and expert approach of Philippa Dickinson, Annie Eaton and the rest of the RHCB team. They were passionate and encouraging, and they made the production of this book a real pleasure. I'm especially grateful to my editor, Shannon Park, for her friendly professionalism in filing the many rough edges off the text, and to James Fraser for being patient with my overzealous design input.

And finally, a big thank you to The O'Brien Press in Ireland and to all the people who have taken such an interest in my books over the last couple of years and helped to get me this far. I am indebted to all of you.

Section I/24: Accident

The eight teenagers waited excitedly for their chance to be dangled from the giant's arm. Solomon Wheat stood apart from his classmates, his face hidden by the hood of his black tracksuit top, his gaze lost in the latticed shapes of the gantries silhouetted against the white light of the dome above them. It was to be their turn next; they could see the arm of the tower crane swinging towards them, the glass and denceramic carriage starting to descend. Except for a single figure, it was empty, the rest of their class having already been deposited on the far side of the complex.

Despite his withdrawn posture, Sol was as excited as the rest of his classmates. He had never been up in a crane car, and this was a luxury model, normally only used by the big-noise industrialists and planners. As a school tour, this was going to be hard to top. The carriage was being lowered towards its cradle. Large enough for ten people to sit around its richly upholstered seats, its smooth, classic, graphite-coloured curves spoke of sheer class. This was how the other half travelled – archaic, but majestic. The figure inside was Vincent Schaeffer, the main man, head of the Third Quadrant, responsible for the very air they breathed. The whole thing was a blatant PR stunt, an attempt to show how the company was 'in touch' with young people. But as long as he got a ride on the crane, Sol wasn't going to complain.

The carriage's cradle, a steel-framed platform, rose to meet the carriage on hydraulic arms as it was lowered the last few metres, magnets activating to pull the swinging load into line and control its touchdown with impressive accuracy. The five girls and three boys surged forward, each of them eager to be the first on board and grab the best seats.

'Hold on!' Ms Kiroa, their teacher, called them back. 'Wait until Mr Schaeffer says it's all right. That includes *you*, Faisal Twomey.'

Ana Kiroa was young, and pretty in a strict, teacher kind of way, but her voice already had the tone of authority, and the students reacted, stumbling to a reluctant halt. They waited, slowly edging closer to the door, while trying to look as stationary as possible. Sol hung back near the teacher. He would try and sit near her if he could, but not so close as to be obvious.

Schaeffer opened the door and waved them aboard, stepping aside to avoid being knocked over in the rush. Ms Kiroa smiled an apology, shrugging helplessly as the students poured up the platform's steps and through the door. Sol shifted the strap of his bag onto his shoulder, stuck his hands deeper into his pockets and nodded to Schaeffer as he passed him. There were three seats left together, and he took the middle one, relishing the knowledge that Ms Kiroa would have to sit beside him. He stuck his bag on the floor and twisted to look out of the window behind him.

They were surrounded by the Ventilation Complex, which made up the centre of the Third Quadrant. Most of the girls hated the complex – they thought it ugly and cold – but to Sol it was interesting, an insight into how the city worked. A stacked maze of metal shafts, ducts, filtration systems, tall dispersal fans and many other unidentifiable constructions served to feed air into the city from the frozen world outside. Beyond, the tops of the poorest apartment blocks in the quadrant could be seen; their windows looking out on this industrial spread.

'Welcome to the Schaeffer Corporation. Unfortunately, at this early stage, I'm going to be leaving you,' Schaeffer told the class, interrupting Sol's thoughts. 'I have a few things to attend to, but I'll meet you on the other side. I'm sure Ms Kiroa can talk you through the trip. Just a few safety messages – sorry, I have to, you know what these safety people are like!'

He was a short man, in a slightly rumpled suit, with a potbelly, long white sideburns and a chubby face. He didn't look like a big-shot businessman, Sol thought, and he was obviously ill-at-ease around young people. Knowing the young people around him, Sol couldn't blame him.

'There is a safety lock on the door that operates while the carriage is in motion, but don't touch the door anyway. Keep your weight distributed evenly for a steady ride; don't all crowd over one side of the carriage – it won't lean, but it could increase the amount of swing. If you feel sick, there are bags provided under the seats. Please use them. Oh, and no eating or drinking in the carriage.' His face expressed boredom at the tiresome rules. 'Right, that's my duty done. Enjoy the ride, and I'll see you over the other side!'

Some of the students started talking softly under their breath as Schaeffer finished. Sol didn't join in. It was funny how people lowered their voices when they were excited. Ms Kiroa sat down beside him, and he pulled his hood further up over his face, feeling suddenly tense.

Schaeffer stepped out of the carriage and closed the door firmly behind him. Sol turned to watch him; the man waved at them as if they were children, and then turned to walk towards another carriage on the far side of the yard. Sol turned back as the seat shuddered underneath him, and he pressed his feet against the floor in reflex.

'This is such a rush!' Cleo, one of the girls across from him, muttered to a friend. 'Feel my arm; I'm all goose-bumps!'

She was an odd-looking girl – cute enough, with her oriental eyes and blonde hair. Cleo and Sol had been friends when they were younger. But now she was just another loud-mouth teenage ditz, a singer for some wannabe band. Sol looked away: he had no taste for girls his own age; they were all so flighty. The carriage jerked slightly, creaked, and then he felt his stomach lurch as they were lifted from the ground. There were a few whoops and squeals, and suddenly everybody was standing up and looking out of the windows.

'Sit down, please!' Ms Kiroa called, but it was half hearted, and she stood up herself to make the most of the view. Sol positioned himself at her shoulder; he was taller than her and, with her head by his nose, he could smell her hair. He breathed in the scent, then moved away slightly, suddenly embarrassed by how close she was.

The city fell away around them, and they rose high over the quadrant, above the Ventilation Complex below, above the surrounding buildings, until they could see clear across the city. Above them, the tower crane's jib began to turn, swinging them out and round, heading towards the Second Quadrant, where they would connect with a gantry crane and be carried over into the Food Production Complex. Between the tops of the four looming tower cranes – one in the centre of each quadrant – and the domed roof of the city, there was only the gantry grid. Each with four arms, the tower cranes' resemblance to a force of protective metal giants was now a permanent part of their image.

'We must be over a hundred metres up,' Cleo said, a tremor in her voice. 'It's like we're flying.'

The city of Ash Harbour looked spectacular. Built inside a hollowed-out mountain five kilometres across, its top roofed with a massive dome to keep out the ferocious elements, this was their whole world. Beyond those walls, deadly storms and freezing temperatures had stripped the planet bare. Sol gazed out at the city, and realized for the first time just how small their world was. His window was facing towards the body of the crane, and his eyes followed it down to the bottom, a long, long way below. The crane's perspective heightened the feeling of being hung out in the sky and he experienced a moment of dizziness.

He caught sight of the carriage that Schaeffer had boarded. It was hanging from another arm of the crane. It was going to pass inside the path of the school's carriage, overtaking it as the students took the scenic route. It was moving jerkily, as if something was wrong.

Sol leaned harder against the glass. He could see two figures inside. One was on the nearside of the carriage, looking anxiously towards the ceiling. He was a young man, dressed in the suit of a businessman or industrialist. Sol couldn't see the other person very well, but knew it must be Schaeffer. Ms Kiroa saw what he was looking at, and leaned in closer beside him, her shoulder touching his.

6

'Why is it shaking like that?' she wondered aloud.

'Maybe just worn bearings,' he replied, wanting to sound knowledgeable. His gaze was locked on the scene before him.

'They should lower it down. It doesn't look safe.' The obvious alarm in her voice carried around the carriage.

All of a sudden the entire class was pushing in around them, staring out at the shuddering crane car, which was coming ever closer.

'Maybe it's going to fall!' Faisal Twomey said, from behind Sol.

'Shut up, you grit!' Cleo snapped.

'Quiet, all of you,' Ms Kiroa said calmly.

Sol felt queasy. Seeing the unstable carriage dangling so high above the ground made him all the more conscious of their own situation. His eyes locked on the face of the man who was less than fifty metres away. This was a man who presumably travelled in these carriages all the time. Sol was close enough to see the barely suppressed panic on his face. Something was badly wrong. Above and beyond the other crane car, beneath the arm that held it, he could see the cabin where the controller sat. He must notice that there was a problem. The carriage was only twenty metres away, but it had stopped swinging past them now and, glancing up at the trolley beneath the arm, Sol could see that the winch had started up – it was beginning to lower the car.

There was a jerk in the doubled cables, and the carriage dropped slightly, shaking back and forth. Sol looked back up at the arm.

'Jesus,' Cleo gasped. 'Look . . . The thing . . . The trolley's come off!'

The trolley holding the winch was hanging off at one end. As they watched, another of its wheels gave way, and now the entire weight of the crane car was suspended from only one corner of the trolley's welded steel frame. The rail holding the wheel was already buckling.

One of the girls started crying. Somebody else joined in.

'Get a grip, for God's sake!' Cleo exclaimed.

With everyone on one side of their car, it was unbalanced, and swinging ever so slightly. Ana had her hand over her mouth; she was holding her breath. Sol spared her a glance, but quickly brought his eyes back to the man in the other carriage. The young man was clutching a rail beside the window, holding onto it for all he was worth, as if that would help support the dangling carriage. Sol felt the floor under his feet tremble, and he looked down in alarm. But it was a normal movement. Their carriage was starting to creep in along its jib to reach the other car.

'What the hell's goin' on?' Faisal growled. 'What's he doing?'

'We're going to get them out of there,' Cleo told him. 'But we're going too *slowly*.'

'Vibrations,' Sol hissed through tense jaws. 'He doesn't want to knock the other car loose.'

The man could see them approaching. He looked out at them, shouting something. Letting go of the rail, he pressed both hands against the window. Growing more frantic, he started hammering his fists against the glass. On the other side, Schaeffer was still looking towards the two control cabs. The dangling carriage jerked again, the trolley's rail pulling bolts free from the crane's arm. The young man behind the glass was talking again, pleading, urging them on. They were very close now. Sol thought he could have jumped the gap, if he'd been able to take a run at it. They were almost within reach.

Sol looked up at the trolley and saw it give, feeling it part from the arm with a jolt like a physical blow. The carriage dropped away, almost seeming to suck them after it in its wake. He saw the young man for an instant before the carriage turned into a tumble, saw him open his mouth in a silent scream behind the glass as he fell. The moment was perfectly silent, and then the cable, snaking past them, smacked the broken trolley against the side of their carriage and everyone screamed.

Their carriage swung from side to side, and the other car was suddenly forgotten. They all clutched at the rails on the walls over the seats; those who missed were thrown onto the floor. Sol had a firm hold on a rail, his eyes shut tight. Ana had seized his arm and was squeezing so hard it hurt, her fingernails digging into his flesh. The swinging subsided, but it was difficult to tell – his head was all over the place, and his stomach was trying to climb out of his mouth. He smelled the sharp, rank scent of urine and knew somebody had wet themselves. Everybody was gasping and sobbing.

'Get us down!' Amanda Yan shrieked. 'Get us down from here! I want to get down!'

They were dropping towards the ground . . . slowly. Ana let go of his arm, struggling to regain her composure. Around the carriage, everyone was sitting down, some trembling and crying, some silent, scared and embarrassed. Sol was surprised to find himself shivering, his heart pounding fit to burst. Steeling himself, he looked out of the window.

His stomach had a hard time dealing with the height, but it was the sight of the other carriage that finally did it. The car lay, crumpled and shattered, about fifty metres from where they were going to come down. He could see the bodies of the two men. Reaching under his seat, he barely got the sick bag out in time.

Sol wandered back and forth by the landed carriage, feeling horribly numb. They could see the crash site, but there were already men swarming over it. Blue-uniformed policemen were cordoning off the scene. He had a blanket over his shoulders, but had no idea how it had got there. An ambulance passed him by, its electric motor whining as it sped towards the wrecked carriage. The two men would not need it.

'Are you all right, son?' a voice said to him.

Sol turned and felt his stomach lurch again. Vincent Schaeffer was standing before him, flanked by two other men.

'I thought you were dead.' Sol frowned, staring in open confusion at the middle-aged man. He had the strangest feeling that none of this was real.

'I almost was, son. I almost was.' Schaeffer was pale, and looked badly shaken. 'It was only pure, blind luck I was called back before the car lifted off.'

He turned to one of the other men, his voice now steady, in command.

'Get these young people to a hospital. They're all in shock. See that they're given the best of care. I want to know how this happened – and I want to know soon.'

They started to walk away, and Sol watched them with dazed interest.

'Arrange meetings with Falyadi and Walden's families,' Schaeffer continued. 'I want to deliver my condolences in person . . .'

An accident, Sol thought. His father had talked about the accidents that had been happening. He had a theory about them. Suddenly Sol wanted to go home; he wanted to talk to his dad. Turning in the direction of the West Wall, he started walking.

'Sol? Solomon! Come back here!'

Ana hurried after him and took his arm.

'Everybody's going to the hospital, come on.'

'I'm fine, I just want to go home,' he told her.

'We'll just get you checked out, then we can all go home.'

He liked having her attention, and let her lead him towards one of the waiting ambulances. His classmates were sitting in and around them, their faces drawn, staring into nothing. Cleo had her arms around Amanda, talking quietly to her. Beyond the ambulances, on an overpass that looked down on the Ventilation Complex, he saw a group of six or seven figures clad all in black; thin shapes in trenchcoats, their long hair hanging down over their faces. Dark-Day Fatalists. It hadn't taken them long to show up.

'Vultures,' Ana muttered under her breath.

Sol regarded them with disdain. She was right; they flocked to the scenes of disaster like scavengers. It was as if they thought that every death proved them right.

A long black car pulled up and two more men in suits got out. But these were not businessmen; with them was the mayor, Isabella Haddad. Her face was carefully drawn in official sorrow, her every movement appropriate to the occasion. Solomon's father had plenty to say about her too, but Sol thought the mayor was okay, or at least the best of a bad lot. He had little time for politicians or politics. None of it ever seemed to make a difference.

Still, somebody had to say something at a time like this. Haddad would have the right words. Sol stopped for a moment, swivelling to look up at the arm of the crane, to where the wrecked carriage had once been attached. The immense machine loomed over them, its image as a protective giant lost in the fall of the ill-fated carriage. Sol realized he was trembling, and wrapped the blanket tighter around his shoulders, turning away from the mechanical tower.

Section 2/24: Debt

It was late afternoon by the time Solomon got back to his apartment complex. Along the maze of narrow corridors and up one flight of steps after another, he made his way through the block of flats to the three small rooms that he and his father called home. He opened the door and checked his father's room. Gregor had not come back the night before; it was Thursday, yesterday had been payday, and he had probably spent the night out with his buddies, playing cards or laying down bets at the ratting dens. He would have gone straight back to work, and would not be home until later. Sol dumped his bag on the sofa-bed and strode into his room, throwing himself down on his own bed.

The room was barely big enough for the narrow bunk and a bedside table. The wall was plastered with posters of late-twentieth-century boxers from the Golden Age of the sport: Ali, Liston, Marciano, Leonard, Tyson, Lewis – great fighters. Every square centimetre of space was taken up with his junk: boxing memorabilia, his gloves, weights, as well as piles of books and his underused bongos.

He stood up again, feeling antsy, restless. The crane accident had left him feeling disturbed, and now he couldn't get the last few moments of the doomed carriage out of his mind. Pacing the living room for a minute or two, he decided to go out for a run. Gregor could be hours yet, and Sol needed to talk – either that or do something active. He couldn't stand just waiting around. Changing into his running tracksuit, he slipped on his trainers, strapped some small weights around his wrists and left the flat.

It would take him ten minutes to get out by going downstairs, so he took to the rooftops instead. The sunlight from the dome was already fading, and the city lights were being lit; tall, denceramic posts topped with glass lenses glowing with sewer-gas flames. The roofs of most of the apartment complexes were flat and paved – with no elements to worry about, people used the rooftops as gardens and gathering areas, and there were routes that dropped in blocked steps to the first level of streets. It was easy climbing for an agile young man. Even without descending to the street, he could run for kilometres across the interlocking walkways and clustered rooftops. But he needed noise and life, things to watch to take his mind off the accident. He pulled up the hood of his top, and set off at an easy jog, swinging his weighted arms in gentle punches to warm them up.

Music drifted across from somewhere, and he followed the sound. There was a party going on. There was always a party going on somewhere. Ash Harbour was a crowded place, and often there was little to do but get drunk, or high, and play music and dance. Sol wasn't into it – he liked to keep to himself – but sometimes he wished he could just let loose and go nuts on the weekend like his classmates. Other times, he just thought they were stupid. But then, they did get more girls that way.

There was graffiti everywhere. There were three gangs on this block, but these weren't territorial marks, just the usual scribbling:

CALL HOPHEAD FOR GOOD BOOZE.

AMANDA YAN GIVES IT UP FOR MONEY.

LIFE'S CRAP, AND THEN YOU DIE.

STOP THE RIDE, I WANT TO GET OFF.

TODD WOZ 'ERE '73. WASN'T IMPRESSED.

WHO ARE THE CLOCKWORKERS?

He gave that last one a second glance, wondering about it, but kept running. The walls around him were coated with the frustrated scrawling of bored kids. Tired of being crammed into this city, with nowhere to go but old age.

The music was louder now, and he slowed down, coming to the edge of a roof that looked out onto a small square lit in moody party colours. Putting his foot up on the low wall while he slowed his breathing, he gazed down at the scene. There was a band playing: two drummers, somebody with an old guitar – a real one – and a few guys on home-made horns. Most instruments were home-made these days. The crowd was in a lively mood, and the music was good, catchy. Solomon toyed with the idea of going down – the gig looked open enough – but he contented himself with watching from up in the darkness for a while.

He recognized the guitarist – it was Cleo. She was pretty handy on those strings, and was leading the singing of some raucous, anarchic anthem. At the centre of the pack, as usual. She was rarely without a boyfriend – there were rumours she'd had a girlfriend once too, but he suspected it was just malicious gossip. Music was such a social thing, he thought. Musicians always seemed to have loads of friends. In boxing, you had your team-mates, the guys you trained with, but it was different. At least for him. To stay sharp, you had to keep training separate from everything else. He turned away from the square and started running again. Climbing over a firewall, he descended some steps, balanced along a jutting wall and then down a ladder to the uppermost street. Watching the world around him from inside his hood, he ran for another half an hour, taking a circuitous route home. The evening light was gone, and the busy streets were lit only by store windows and the gaslights. He climbed up to the roof again, taking a different path back to his flat, one that led to the single window in the sitting room. He had left it open when he left.

He unstrapped the weights from his wrists as he dropped down to the floor . . . and was immediately aware that there was someone in the darkness with him. Bunching up in a defensive stance, he ducked away from the low light of the window, but it was too late. He felt a blow of something hard and heavy across his left hand, knocking away his guard and sending shooting pain through his wrist. From somewhere there was the scent of an acidic aftershave. Striking out with the weights in his right hand, his knuckles brushed against the fabric of the man's jacket. A foot came down heavily on the back of Sol's knee and he realized he had two opponents. As he fell to his knees, a hand grabbed his hair, pulling his head back, and a fist landed square on his nose. Pain burst across his face. Something hit the back of his neck, and he crumpled to the floor, stunned. He was dimly aware of two men clambering out of the open window, and then there was silence.

He lay there for some time, tenderly clutching his broken nose, his eyes full of tears. As he waited for his head to stop spinning, he took a woozy glance around the room. It had been completely ransacked.

'Dad'sh goin' to go nutsh,' he muttered.

'You've been broken into,' the policeman confirmed. 'Sure as shootin'.'

'I know,' Sol acknowledged sourly.

He had an ice pack in each hand, one held to his nose, the other pressed against the back of his neck. His voice sounded as if he had a cold, and every time he moved his head a furry headache rolled around inside it. The officer, who had introduced himself as Carling, had made a cursory examination of the door, the window and the overturned room before delivering his verdict. He did all the talking, in an official, monotonous manner, as his partner gazed out of the window.

'Anything missing?' he asked, his erasable notepad out.

'Not that I can see.' Sol looked around. 'I think I scared them off. Look, aren't there tests you're supposed to do? Fingerprints and stuff?'

'Nah, they'll have been wearing gloves.' Carling shook his head. 'We get called out to break-ins like this every day. Nothing to look for.'

Sol scowled. 'Thanks for dropping by, anyway.'

'Not sure I like your tone, son.'

'Sorry, Officer. I'm sixteen. It's the only tone I've got.'

Carling chuckled drily.

'Wife an' I used to live in a place like this, had a window just like that one,' he mused. 'Got broke into five times. *Five* times! And me an officer of the law. We moved out, got an internal flat, no windows. Haven't been broken into since. Place isn't as nice, no natural light or nothin', but it's *safer*, you know what I mean?'

Sol stared at him over the ice pack. 'So, what you're saying is: if we moved to a worse flat, if we didn't have any windows at all, it'd be harder to break into?'

'You've got to have security, son,' Carling told him.

'By that reckoning, then, if we didn't have any doors into the flat either, we'd be completely safe.'

'That's being a bit extreme, son.'

'We had to wait four years to move to a place with a window. We kind o' like it.' Sol took the pack away from the back of his neck and looked at it. There was a little bit of blood on the cloth.

'That bent out of shape?' Carling nodded towards Sol's broken nose.

'I think it's just the cartilage,' Sol muttered. 'I'll have my coach look at it tomorrow – he sees these a lot.'

'You should think about personal protection, then. The wife and I have a selection of personal-protection measures aside from my regulation weapons. She favours pepper spray – not that I can officially recommend it, you understand, but it's not illegal, you know what I mean?'

Sol was going to point out that he was a pretty handy boxer, but then remembered that he had been floored without getting in a single blow. So much for all his training. He stayed quiet.

'Other things I can't recommend,' Carling continued, 'would include knuckledusters, coshes; small, easily concealed knives; a bag of ball bearings; or even that timeless classic, the rock-in-the-sock. I must urge you not to resort to any of these measures, but if you have to, there is a good range to be had at reasonable prices down on Buccaneer Street. Don't go there after dark.'

'I'll be fine as I am, thanks,' Sol reassured him.

His father had firm ideas about weapons. Like most boys his age, Sol had gone through a stage of playing with knives. Gregor had taken one of the blades and cut up his favourite Muhammad Ali poster with it. Sol didn't want to think about what he'd do with pepper spray. Or a rock-in-a-sock.

'I think we're done here, Jim,' Carling said to his partner. Then, looking one last time at Sol: 'Stay safe, son. There are some real nut-jobs out there.'

'Yes, sir.'

The policemen departed, leaving Sol to survey the bombsite that was his home. First the accident at the crane, and now this; it had been a hell of a day. The mess was going to take some clearing up, but it would be best to get it done before his dad got home. Gregor would be a pain in the neck as it was, knowing his son had been attacked. Seeing the flat wrecked too would mean an evening of ranting about the state of the world. That, Sol could do without.

He leaned into the tiny open-plan kitchenette, throwing the sodden ice packs into the sink. Heaving a sigh that made his aching head throb, he started straightening up the living room. With the worst of the mess cleared up there, he went into his father's room and pondered on whether to leave it and let Gregor clean it up himself. Sol shrugged – he would tidy up the big stuff. Bending down to right the bedside table, he caught the drawers before they fell out of it, and was pushing them closed when something caught his eye. In the bottom drawer was a stack of betting slips from Cooley's, a ratting den in the Fourth Quadrant.

Sol sat down on the bed.

'Ah, Dad,' he breathed.

Gregor normally kept his gambling under control; he was always saying you had to keep a firm grip on your vices, or they'd grip you. But times had been tight recently, and Sol knew how the hope of a big win could push gamblers over the edge just when they could least afford it. There were a lot of slips here, and no way of telling whether they'd been paid off or not. Sol began to wonder if their two recent visitors had been burglars at all. He wondered if they'd been trying to collect on a debt.

'What do you mean, we've been withdrawn?' Cleo demanded. 'We're the main act!'

'I'm sorry, Cleo, but it's at the request of the sponsor.' The school principal, Mr Khaled, held his hands up helplessly. 'They had someone at one of your performances recently, and found some of your lyrics . . . inflammatory. They said that we'd either have to drop your band or lose their sponsorship. What could we do?'

'You could stand up for your students, is what you could do—'

'Now, mind your tone, young lady,' he warned. 'It's the students I'm thinking of – all of them. They've been promised this ball and we're going to give it to them. But we can't do it without money. Internal Climate is our sponsor, and we have to respect their wishes—'

'You have to kiss their small-minded *asses*, is more like!' Cleo retorted.

Khaled's pale brown face stiffened, and Cleo saw the beginnings of a storm brewing. She didn't like the man, but he tried hard to win the students' respect. It was his temper that let him down most of the time.

'I have to go and tell the guys,' she said in a softer voice. 'Just out of interest, who's going to headline it now?'

'Iced Breeze,' Khaled supplied.

'Aw, good grease, not those saps—'

'Get to class, Miss Matsumura.' The principal's tone left little room for argument.

Cleo angrily shifted the strap of her bag onto her shoulder and headed for her classroom. Freak Soup, her band, were the most popular group in the school, which was why they'd been the obvious choice to headline the end-of-year gig. It was going to be their biggest-ever audience, and they'd been really keyed up for it. She was nearly crying with frustration as she entered the classroom. They had Ms Kiroa for civics.

The teacher took one look at Cleo's face and just waved her to her seat. Everybody knew that she'd been called away by the principal; now everybody could guess why.

Cleo slumped down in her chair with burning cheeks, avoiding the eyes of those around her. The open roof let in the light from the dome, but it was dull and grey, and the electrical lamps had been turned on. Sol Wheat sat across from her, his hood up. He was trying to hide it, but she noticed his nose looked badly swollen, and she wondered if he had banged it somehow in the crane carriage.

'We were about to have a minute's silence for the two men who died yesterday,' Ms Kiroa told her. 'By the way, if any of you feel you need to talk about what happened, you're welcome to come to me after class. So, if you could all stand . . .'

Cleo stood up with the rest of the class. She breathed in and out slowly, subduing the sobs that wanted to come out. It was so *unfair*. She couldn't believe the nerve of those snides. Those welshing, backstabbing little snides. Well, if they thought her lyrics had been inflammatory before, just wait until she came up with a number about this . . . She'd write stuff that would make their hair stand on end.

'Thank you, you can sit down now,' Ms Kiroa told them. 'Sol, take your hood down, please. You know I don't like you wearing it up in class. So, to recap on last week, why is it necessary for the bulk of us to travel to work or school on the clockwise route, and then complete the circle on the homeward journey?'

Cleo snorted quietly. They'd been learning this since primary school. Right turns to school, and right turns home. Hands went up.

'To generate the kinetic energy for the Heart Engine, miss.' Ubertino Lamont, one of Freak Soup's drummers, spoke up as the teacher pointed to him. 'To keep the flywheels turning.'

'Duh,' Cleo mumbled.

'All right, that was an easy one,' Ms Kiroa said. 'And we know that during the working day and early evening, the flywheels are driven by the tram system, and by the foot stations. Something most of you can look forward to when you leave school. One hour a day every fourth week. Unless you get to fill some vitally important role, such as a . . . oh, a *teacher*, say.'

She struck a glamorous pose, and some of the students smirked.

'But who can tell me this?' she went on. 'In the fourth year of its operation, the generators were already online and feeding the city much of its heat, but most of the works were still not connected up. That was the year the Heart Engine failed. Can anybody tell me why?'

There was hush in the classroom. Few of them had even heard of the event, over two hundred years ago.

'Too much fat in its diet?' Cleo muttered beneath her breath, prompting a chorus of sniggers.

25

'The construction workers went on strike,' Ms Kiroa told them, still trying to ignore the aggrieved young upstart in the second row. Cleo was upset, and she was looking to start a fight with her teacher in order to blow off some steam. Ana wasn't going to fall for it. 'The workers went on strike and, as a result, the entire city nearly froze to death.'

Most of the rest of the lesson was about all the systems that the Heart Engine supplied energy to, which was pretty much everything in the city. Any major works that didn't get energy from the generator, supplied power to it. It was engineering stuff, and it tended to put Cleo to sleep. She was surprised Ms Kiroa had any enthusiasm for it, but the teacher seemed as entranced by the city's works as some of the guys. But then, rumour had it she was going out with someone from Ventilation. Cleo feigned interest, and managed to make it to the end of the class without yawning too much.

The other guys from the band were waiting for her when she came out after the bell rang for break. Flipping her hair over her shoulders, she leaned back against the corridor wall with her hands on her hips, heaved a sigh and looked at each of them in turn. She could see no reason to break it to them gently.

'We've been dumped,' she said.

'Why?' Faisal, their bass-horn player asked.

'Internal Climate says our lyrics are inflammatory.'

'What do they mean, "inflammatory"?' their treble

horn, Amanda, said, frowning. 'They think we're a fire hazard?'

'That's inflammable, Am,' Cleo explained patiently. 'Inflammatory means . . . like, we ignite passion. Get a rise out of people.'

'Isn't that what music's supposed to do?'

'Not according to Internal Climate, it's not.'

'Slimy grits.' Ube Lamont, the drummer, shook his head. 'This is all just part of the corporate monopoly of everyday life. Every day it gets harder to draw a free breath into your lungs; this place is being taken over by the cranks who want to stamp their ownership on the world.'

The others stared silently at him.

'You're sounding more and more like a Dark-Day Fatalist all the time,' Cleo told him. 'You should lay off the smoke, it's making you morbid.'

'I'm not fatalistic, I just object to being a cog in the machine,' Ube replied, looking defensive.

'We *live* in a machine,' Cleo sighed. 'Get used to it.'

'You should be careful how you talk, anyway,' Faisal told him. 'You mess with the machine, and the Clockworkers'll come for you. I know somebody whose uncle disappeared after he said the wrong thing.'

'That's bullology,' Ubertino sneered. 'The "Clockworkers". A myth started by the men in power, a cynical ploy to keep the masses cowering—'

'What the hell have you been reading lately?' Cleo asked, wincing. '"Keep the masses cowering"? Jesus, Ube.'

27

'I just know what I've heard,' Faisal added vehemently.

'You're a scaremonger, a servant of the rumour-mill.'

'I'm goin' to belt you in a minute . . .'

'Enough!' Cleo placed herself between the two boys, her lips pressed into a thin line. Her nerves had been a bit raw since the crane accident, and she was ready to have a go at the pair of them. 'It's not worth knocking heads over. We all need to chill out.'

She glanced around. They were alone in the corridor.

'Anybody got some stem on them?'

Section 3/24: Power

Coach Assagioli – Saggs, to his boys – pressed Sol's nose gently between his palms, causing a spark of pain that made Sol flinch slightly. Around them, the sounds of a busy boxing club filled the air: grunts, thuds, panting breaths, skipping ropes tapping and whirring, feet gliding back and forth across the floor. But he could no longer get the smells; no liniment, or warm rubber, worn leather or fresh sweat. It was difficult enough to draw breath through his nostrils. The gym was well lit, but the equipment was old and overused, like so many things in Ash Harbour. He still loved it here, his second home, his temple.

'You're lucky,' the coach grunted, nodding to himself. 'They just broke the cartilage. Bridge is fine, nose is even straight – they haven't spoiled your good looks.'

Sol sniffed, then put his hand up to his swollen nose and wiggled it gingerly. He could feel the two edges of the cartilage rub together.

'No sparring for you for a couple of weeks,' Saggs told him. 'Do some work on the bag today, and take it easy. Join in the circuit training if you want.'

Sol tutted. He'd been looking forward to letting off some steam, and the bag just wouldn't do it for him. Gregor had not come home last night, and Sol was starting to get worried. He had phoned the depot, but his dad had not shown up for work since the crane accident. Sol was considering reporting him missing. His father rarely stayed out two nights in a row, and if those two heavies were after him, Gregor might be in trouble. The ease with which they'd beaten him rankled Sol as well. He would have come off better in a fair fight.

'I need a few rounds, Saggs,' he pleaded. 'This thing with the crane's been driving me mad. Just a couple of rounds to loosen up, take my mind off it . . . please?'

Saggs regarded him for a moment, and then nodded.

'All right, you're in with Nestor. Take it easy.' He turned to the thin-figured, pale boy working on the punchbag. 'Nestor! You're in the ring with Wheat! He's got a broken nose, so I just want to see body shots from the pair of you. Touches to the head, nothing to the face. And I want to see you moving those feet, Nestor!'

Once he had his head-guard on, one of the guys helped Sol with his gloves, pulling them on over his wrapped hands and doing up the laces. They were Gregor's old gloves – real leather, not like the synth-fibre most of the other guys used. Climbing through the ropes, he bounced around on the sprung floor, shaking his arms out. Nestor was an easy opponent; a slight white boy, he'd taken up training about a year ago because he was being bullied. He was a bit of a drip, but he was all right. He'd never be a fighter, though. Sol watched him climb in, his thin legs sticking out of baggy shorts, his T-shirt covering his scrawny body, but not his long, skinny arms. Good reach, but no power. Sol was a bit shorter, several kilos heavier, and a lot more muscular, even for sixteen. By the time he was eighteen, he'd have the build of a real middleweight, and would be fit for serious competition.

Saggs called the start, and the two opponents circled each other, both up on the balls of their feet to constantly change stance, trying not to signal their intentions. Nestor was nervous, defensive, and every time Sol moved, his guard twitched. They traded a few easy shots, Sol dodging Nestor's blows with an easy grace, not even needing his guard. A right hook forced Nestor to cover up, blocking his own view, and Sol followed up with two neat uppercuts to the kidneys. Nestor danced away, but Sol followed. Jabbing into Nestor's guard, he brought his left round in a hook – Nestor covered his head, and lashed out in fright.

His glove caught Sol straight in the nose.

Sol bellowed in pain, his face suddenly on fire, and something snapped. He rained a combination of punches in on Nestor's head and body, restraint lost in a blind rage. The lighter boy crumpled under his assault.

'Sol! Break it up!' Saggs shouted.

Sol pounded Nestor's guard out of the way, hitting him hard across the sides of the head, once, twice, three times. He followed his final right hook through with his elbow, catching Nestor on the temple. The other boy's headgear was the only thing saving him from serious injury. Nestor collapsed to the floor and went limp.

'Solomon!' Saggs roared. 'Get the hell out of there, now!'

He ducked through the ropes and shoved Sol back to his corner.

'You part when I say you part!'

Backing against the post, Sol looked past the coach at his fallen opponent. Breathing hard, he felt the animal glory of beating an enemy; but as the pain in his face faded, a sense of shame descended on him. Nestor was struggling to his feet, his nose and mouth bloodied, one of his eyes starting to swell. They'd been training, just helping each other out, and Sol had lost his head and pummelled a weaker opponent. He started forward to apologize, but Saggs stopped him angrily, and Nestor glared at him and turned away.

'You're out of sparring for three weeks,' Saggs snapped at him. 'It was an accident that he tagged you. You should've seen that. Hit the showers and cool off – I don't want to see you back here till Monday.'

'Yes, Coach.' Sol slipped through the ropes and jumped down to the floor of the gym.

Undoing the laces of his gloves with his teeth, he stuck them under his armpits and pulled them off. Then he took off his head-guard and threw them all into his bag. There were a few curious glances from some of the others working out in the gym as he headed for the changing rooms.

Sitting on one of the benches, he unwound the wraps from his hands and dropped them into his bag. Then he stripped off and stood in the shower, letting the water pour over him. Looking at his hands, he thought of how his father had shown him how to punch against a pillow as a child. That was how he'd always worked out his aggression, punching a pillow, or the mattress of his bed. He leaned against the wall, and let the soothing water fall on the back of his swollen neck.

Two of the other guys, Teller and Gant, came into the changing room.

'See the red mist out there, Sol?' Teller called.

'Beware the red mist!' Gant chimed, pulling off his shorts and then his groin-guard, before scooting from the chilly room into the showers.

Solomon looked up into the spray, running his hands over his face, and then stepped out of the shower and towelled himself down. Walking past Teller to his bag, he started getting dressed.

'Hear you were at that crane wreck,' Teller said in a quieter voice. 'What was it like?'

'High,' Sol replied, pulling on a fresh T-shirt.

33

'Come on, talk to us, man! Did you see the bodies? What's it like seein' someone die?'

'Tell, get a life, will ya?' Sol rolled his eyes. 'You're like a kid—'

'Aw, go on!' Gant urged him as he spat out water. 'Were they in pieces? Did y'see bits of 'em? I hear you *burst* when you fall from that high up . . . like a bag of guts!'

'Sick grit!' Teller laughed. 'Hey, did you guys hear about Harmon Effram? The big Jew who used to train over at the Fourth Quad gym?'

Sol remembered him, a regular worshipper at the same temple his mother used to go to. A religious type; there weren't many full-on Jews left in the city. Most people in Ash Harbour were a mix of races – with everybody living on top of each other, you couldn't help it. Effram had been a decent fighter – slow, but tough.

'What about him?' he asked.

'Big yid got squashed last week,' Teller informed them. 'He was working in the hydroponic gardens over at the fertilizer plant. The balcony above him collapsed, dropped a ten-ton fertilizer tank on him. It was like he was stamped on by a huge foot or something. Like somebody'd painted a huge, wide Harmon all over the floor.'

Sol felt mildly ill.

'Kind of like what you did to Nestor, eh, Sol?' Gant chuckled.

34

'That was just stupid,' Sol muttered.

'Ah, nobody likes the little weed anyway.' Gant wrinkled his nose. 'Maybe he'll get the message now.'

The door of the changing room was opening as he said it, and there stood Nestor, bag in hand. They lapsed into silence, but he was already turning round and heading out of the door.

'Nice one, Gant.' Teller shook his head. 'What did ya have to say that for?'

'It's the truth.' Gant shrugged.

Sol cursed to himself, quickly lacing up his trainers. Gregor was always checking in with Saggs to see how his son was doing. If Nestor quit training because of the beating Sol had given him, there'd be hell to pay. And Sol was feeling guilty enough already. He grabbed his bag and hurried into the gym. Glancing around, he strode to the far door and stepped out into the alley. Nestor was nowhere to be seen. Shifting his bag onto his shoulder, he pulled up his hood, jammed his hands in his pockets and started off home.

By the time Anastacia Kiroa got home to the apartment she shared with two other teachers, it was after ten. She walked in to find the place in darkness, and reached for the hall light switch. Nothing happened. Another blackout. Clicking her tongue, she found the small methane lamp in the hall cupboard, lit it, and used it to find her way through the dark apartment to her room. She knew the place inside out, but Candice, one of her flatmates, still hadn't grown out of her student lifestyle. She tended to leave stuff sitting in the middle of the floor where you could trip over it.

The blackouts seemed to occur much more frequently than they had when she was a child. But maybe that was just her being nostalgic as she glowed from her evening out. She had been out with Julio, walking in the gardens on the upper levels. Changing out of her tight red skirt and lacy black blouse into her worn old dressing gown, she hugged herself as she remembered how he had kissed her on the balcony overlooking the lights of the promenades. She'd never met a man with so much passion. He was an engineer, working in Climate Control, and he talked about the city as he knew it – from the inside out.

Pulling back her dark brown, shoulder-length hair, she tied the belt on her gown and wandered into the living room. They had a decades-old webscreen but, with no electricity, it was useless. They had a little rechargeable radio, and she switched it on, listening to the news as she made a hot cup of spirulina soup. She hadn't taken her supplements that day, but she'd do it later. The diet in Ash Harbour left a lot to be desired. Spooning the powder into a mug, she lit the small gas stove that they now kept for these occasions, and put some water on to boil. It heated noisily as she listened to the headlines. There had been a murder, a man from the Fourth Quadrant. A daylighter – one of the men who worked to clear the dome's surface of ice and snow. Ana put a hand to her mouth; Sol Wheat's father was a daylighter. But he lived here, in the Third Quad. The water on the stove came to the boil, and she took the steaming mug to the couch, curling her legs under her and pulling a cushion onto her lap. The apartment was cold, and they had used up their heating quota for the month.

Solomon Wheat. He had a real crush on her. It was flattering, if a bit awkward sometimes; particularly as she was only a few years older than her students. She wished he'd get over it, though; it must be so obvious to the others in his class. Or maybe not. Even so, it might be a good idea to talk to him. Ana bit her lip. He was becoming a fine-looking young man; muscular, physically confident, with those Slavic cheekbones and a bright smile that he rarely showed. The girls liked that – but he kept to himself so much. Ana sipped at her soup and idly wondered what it would take to bring Sol Wheat out of his shell.

The walls were thin in the apartment block, and by the sounds of things, most of her neighbours were still awake. Directly overhead, somebody was playing a clarinet; she heard it sometimes in the evenings and loved the sound. Despite the chill, she switched off the radio and opened the living-room window to see if she could hear it any clearer. A few of the windows around her were weakly illuminated with light from the same kind of gas lamps that she was using.

The clarinet music – some blues number – carried

down from above. She could only guess at how old that instrument must be. Surely older than Ash Harbour itself; she had never heard of anyone here who made clarinets. Hands clasping her warm mug of soup, she looked out over the sector below her. Tightly packed buildings – some housing branches of the Machine itself – everything linked by ducts, cables, pipes and drive-shafts, all entwined around the multi-level roads, used by pedestrians, cyclists and mopeds more than cars these days. Private cars were becoming a thing of the past, having become too expensive for most people to maintain. Spare parts were at a premium, as was the electricity to power the vehicles themselves – most motor vehicles were many years old, and had a cobbled-together look about them. A few commercial trucks and vans passed from time to time.

The lights of the apartment block would be out until morning now. She could see that the other buildings on the grid were dark, and even the lights on the tramlines had gone off. Closing the window, she went into the kitchenette to rinse out the mug and found the water had been cut off too. The tap released a last spurt and then nothing. Swearing under her breath, she checked the hot water, but it was gone as well. The people at Water First had sworn that all the problems had been fixed. This was the fourth time in a month, and the bills were going up all the time. There were numerous underground streams running into Ash Harbour, and they were surrounded by the ocean that lay under the pack ice. It was farcical that they couldn't maintain a water supply. The water company could expect a short, sharp phone call in the morning – not that it would make any difference.

She dropped the cup into the sink, took a tumbler from the cupboard and went back to her room, bringing the lamp with her. There was a canteen of schnapps and a well-thumbed copy of *Lady Chatterley's Lover* in the drawer beneath her bed. A *proper* copy, from back when books were made of paper. Once again, the new world had failed her, forcing her to seek comfort in the simplicities of an older, more vital time.

Section 4/24: Weapon

Solomon woke with a twitch of his body, caught in the confused world between sleep and wakefulness, trapped for a last fleeting moment in the falling crane carriage. Looking at the clockwork alarm clock, he saw it was after seven a.m., but there was little trace of light from under his bedroom door. He got out of bed and opened it to find the living room in darkness, even though the shutters were open. Peering out at the dome above the city, he could see only a grey glow. There must have been a heavy fall of snow during the night; the daylighters would be busy today. The flat was cold; pulling on his tracksuit, he slapped his arms around his body.

It was Saturday, but the weekends rotated for all the schools, and he had classes today. His school would be off Sunday and Monday. This system ensured that people kept moving through the city, one of the main sources of power for the Machine, and a key to its flywheels maintaining their momentum.

Gregor's bed was still made, but that was not unusual – his dad was particular about neatness, so he could have come home and left again. But Sol could not see any sign that his father had returned; after two nights away he would have wanted to say hello to Sol before going back to work. Surely he'd heard about Sol's class witnessing the crane disaster? Sol shivered, blowing warm air into his hands as he put a mug of water in the microwave to heat. He always started his morning routine with a drink of hot water. The microwave didn't come on. He checked the light switch; the electricity was gone. Shaking his head, he left the mug where it was, picked up his skipping rope and walked across the frigid floor to the middle of the living room. He had spent the previous evening doing a proper clear-up of the flat, needing activity to ease the guilt of the beating he had given to Nestor. As he warmed up with some gentle skipping, he wondered if he should report his father missing. Gregor had never been away three nights without telling him. At least, not since the bad old days after he'd lost his previous job.

Sol's eyes fell on the leatheresse upholstered chair in front of him, and the rope caught on his ankles. There lay his father's scarf. Gregor had been wearing it when he'd last left for work. So he *had* been home. The scarf was wrapped up in a bundle, and Sol bent forward to pick it up. It was heavy and, as he unwound it, he fumbled with it and dropped what was inside. A dark grey gun hit the floor, clattering across the coated concrete.

Solomon stared at it in disbelief, kneeling down and touching it tentatively before taking hold of it. It was heavy, a solid weight in his hand. He had never seen a real gun before, but there were plenty in the old films on the web. It was an automatic and, remembering from countless action films, he checked that the safety was on. It was a little switch on the left side of the pistol. Another catch on the bottom of the handle made the magazine – the clip – spring free, and he nearly dropped it. Through a slot on the side of the clip, he counted thirteen bullets. It was fully loaded. He slid the clip back into place in the handle of the gun, pushing it home with a satisfying click. Pointing it at the window, he aimed down the sights. He could see the top of his school, and he fired a few imaginary shots through the windows.

It looked fairly new; not manufactured like most things that were made before Ash Harbour, but machined, the angles and curves handmade. What was it doing here? The scarf was lying discarded on the chair, and in its folds he saw a piece of rice paper. He had been so entranced by the gun, he hadn't noticed it. Unfolding it, he found a note, hastily scribbled in his father's handwriting.

Sol. Keep this close to you. You're in danger. Steer clear of the police, they can't be trusted. I'll come back for you soon.

Gregor.

Solomon sank onto the chair, trying to imagine what could possibly make his father give him a gun. Gregor despised guns. Sol was sure that he'd never used one himself, and yet here he was giving one to his son. Where did he even get it? He crumpled up the note and threw it into the recycler in the kitchen. Then he wrapped the gun back up in the scarf, pushed it down into the bottom of his bag and got changed for school.

Ana sat on the seat in the tram, half asleep, her head leaning against the pole that she held as the vehicle hummed down the street. It was crammed with people, and she knew that beneath the wheels the weight of the morning trams would be tilting the enormous gyroscopes that made up the central circles of the city. The trams worked in pairs, each moving up and down through different levels like a barge through a lock; the weight of each full one heading into the city helping to lift an empty one up to a higher level as it descended.

In other parts of the city, bridges and elevators carried people in the same way. Each person's home was set a certain distance from their workplace, and their trip to and from work was roughly timed for best effect. It was part of a massive and intricate operation that kept energy running through Ash Harbour. Everything about the original parts of the city was carefully co-ordinated to produce and save that precious energy, the electricity and heat that made their way of life possible – just heating the freezing air pumped in from outside was an enormous drain. It all required careful timing and co-operation; but the people of Ash Harbour were well trained, the system having always been a part of their lives.

Ana looked out of the window, up at the dull light falling through a small section of the dome's grey hexagonal grid. The daylighters were slowly clearing the snow, and there would be better light soon. Pigeons, one of the only breeds of bird left in the world, whirled in flocks under the dome; at night, bats would take their place. The dark morning depressed her, and she imagined what it must be like to live in some of the other domiciles around the planet. If there were any left – there had been no contact with anyone for years. Ash Harbour was the only one with a dome; all the rest were underground. Ana shivered at the prospect. The thought of a life without daylight was too awful to contemplate. The suicide rate in the city doubled whenever the light from the dome was completely blocked out by snow or cloud.

The architects of Ash Harbour had known the importance of sunlight. The catastrophic climate that had driven mankind into these protected enclaves could last for generations, and humans would need daylight to give them hope, and they would need a purpose to survive. And so the architects had created the dome . . . and the Machine.

The tram reached Ana's stop, and she pushed through the close-pressed bodies to the sliding door. Hitting the button, she hopped down, feeling the bite of the cold air on her face. For a place with an artificial climate, the city could get a bit frigid at times. She must remember to ask Julio why that was. The Machine was running at close to full capacity; how could there not be enough heat? She didn't remember it being this cold when she was young.

Alan Turing High School was a beige, utilitarian complex of reinforced concrete. Riddled with small windows, it was built to be well-lit and permanent. The outer walls were daubed with the colourful remonstrations of yet another generation of mis-understood youth. Two men dressed in conservative dark grey suits and long coats were standing across the street from the entrance to the school. They did not look like normal visitors. Shooting a glance at their faces, Ana saw that they were watching her as she made her way inside. Something about them made her nervous, but she shook the feeling off, annoyed at herself for being so paranoid.

The school was only one storey, but it nestled above several levels of streets and apartment blocks. The city's architects had shown remarkable foresight in their construction of the building; whereas many blocks on the top levels had paved roofs that were used as yards and meeting places, the school had no roofs at all, except for the insulated awnings that could be drawn across. The students could look straight up at the dome, but the walls around them stopped them being distracted by the sights of the city. Wherever possible, the schools in the city were on the highest levels. Children were judged to be in greatest need of the sunlight. This privilege was one of the advantages that had drawn Ana into teaching.

She was always in before her students; she found they were more punctual if they knew she saw who arrived first, and who showed up last. Opening the register in readiness, she turned to the carbon board and started writing with her stylus. Her first class was 8C, for mathematics. They started to wander in, clumped in groups, or in ones and twos. Some of them muttered teenage greetings to her and she replied to each of them as they sat down at their desks. No class was ever in a good mood for the first lesson of the morning.

When the bell rang, they were all in, except one. She didn't need to check the register to see who was missing.

'Does anybody know where Sol is?' she asked.

The police were waiting for Sol at the school entrance. Two serious-looking men in suits approached him as he walked up to the door.

'Solomon Wheat?' one of them asked.

'Yes?'

'Inspector Mercier – Criminal Investigation

Section.' The man showed him a badge. 'I wonder, young sir, if we could ask you some questions about your father?'

Sol looked the man up and down, trying to show some attitude. His heart was pounding. Would they search him? How could he explain the gun in his bag? The policeman was a little taller than he was; clean cut, pale and weak in the chin. He had a neatly trimmed moustache, mousy hair parted on one side and slightly sunken eyes. The other man was larger, with a lantern jaw and no moustache, but otherwise the same. They probably even bought their clothes in the same place.

'This is Sergeant Baiev.' Mercier tilted his head in the direction of the second man.

'I haven't seen my father in three days,' Sol told them. 'Do you know where he is?'

'I wish we did, young sir. You see, I'm sorry to tell you that we have a warrant for his arrest. For the murder of a Mr Tommy Hyung, a fellow daylighter. Would you mind coming with us?'

'Murder?!' Sol exclaimed, stunned. 'He can't be . . . I mean . . . Murder?'

'I'm afraid so, Mr Wheat. Now if you'd just come with us—'

'I have a class—'

'Your teachers will be informed. I'm sure they'll understand.'

They led him to an unmarked black car parked on the corner. Baiev got behind the wheel, while Mercier sat beside Sol in the back. It was a black, blocky machine, and the engine sounded more powerful than a normal electric motor. Pulling away from the kerb, Baiev steered it into the road, skilfully avoiding a group of teenagers on mopeds, and soon they were on the main western route, heading towards the closest section of city wall.

'When was the last time you saw your father?' the inspector asked him.

'Wednesday morning . . . aren't you meant to be recording this or something? I thought there was supposed to be a—'

'You're not under arrest, Mr Wheat. You're just assisting us with our inquiries. Have you had any contact with your father since then?'

The school bag holding the gun was a heavy weight in Sol's lap. The note had said not to trust the police.

'No. I don't know where he is.'

Mercier eyed him thoughtfully.

'You have no need to be worried about our intentions, young sir. It's merely our job to bring your father in. If he's innocent, then he has nothing to fear from us.'

'I don't know where he is,' Sol repeated. 'Where are we going?'

'To the station – this won't take long. We'll return you to school when we've completed the interview.'

'I'm under eighteen. Shouldn't I have somebody with me or something?'

'We can assign you a social worker if you like. There's

a lot of red tape involved, though. Your mother's deceased, isn't that right? A tram crash? You lost your older sister in the accident too, according to the ISS file. A tragedy. I lost one of my sisters to cancer recently. Melanoma, very ugly. They used to be able to cure that, you know. We just don't have the drugs now. But at least we were ready for it. A tram accident – now, that's *very* sudden. Hard to take, I imagine.'

Sol hadn't thought about Nattie and his mother for some time. It had been years since the accident. Gregor was his only family now. He hated this cop for bringing it up like this. His memories of his sister and his mother were fading treasures, recalled on quiet nights with a bitter mixture of fondness and distance. They were not for blunt discussion in the back of a police car.

The police station was twelve storeys high, with an observatory on the top floor and metal grids on the windows. This was not a local branch, it was the CIS headquarters; centre for all the major criminal investigations. Its grey and blue walls rose out of the clustered buildings around it, tall and imposing. The road took them up to the fourth floor, and Baiev stopped outside the door. Mercier gently ushered Sol from the car. For a moment Sol felt trapped. Some of the guys he trained with in the boxing club were regular visitors to police stations. They said there were weapons detectors on the doors.

'You can leave your things in the car,' Mercier told him.

Sol was not reassured; he was certain they'd search his bag. But they could do that anyway. He left the schoolbag on the back seat of the car and let the inspector lead him into the station.

The interior of the building was a straight-edged warren in light cream and white, with green tiled floors. Like most buildings in Ash Harbour, it was compactly constructed. The corridors were well lit, and there were notices up everywhere. Mercier led him past the front desk, where two officers were arguing with an enormous, pale-faced gangland type from the bottom levels, and a pair of irate Filipinos. The five raised voices echoed down the hallway as Sol and his guide made their way deeper into the building.

'You will be safe here, Mr Wheat,' Mercier told him. 'Don't let the atmosphere of the place alarm you. Or some of the people you see here, for that matter. There is nothing to be scared of.'

This did little to put Solomon's mind at ease. There were holding cells along this corridor, and the heavy doors, with their small apertures, were an intimidating sight. At the end of the corridor Mercier opened a door and waved him in.

'Ah, thank you, Inspector,' a voice greeted them.

Beyond the door was a grey room with no windows, lit by a single diode cluster hanging from the ceiling. There were three men in the room, all in the dark red uniform of the ISS – the Industrial Security Section. These people had authority wherever affairs of the

Machine were involved. Which was pretty much everywhere. If you were to believe the rumours, there was no love lost between them and the CIS. One of the men, obviously of the highest rank, gestured to Sol to sit at the bare table that occupied the centre of the room. Controls for a recorder were set into the top of the table at one end, and there was a chair on either side.

'Thank you, Inspector,' the first man said again. 'We'll take it from here.'

'I'd like to sit in, if you don't—' Mercier began.

'That won't be necessary, thank you.'

Sol glanced back at Mercier, understanding the insistent note. Mercier – an inspector in the CIS – had just been tasked with delivering him. It was the Industrial Security Section that was in charge here. That must be pretty demeaning. The inspector's face was frozen into a carefully neutral expression. He nodded and left, closing the door behind him. Sol turned to face the three men.

'Have a seat, Mr Wheat,' the first one told him. 'I'm Inspector Ponderosa, this is Sergeant Koenig and Detective Collins. We just want to have a word.'

Sol sat down in the chair nearest him; the sound of its legs scraping across the floor was very loud in the small room. Sizing the officers up as if they were opponents in the ring, Sol let his eyes wander from one to the next. Ponderosa was a middleweight; his athletic build accentuated by the wine-coloured

51

uniform and its black and silver trim. Under close-cropped, dense black hair, his rugged, good-looking face was spoiled by a mouth with the thin lips of a wound. Koenig was a light heavyweight; narrower than Ponderosa in build, but taller and with blond hair. Collins ·was red-haired, short, squat and burly; a heavyweight barrel of a man. The three officers studied him as if he were some mildly interesting subject in a laboratory. Then Ponderosa gave him a warm smile and took the chair opposite. He leaned forward, putting his elbows on the table.

'As I'm sure Inspector Mercier has told you, we're looking for your father,' he began. 'When was the last time you had any contact with him?'

His voice had a slightly high-pitched quality to it. Sol could imagine it getting annoying very quickly.

'Wednesday morning – I told Mercier that already. I haven't seen him since then. Who's accusing him of murder?'

'I'll ask the questions,' Ponderosa chided him gently. 'Can't have you stealing my thunder, now can I? You saw him Wednesday morning, before you went to school, is that right? He was on his way to work? And, if I'm not mistaken, he didn't come home that night, or the following night. Am I right?'

Sol nodded.

'What about last night?'

'He . . . he didn't come home either. I didn't see him.'

Ponderosa's face was almost expressionless. There was still a smile playing on the corner of that slit of a mouth, but it was no longer a friendly expression.

'Have you had any contact with him at all since Wednesday? A phone call, a note to say where he was? Nothing?'

'No.'

The room was stifling. There was nowhere to look that wasn't solid and grey. Only the door: flat and featureless, and closed.

'You must have been worried when he didn't show up.' Still the semi-smile from Ponderosa, with no trace of humour in sight.

'He stays out some nights,' Sol said softly.

'Ah, yes. The ratting dens. I believe he's a regular visitor to the fights in the Filipino District as well. Likes to bet a bit, your father, doesn't he?'

Sol looked down at his hands, then glanced towards the door. They weren't supposed to be allowed to interrogate him on his own like this, he was sure of it. He knew he should challenge them, but he couldn't summon up the nerve.

'We don't care about that kind of crap, Solomon,' Ponderosa said with a dismissive wave of his hand. 'We're just interested in anything your father might have said to you in the last few days. I can't believe he wouldn't have sent you some kind of message in that time. Not even a note? No phone call?'

'I said *no*.'

'What about his friends? Have you talked to any of them?' The ISS man stood up, walking round the table to bring his face closer to Sol's. 'Who is he most likely to confide in, do you think? I'd like you to give us a list of his friends, workmates – anybody your father trusts. He's in real trouble here, Solomon. We can help him, but we have to find him first. We think he's fallen in with some very nasty people. Help us find out who he might have talked to, and you'll help him.'

His father didn't trust anybody. Not really. He had a few friends, gambling mates, but Sol couldn't think of anyone who . . . Murder. His father was being accused of killing somebody. It hit home for the first time. Sol couldn't believe it; Gregor got into fights sometimes – he was difficult to get on with – but he wouldn't kill anybody. At least, not on purpose.

'How did it happen? The . . . the death,' Sol asked falteringly. 'How do you know it was my dad? He wouldn't kill somebody, he just—'

'At four sixteen p.m. on Wednesday afternoon' – Ponderosa cut him off – 'three witnesses say they saw your father severely beat Tommy Hyung – a fellow dome-maintenance technician – before throwing him off a catwalk into a piston well. The pistons were not operating at full speed, which is how they were stopped in time to save enough of Mr Hyung's body to be positively identified. Well, from his dental records, anyway.'

The other two men were standing against the walls

54

on either side of Sol now, and he threw furtive looks up at them. He glanced at the door again. It was the only way out of the room, and all three men were between him and it now. The balls of his feet were pressed against the floor, his legs bouncing up and down restlessly. He had his fingers knotted together and he stared down at his hands, crushing his fingers against each other.

Mercier had said there was nothing to be scared of. Why had he said that? Sol wasn't being accused of anything; why would he be scared? His swollen nose itched, and he scratched the bridge of it, trying not to touch it where it was broken.

'I'm asking you for names, Solomon.'

When he didn't look up, Ponderosa grabbed his chin and forced his head up.

'Listen to me when I'm talking to you!' the inspector snapped.

There was the sound of angry voices outside, and the door swung open. There was Ana Kiroa, with outrage written across her face. Mercier stood behind her, looking sheepish.

'What the hell is going on here?' she snarled. 'This boy is sixteen years old! Who do you think you are, interrogating him without a guardian present? I'm going to have you all up on charges, you goddamned fascists! I want the name of your superior – I'll have the mayor herself down on you for this! Come on, Sol. You're getting out of here. These goddamned bullies can't question you without an adult here to represent you and they know it. And I'll be damned if I'm going to give them the chance after this.'

Sol was already standing up. Ana looked young and small, standing among all these men, her outrage fierce but brittle. Her voice was shaking as she spoke. She could only be a few years older than him and yet she had put them all on the defensive.

At first he couldn't understand how she had got there, but then he realized Mercier must have led her through.

'A clerical error, miss,' Ponderosa said, unabashed. He threw a hostile glare at Mercier. 'We're sorry if there's been any misunderstanding. The boy was just—'

'The *boy* was just *leaving*!' she barked. 'Come on, Sol.'

He let her lead him out, looking back just once at the three policemen.

'Keep walking,' Ana muttered under her breath.

'We'll be in touch, Mr Wheat,' Ponderosa called after him. 'Once all this has been cleared up.'

'Keep walking,' she repeated.

She had her hand on his elbow and was striding towards the entrance. They passed the desk, drawing a few curious looks, and then came out onto the street.

'Mr Wheat!' Mercier shouted, and Sol turned round. The inspector was holding his school bag.

'Your bag, young sir. You mustn't forget your bag.'

'Thanks,' Sol mumbled, taking it from him.

The gun was still in the bottom of it – he could tell by the weight. They hadn't searched it.

'Apologies about the, eh . . . the mix-up,' Mercier said humbly. 'Should've ensured a proper procedure. I was assured that the ISS had permission from the school and it was all above board. Regrettable mistake. It won't happen again.'

'You've got that right!' Ana snorted.

They walked away, looking for a tram stop.

'Thanks,' Sol breathed. 'I wasn't sure what to do. I mean, they were police . . . and I . . .' He was shaking, and his voice was catching in his throat. 'They said Dad killed somebody.'

'Jesus. Those gutters really did a number on you.' She shook her head. 'They can't question you about a library fine without a guardian present, let alone a goddamned murder! Goddamned fascists!'

He suddenly noticed that she was breathing hard too, and she was sweating. She was frightened. He realized it must have taken some nerve for her to barge right in there and confront those cops in their own station.

'How did you know where I was?' he asked her.

'A man called the school – said you'd been picked up. He said you'd been taken here.'

'Who? A cop?'

Ana frowned.

'I don't know; at the time I assumed he was, but now I'm not sure. He didn't sound like somebody who thought much of the police.'

Sol thought about the gun in his bag. And the note from his father. They came to a tram stop and looked down the road. Sol slipped his hand into his school bag and found the hard shape of the gun wrapped in the scarf. Its weight was reassuring, for all the good it would have done him in the police station.

'Where *is* your father?' Ana enquired. 'I presume they haven't got him?'

'No. And I haven't seen him since Wednesday. That's when they said . . . they said he did it. He killed a guy.'

'We'll go back to school until going-home time,' she told him. 'You shouldn't be on your own. Do you have any family you can stay with?'

Sol shook his head.

'Well, you'd better stay with me then. Those thugs might try to pick you up again. They're not above tossing your rights aside if they think they can get away with it. You can sleep on the couch.'

'Okay. Thanks.' Her back was turned to him as she looked down the road for the tram, so Sol allowed himself the barest hint of a wry smile as he spoke. He was finally getting to spend the night at Ana Kiroa's, and all it took was his father to be accused of murder. It was turning out to be an insane week.

Section 5/24: Rumours

With Ms Kiroa gone, her students had a free class. The principal had told them to study, and as soon as he left, they had proceeded to have a lively discussion about why Sol Wheat might be helping the police with their inquiries (or busted, as the boys put it).

'This is a symptom of the authoritarian system,' Ube Lamont declared.

'My ass,' said Faisal. 'I bet he's been done for dealing.'

'I've never even seen him *smoking*, let alone dealing,' Cleo responded.

'Not stem, I mean gulp. I bet he's running a still. Or his dad is. His dad's into all sorts of stuff.'

'You don't even know his dad,' one of the other students put in.

'My uncle knows one of the guys his dad works with,' Faisal replied. 'And he says Gregor Wheat's always down in the lower levels. They all are, those daylighters. They work hard and they play hard. I say more power to 'em.'

'Who'd believe what your uncle says?' Ube grunted. 'I've seen him out on the dome platforms on Sundays. He's a Dark-Day Fatalist.'

'So what if he is?' Faisal snapped defensively. 'Doesn't mean he isn't right!'

Cleo listened to the discussion bounce back and forth across the class as Solomon's reputation was remoulded to suit his new place in the criminal fraternity. There was an unmasked respect for his new status as a wanted suspect, but also a malicious glee at the trouble he was facing.

She and Sol had been proper friends once, back when they both did gymnastics. Not childhood sweethearts or anything like that, just two kids who had a good laugh together. But he'd changed after his mother and sister died. These days he was . . . well, he was all right. He just didn't really click with anyone, didn't trust anyone. Which made him all the more mysterious now that he had been busted.

She couldn't help herself, she was dying to know the full story. That didn't mean that she had to take part in this gossiping, though.

'Listen to you, all of you!' she cried out, standing up to get their attention. 'You're like a bunch of old women, the way you're going on! Sol's probably just broken one of the thousands of faggin' rules they stick us with, and they've dragged him off to make an example of him as a warning to the rest of us. It could have been any one of us. They just want everyone to be scared, so we'll behave the way they want us to. It's not about *him*, it's about controlling the way *we live.*'

Some of the others nodded. Many of them felt that their lives were being manipulated by the people in authority. It was a common subject of Cleo's music, and she knew it always touched a nerve. She loved the way they looked at her when she talked like this; with passion and respect in their eyes.

'Look at the way we were cut out of the end-of-year gig,' she continued. 'Why? Because they don't like our music. And why don't they like it? Because when we're singing our songs, we can say what we damn well please. Sol's just the latest victim.'

'Maybe it's not the police at all.' Faisal spoke up. 'Maybe he's been "disappeared" by the Clockworkers.'

'Oh, shut up, Fai. God, you're worse than Ube sometimes.'

There was a lull into silence as the class tried to come up with a new subject for conversation.

'Hey, you said Sol's dad was a daylighter?' somebody piped up.

'Yeah.' Ube sighed.

'Wasn't there a daylighter murdered the other day? Somebody threw him into a piston well. He got all mashed up!'

Suddenly the subject had been reopened, and a new flurry of theories ricocheted around the room. By the time Ms Kiroa had returned with Sol, the image of his father had already been re-formed: a player in the twilight underworld who had crossed the city mafia and earned himself a swim with the pistons. And now his son was carrying his debt, his card marked, his days numbered, his life lived by the ticking of a clock.

When he walked in with Ms Kiroa, the class looked at him with a new-found respect and a profound sympathy.

Solomon circled his father in a clear space on the roof of their building. Barely twelve years old, he was already up to his dad's shoulder, and strong for his age. He had his guard up, chin down, elbows tucked, as he darted back and forth, trying to find an opening in Gregor's guard. Once, this would have been a one-sided game, but his father was having to work now. It was just touch-sparring, and Sol was getting quicker. They weren't wearing gloves, and Gregor's big meaty hands were open and loose. Sol tried a jab, and then an uppercut, but Gregor knocked them away.

'You're too tense,' he told his son. 'It's slowing you down. Loosen up.'

Sol feinted a left hook, and nearly got a right hook to Gregor's temple.

'Better!' said his father, smiling.

They moved around each other, both light on their feet, both relishing the game. Solomon pulled his fist in close to his head, and Gregor's left hand whipped out and slapped his son's right. Sol's hand caught his own temple, and he winced.

'Don't hold your hands too close to your head, especially when you're not using gloves,' Gregor told him. 'They can

hurt you as much as your opponent's can. It's all very well if you're both wearing nice big soft gloves, but with bare knuckles, give yourself space. Got it?'

Sol nodded. He loved this; it was only when they were training that he got to spend time alone with his dad. The flat was so small, he and Nattie were still sharing a room, even though she was fourteen now, and showing far too much interest in boys. Gregor would come home after work and they would have dinner, and he would sit down and browse the web for a while. He might talk to Sol, but it wasn't the same. It was family talk: 'How was school?' or 'What did you get up to today?' And he never talked about his day at work. They didn't ask, either; nobody was very interested in what a crane driver did all day. Sol moved his hands out from his head a little, and they circled for another minute. Then he aimed a touch at Gregor's exposed forehead.

Gregor's head came forward at the same moment, and Sol's knuckles cracked painfully against the bone of his father's brow.

'Ow!'

'Oh, sorry, son. Show me your hand . . .' Gregor examined his knuckles. 'You'll be all right. You have to be careful hitting the forehead — it's the hardest part of the head. You can break your hand on it. In the prize-fights, some of the guys actually head-butt fists to do just that. Maddest thing you ever saw. Come on, let's call it a day. Your mother'd have my guts for garters if you came down with a broke-up hand.'

Putting an arm around his son's shoulders, Gregor steered him towards the stairs.

'Have you ever been in a prize-fight, Dad?' Sol asked.

'Naw, fighting for money's a mug's game, son. You'll always lose more than you gain. Always use your head first; I don't want to hear about you using this stuff in school, you hear me? You only fight when you have to, but you need to know how, and that's why I teach you.'

Sol nodded. He'd already been in a few fights in school, and he'd won them all, but now he thought it would be better if Gregor didn't know about them.

'You have to learn to look after yourself, because nobody's going to do you any favours in this life,' Gregor went on. 'You've got your family, but apart from that, you're on your own. You can't rely on anybody. You should never give your trust freely, Sol. You've got to make people earn it. You hear me?'

'Sure, Dad.'

'That's another thing. Don't let me see you fighting with your sister, either. You nearly gave her a black eye that time in the kitchen.'

Four years later, in Anastacia Kiroa's flat, Solomon lay awake, smiling at the memory. His sister had kicked his backside while he was feeding Tyson, their pet rat. He'd retaliated in an apoplectic rage, hurling punches at her. Natasha – an early student of their father's boxing techniques – had lost her temper in reply, and they'd gone at it in the kitchen, tearing chunks out of each other. Sometimes they just needed to let off some steam. He lay in the bed that folded out of Ana's couch, his mind racing. Mixed in with older recollections were tumbling images of the events of the last few days: the crane accident; the attack in his flat; the interrogation at the police station; and, most of all, his father's crime. Or 'alleged' crime.

Part of him believed it. Gregor got into fights sometimes, he knew that. He took arguments seriously, and he hung around with men who got physical when things didn't go their way. Maybe this one had gone too far; Gregor wouldn't murder somebody, but if that guy, Hyung, had pulled a knife or something, then Gregor might have had no choice. Sol could imagine his father killing under those circumstances, and despite himself he felt a little thrill of excitement at the thought. His father could be a killer. Part of Sol had always wanted that kind of reputation: the reluctant killer. 'I didn't want to kill that man, but it was him or me.' That was what it meant to be hard. And he had always known Gregor was a hard man.

Sol was always a little uneasy sleeping in somebody else's place. It wasn't insecurity; it was the idea of being indebted to somebody. Accepting hospitality meant you weren't going it alone. And going it alone was important to Solomon. He thought of Ana, asleep in her room, and tried not to let his imagination run away with him. It had been awkward earlier in the evening, with her flatmates here. An evening with three teachers. One of them, Candice, was quite cute. Dark, and with a mass of black hair around a lively face. But not as beautiful as Ana. He had hoped he'd be alone with her, but he should have known better.

They were funny, the three women. At first they'd tried to act like teachers, all strict and proper. But being at home was obviously too much for them, and they'd relaxed and changed completely; chatting and making each other giggle. Maybe living with Gregor meant he was only used to a man's world, but really, they were so . . . *girlie*.

He thought back to the time when he'd first seen Ana like that. He'd been out running late one night, and as he passed a nightclub, he'd seen her coming out of the door. She was dressed in a tight short skirt and a white blouse that showed her full figure. She was laughing with friends, all of them sweating from dancing in the hot atmosphere of the club. He had watched them walk away as he hid in the shadows with his hood up. That was the moment when he'd fallen for her.

Memories continued to weave through his mind as he slowly drifted off to sleep. It was Sunday tomorrow. He would go up to the West Dome Depot and talk to some of the people his father worked with. Maybe they would be able to tell him what had happened to Gregor – perhaps one of them was a witness to the fight. Sleep came in an unsettled churning of wrecked machinery and claustrophobic, grey walls. Dark figures silhouetted against his living-room window faded to nothing, but the sense of their presence continued to hang there, long after they were gone.

Section 6/24: Music

Sitting on the edge of her bed in her nightgown, cradling her guitar, Cleo was plucking out a tune that had come to her in her sleep. She struggled to remember it, trying different notes as she sought out the melody. She still had not learned musical notation, so she used a digicorder to record the tune once she had worked it out on the guitar. The lyrics would get written down later, with the chords scrawled above the words. Her sister, Victoria, who shared the room with her, eventually woke at the sound of the experimental notes, turned to look over at her and scowled. She put her face in her arms, covering her ears.

'It's Sunday morning!' she protested. 'Do that somewhere else!'

'Go dangle,' Cleo retorted.

'Stick it up your bum!' Vicky snapped back, with a grin on her face.

'When I'm famous, you're going to have to show me some respect.'

'When you're famous, I'm going to have to *wake you up* and show you you're dreamin'.'

'I'm going to make some breakfast,' Cleo announced, prodding her sister's huddled figure. 'You want some?'

'No, thanks. In case you hadn't noticed, I'm trying to *sleep*!'

Cleo giggled and took her guitar with her, through to the kitchen. Her mother was reading some old book, while her father watched the sports on the web.

'Cleopatra, darling, put on something warm – you'll catch your death,' her mother told her.

'I'm fine, Mum. Is there any water?'

'Yes, it came back on this morning . . . eventually.'

After a breakfast of papery waffles and egg sauce, Cleo sat down on the couch beside her father, humming to herself and searching for the elusive tune on her guitar. Ever since losing the end-of-year gig, she had been playing with some new lyrics. She sang them haltingly as she put the riffs together.

> '*You can stitch my mouth,*
> *Nail my tongue to the table,*
> *I'll keep shouting out,*
> *For as long as I'm able,*
> *You won't shut me up—*

'Damn it!'

The A-string broke with a twang, and she sighed in exasperation. It was her last one.

'Should get a synth one,' her father murmured, referring to the electronic guitar synthesizers, his attention still focused on the basketball.

'It's not the same, Dad,' she told him, for the hundredth time.

'No strings, though,' he replied.

'Well, who'd pay for it, if I did?' she said, and then immediately regretted it.

He had lost his job in Plumbing Maintenance three months previously, in a 'streamlining drive', and had not been able to find more work. Now they lived on her mother's wages from the part-time library job, and his welfare payments. They never had enough money now, and his pride had been hard hit.

'Sorry,' she muttered.

Cleo undid the broken string and wound the two pieces around her fingers, tying them into a coil. She would need to get some more – and there was only one place to do that.

The trams did not descend into the guts of the city. To reach the lowest levels you had to take a tram to a point above your desired destination, and take steps or an elevator down. Cleo preferred the stairs – the elevators were becoming unreliable. From her tram stop, she descended one hundred and fifty-eight steps to Sub-Level Three of the Fourth Quadrant; one of the several levels occupied by the Filipino District.

On the way down, Cleo passed the exposed workings

of the city. Drive-shafts carrying the city's power whirred, causing the steps to tremble beneath her feet; pneumatic shock-absorbers caught much of the vibrations from the engineering, and the heated air was drawn out and along radiators that kept the ambient air temperature at the required level. Pipes wove through the infrastructure, carrying hot water, near-freezing water, steam, or sewage, contaminated air and carbon monoxide as well as methane from the sewers. Heavily insulated electricity cables followed the catwalks and stairs for ease of maintenance. In more concealed areas, Cleo knew, enterprising individuals tapped the lines, drawing illegal power from the city for personal use.

It got dark as she descended. There was little light from the dome down here. Dust grew thicker, with no winds or rain to clear it, and cockroaches thrived. The walls were thick in the sub-levels: load-bearing reinforced concrete and denceramic architecture. Ash Harbour's most abundant mammal, the rat, had made its home in the countless nooks and crannies. Cleo had learned once in history that the rat had conquered the world right alongside mankind. If the elements won out, rats, not humans, would be the last mammal to die. And the cockroaches would be around a long time after that.

Ash Harbour was in what had once been the South Pacific, before most of the ocean had become a vast plain of pack ice. The Philippines had been one of the last refuges of the Old World as the city was built, and the Filipinos had wielded a huge amount of influence in the last years before people moved in. As the richer countries slowly became frozen wastelands, Southeast Asia had found itself host to its more affluent neighbours, and when the rich and the influential booked their places in Ash Harbour's safe confines, the workers who had built it begged, bribed, bargained and cheated their way in. Many, many more were turned away by force of arms.

In the years that followed, many of those who had been rich on the outside used up what they had to trade, and affluence took on a new shape: those who could affect the running of the city's machinery. But there were still many thousands who had come in on the bottom rung and were forced to stay there. The majority were Filipino, and their culture dominated the sub-levels of the Fourth Quadrant. Of all the cultures that had taken refuge in Ash Harbour, only the Pinoy, as they called themselves, had managed to keep a semblance of their original culture. They had also established a new one; the bulk of the black market in Ash Harbour was run by Filipino gangs, and that was what had drawn Cleo to this area on a Sunday morning.

The Filipino District was her favourite place in the whole city. The same smells always hit her as she drew near: dust, grilled fish, spices and closely packed people. An eclectic mix of stalls and arcades filled the collection of alleys and streets before her, all under the roof of the heavy machinery above. Near the bottom of the steps she spotted a tortoise wandering among the feet of the crowd. She bent down to pick it up, and brought it with her along the street.

The place always seemed to be loud, as if business went on day and night. Cortez's store was a small, incredibly cluttered stall on Sub-Level Three. It was filled with all manner of merchandise, from handmade toys to fertility cures. A webscreen sat on the counter, with a pornographic animated screensaver cycling through a lewd liaison. Behind the counter, a mountainous Pinoy man with a scarred face sat, dozing fitfully. Cleo knew there would be other, more watchful sentries nearby.

Cortez himself was a chubby man in his sixties, who wore old-fashioned half-moon glasses, and dressed as if he were always cold. This morning he had a woman's shawl draped over his shoulders, and a thick cotton hat on his balding head. His flat, wide face split into a smile when he saw Cleo and he stood up from his little stool.

'Ahhh! Little Cleo, come to warm an old man's heart! *Mabúhay!* Come in, come in!' He turned to a little girl with a small mouth and big eyes who was hugging the frame of the door that led to the back room. 'Gátas! Bring some tea for our guest. Be quick now!'

Cleo knew better than to refuse the tea, although she did not want to stay long.

'Morning, Cortez,' she said confidently. 'I'm looking for some strings.'

'Of course, of course.' He waved at her to slow down, as if she were in danger of hurting herself if she spoke any faster. 'All in good time. First, you have to tell me how you've been. Ahh! And you've found Mayon! Good girl, you know what he's like, eh?'

Mayon was the name of Cortez's tortoise. He was always wandering out of the store and into the street. Somebody always found him and brought him back. Everyone knew Cortez's tortoise – he was the safest creature in the Filipino District.

'Now,' Cortez said, putting Mayon on the floor, from where the tortoise immediately set off on another expedition, 'I haven't seen you in an age. You've grown since you were last here!'

Given that it had only been about a month since her last visit, Cleo thought that unlikely, but she smiled gratefully. She reluctantly took a stool beside him and asked how business was. He always had her make some conversation when she came, and she suspected that he harboured some romantic ideas about her. Or maybe he was just a friendly old man.

'Life is always the same down here, in the depths,' Cortez told her. 'We wait for visitors to brighten our day. Tell me, how is young Estella? Such a sweet girl.'

Estella was a Filipino hippy-chick that Cleo had gone out with for a while, just to see what it was like. She had needled Cleo constantly to give up the gulp and the stem and, for the love of God, to please stay away from Cortez. Cleo had broken it off, deciding that she only needed one mother, and anyway, she was definitely more attracted to boys. But they had stayed friends.

'She's fine,' she replied. 'Feisty as ever.'

Cortez nodded.

'And your family? How are they?'

'Very well, thank you.' Cleo was wary of telling him too much about her family. She certainly didn't want him to know that her father was out of a job.

The little girl, Gátas, came in with two mugs of fragrant jasmine tea. Cortez could provide the best of everything, for a price. But he took hospitality seriously. Cleo took a mug and breathed in the fine aroma. Gátas handed the other cup to Cortez and then returned to her position, hugging the door frame and watching the new arrival. Cleo smiled at her, but the girl did not return the gesture, merely looking the other way, into the storeroom.

'I'm looking for some guitar strings,' Cleo urged Cortez gently. 'I'm completely out of As, and I'm running low on Ds too. Do you have any?'

'Not here, at the moment,' he replied, taking a sip of his tea. 'But one of my boys can fetch some. Quiroz, down the way, looks after my musical supplies. Just a moment.'

Without moving from his chair, he shouted into the storeroom, rattling off some Tagalog at an unseen person inside. A tired, overworked voice replied, and there was the sound of a door opening and closing.

'It'll just be a few minutes,' Cortez assured her. 'How is the music coming along?'

'Great,' she responded, warming to her favourite subject. 'I'm working on a new song now. The band's really coming together . . . We were lined up for the end-of-year ball, but the principal pulled us.'

'That's terrible! How could he turn down such an excellent band?'

To the best of her knowledge, Cortez had never heard her play, but it was nice of him to say it.

'The sponsor, Internal Climate, said our lyrics were inflammatory.'

'Aren't young people's lyrics *supposed* to be inflammatory?'

Cleo beamed, despite herself.

'Is there anything else you'd like, while you're here?' he asked. 'Some stem perhaps?'

Cleo shook her head, thanking him with a smile. She didn't have enough money for both the strings and the drugs. Sipping the hot tea, she tried not to think of her dwindling supply of stem at home, hidden up on the roof of the apartment block.

'Is it the money?' he persisted. 'I could give you some on credit.'

'No, thank you.'

Estella said that Cortez was no small-time hustler. Cleo knew that his little store was just a front for his black-market operation. But even that was only the tip of Cortez's personal iceberg. Estella claimed that Cortez was head of the Fourth Quadrant Family, the gang that ran most of the Filipino District. The two short sticks he kept by his chair had a purpose; Cortez was a master of eskrima, the Philippine art of stick fighting, and was rumoured to have battled his way through a hundred street fights to the top of the gang in his youth. It was not a good idea to be in debt to a man like that. He shrugged, giving her a flat grin.

'It's there if you want it,' he said.

The door in the back of the store opened and closed again, and a young man came out to the front. He had some guitar strings in his hand, but leaned down to whisper something in Cortez's ear. The old man nodded, took the strings and dismissed him.

'I'm afraid I'm going to have to leave you, my dear,' he told her. 'Here are your strings. Let's call it twelve credits, if you please.'

She handed him three plastic five-credit coins, and he opened his till to give her change. As he put the money in her hand, she felt a small rice-paper bag folded around the coins. Without opening it, she knew it would be a 'sample' of the flaky brown powder her friends coveted. She was always able to impress them with her street contacts. Before she could half-heartedly refuse, Cortez was up, tucking his sticks under his arm and moving to the back door.

'Give my respects to your family,' he told her,

knowing she wouldn't. 'I'm sorry I have to rush off, but duty calls. I'll see you again soon, Cleo.'

And he knew he would.

Cleo decided to take the elevator back up to the lowest tram level. She should not have taken the stem. That was a mistake. She had to come here for the strings – metal was a precious resource in Ash Harbour, and non-essential items like guitar strings could only be had on the black market. But taking the stem without paying for it was a bad move. Now she was in Cortez's debt.

The first elevator she tried was out of order. So was the next. And the next one after that. Heaving a sigh, she found a flight of stairs and started climbing. When she came to the first walkway, she looked out on the level she had just left. Something was wrong. Water was pouring down the main street, washing around the ankles of the people, causing them to stumble for higher ground; a dirty, foamy water that had some kind of debris floating in it. One of the drainage pipes in the levels above must have burst. As she watched, the electric lights of the stalls flickered and went out. The water had knocked out the electricity supply. Only the gaslights remained, giving the area a haunting glow. All around her, murky, mechanical shadows swallowed up the sparse light.

'God Almighty,' she breathed. 'What the hell's happening to this city?'

* * *

Solomon looked down on the city from the elevator. White light burned down from the dome, its hexagonal lattice of girders casting a delicate web-like shadow over the cityscape. The daylighters would be on normal maintenance duty, with no snow and ice to clear. That would mean they'd be in a more welcoming mood, and more likely to help him find answers. He knew how Gregor felt about the ice. To him, it was a bitter adversary – one he respected, but hated with a passion. The workers would scrape the dome clear one day, and the next day the ice would be back. If it was just the freezing air, it would start as a feathery coating that would grow slowly, like a rock-hard fungus. But a blizzard could bury the glass in snow in a matter of hours. And when the temperatures had risen back to a manageable level – say, around -70°C on a good day – the daylighters would get back out there to clean it off once more, and give Ash Harbour what little sun there was to be had.

The depot where his father worked was relatively quiet. There were a few men in the workshops where the tools were fixed or recycled, and a couple of people in the canteen. But the man he was looking for was on the exit floor. The highest area on the west wall of the city, this was where the men and women went up through the airlock to the outside skin of the dome. Harley Wasserstein was a huge man, with a full, white-blond beard of curly hair that helped compensate for his polished cranium. Two wings of curls rose up on either side of his bald pate, giving him a comical appearance that alleviated his otherwise fearsome stature. Sol was an avid watcher of wildlife documentaries; all those films of animals that no longer existed. For him, Wasserstein was a polar bear in human form.

He sat on a bench, having just come down from the job. His safesuit was pulled down to his waist, and he had taken off the fleece he wore underneath to cool his huge, sweating torso. Hard labour under direct sunlight on glass could heat you up despite the Arctic temperatures. Around him, the twenty-nine men and women of his team were stripping off and changing back into normal clothes. Shovels, picks and barrows and other tools sat neatly in racks; heat-hoses lay coiled on their rigs, and pneumatic charges were packed against the wall.

Sol stole a glance at the webscreen that showed the weather conditions outside. The outside temperature – without wind chill – read $-85°C$. Positively balmy. In weather like this the daylighters from the four depots could clear nearly half the dome in a day. In an ice storm, the temperature could drop to $-180°C$ or more. Even in a safesuit, a man could freeze solid in minutes. Harley waved wearily to Sol, beckoning him over.

'Come about your dad, I expect,' he boomed. 'We haven't seen 'im. You any idea where he might be?'

Sol shook his head.

'I was hoping you could tell me. You know he's . . . They've accused him—'

80

'Don't you mind that crap.' Harley grimaced. 'A heap o' mouthgrease, that is. There's no way Gregor killed Tommy. Hold on there while I change and we'll go down to the canteen. I need to get some food in me.'

The food hall was filling up, and the background sound of voices meant Harley and Sol had to speak loudly to be heard even across the table. The room had a low ceiling, and the busy kitchen gave the air a warm, damp quality. The smell of cooking oil, fish, onions and overcooked vegetables pervaded everything. The walls, once white, were a seedy yellow.

'Haven't seen your dad since Wednesday,' Harley said, over a large plate piled high with vegetables and steamed carp, fresh from the fish farm. 'We were out on the glass, and he just up and left. Didn't even tell me he was going, simply unhitched his safety line and slid down to the airlock. He's never done that before. Your dad's a reliable man – one of my best. Tommy was working nearby; he saw your old man take off and followed after him. Something must have got Gregor worked up, but I couldn't tell you what. That was the last time I saw either of them.'

'Didn't you go after them, to find out what was going on?'

'Sure I did. You don't cut out in the middle of a job. Not on my watch. But by the time I got in, they were both gone. Just dumped their gear where they came in and skedaddled.'

He shovelled some fish into his mouth, chewing as he talked.

'It's just not like your old man to do that, Sol. I mean, he's got his interests outside work, you know . . .' He looked anxiously across the table.

'I know about the gambling,' Sol told him.

'Right, well, that's his own business, y'know? It's never got in the way before. But if this is down to some debt or somethin'. . .'

Sol thought about the betting slips he had found in his father's room.

'I don't know,' he said quietly.

His mind turned to the man Gregor was supposed to have killed.

'What kind of man was this guy, Hyung?' he asked. 'Was he into gambling?'

'Tommy?' Harley looked up at the ceiling. 'Not sure. Didn't know him too well; he was fairly new. Bit of a tough guy, I think. Kept to himself, mostly. He and your dad got on well, though. When the two of them ran off at the same time like that, I just assumed Tommy was going after Gregor to see what was wrong.'

Sol nodded.

'Where were you working?' he asked. 'When they cut out?'

'Third Quadrant, halfway up the grid.' Harley stuck a whole potato in his mouth. 'Didn't see where he actually stopped. It'll be on his marker. Go on up and have a look if you want.'

Sol thanked him and got up to leave. Harley reached across and grabbed his arm. His huge hand made Sol's upper arm look like an infant's.

'Sol, if you know where he is – or if you find him – tell him to come to me if he's in trouble. I'll see 'im right. It doesn't matter what he's done. Debts can be settled, y'know? There's no need for him to get hurt over money.'

'Yeah, thanks, Harley,' Sol replied. 'Appreciate it. But, to be honest, I just want to know what's happened to him. It's drivin' me nuts, not knowing.'

The big man nodded, staring into Sol's face.

'You need any help, just ask.'

Then he turned his attention back to his meal. Sol left the canteen and went up to the changing room. Punching up his father's marker programme on the webscreen, he entered Gregor's password, 'Southpaw', and brought up the last record. It showed a stylized display of the dome, and his father's path across it on the Wednesday afternoon. It stopped at section D63 in the Third Quadrant. It meant nothing to him. He used the cursor to turn the display so that the image of the dome spun around, showing all 360 degrees of the structure. It didn't tell him anything.

He logged out and sat down on the nearest bench. This was starting to get him down. A thought occurred to him, and he stood up and walked over to his father's locker. Tapping in the combination, he opened it and looked inside. It was in a state. Things had been thrown in – clothes, boots and hats were stuffed in as if in a rush.

The old books that Gregor read while he was on standby had been crushed in at the back, their pages crumpled. Solomon took one out, straightening it up and smoothing the pages. It was a real paper book. A copy of *A Clockwork Orange*. There were a couple of his other favourites in here too: *The Name of the Rose* and *Nineteen Eighty-Four*. Sol was shocked at the way they had been creased. Gregor would never have done this, not in a million years. And he never left his locker in this kind of disarray. It went against his very nature to make a mess like this. Somebody else had been through his things. Sol examined the lock, but it showed no signs of having been forced. Maybe Harley had put some of Gregor's gear back in, making the mess in the process, but Sol already knew what had happened.

The men who had turned their flat over had gone through the locker as well, he was sure of it. Sol smoothed out the books and put them carefully back on the shelf, placing a heavy box of loose nuts and bolts on top of them to help flatten the pages. Closing the locker, he tested the door, but it was shut tight. Whoever these men were, they had no problem with combination locks. Sol strode out of the depot, following a walkway that skirted the rim of the crater, just below the dome's base. From here he could see clear across the city. The four huge tower cranes from each of the four quadrants were moving, their various arms swinging loads with delicate precision. On the massive gantries that stretched across the top of the city, smaller cranes swept along rails and, above them, he could see people gathering on the sun platforms. Pigeons wheeled in among them.

These platforms offered the best exposure to the cherished daylight, and a lottery decided who would get the opportunity to spend a few sweet hours on the public spaces. Sometimes they were even used by thrill-seekers for base-jumping with home-made parachutes. Not all the chutes worked.

The government was being forced to sell these platforms off as it struggled with the higher costs of running the public services. Most of the platforms were privately owned now. The one closest to him was one of these; it belonged to the Dark-Day Fatalists. He gazed up at the dark-clad figures in disdain. Every Sunday they gathered to offer prayers up to the elements. He didn't know an awful lot about them, but the gist of their philosophy seemed to be that the Machine was an abomination, that nature would win out, and Ash Harbour was just postponing the inevitable. The platforms had railings, but some of the more despairing DDF members would use the height to make a final, dramatic statement – by throwing themselves off the edges of the platforms. Prices for property directly below DDF platforms tended to be lower than average.

In fact, high falls had become such a popular choice for anybody committing suicide that police had taken to routinely questioning anybody on the upper levels. The DDF maintained that they did not encourage people to take their own lives. But there were those who said that when the Fatalists gathered up on those platforms, they prayed for a disaster that would split open the dome and destroy life in the city. There were always rumours about what the DDF did in their secret sanctums. Some said that they even started false rumours themselves, to give their movement an air of mystery.

Sol just thought they were a sad bunch of losers.

He watched them for a little while longer, then shook his head and walked towards the nearest elevator. The only threat the DDF posed was the damage caused by their falling bodies.

Section 7/24: Corpses

Cleo stopped and looked back the way she had come. In the dim light from the gas lamps, all the walkways looked the same. In front of her, the path forked off in three different directions. None of them seemed to lead upwards. Biting her lip, she looked back again. She was lost. Somewhere nearby, a bank of pistons pumped away, and all around her was the rubbery stink of cats' pee. There were thousands of strays in the city. Seeing a reflective sign with grid numbers on it, she walked up to it, staring at the numbers and trying to work out where she was. But she was no good with the grid system; she needed street names and buildings to find her way around. Even if she could see the dome, it would help. But there was just the damp, musky darkness.

Off to her left, she heard the sound of voices. The left-hand walkway led into a corridor that would take her in that direction. She put her hand in her pocket, her fingers closing around the little canister of pepper spray. This was a rough part of the city, and people were known to disappear down here in the darker sections. A young girl lost in the works would be an easy victim for the kinds of cut-throats who hunted in the shadows. But she could wander around the lower levels for days if she didn't find her way up. Fervently wishing there was more light, she gripped the pepper spray and edged forward towards the dark corridor.

The corridor led out onto an observation balcony that looked down on the level below, three lines of large sewage-treatment tanks. Two men and a woman were dressed in sewage workers' overalls with tool belts and head torches, and were manhandling a large bundle towards the intake hopper of a grinding rig – its massive wheels used to crush any solids in the system into slurry. Cleo crouched down close to the floor, her gaze glued to the scene below her. The more she looked at it, the more the indistinct bundle seemed to have a decidedly *body*-shaped appearance.

They heaved the body over the edge and into the hopper. One of the men – a ghostly-looking man with white hair, white skin and pale eyes – slapped the big button to start the machine. It didn't start. He pressed the button again. Nothing. They all leaned over the edge to look down into the bottom of the hopper.

'It's not faggin' working,' he announced.

'Do ya think?' the woman said sarcastically. She was an Oriental with the grey pallor of somebody who rarely saw daylight. 'I can *see* it's not working! We'll have to try another one.'

'How we going to get it out of there?' the white man asked.

'You're going to have to go down there and get it.'

'The hell I am. I've seen what happens to bodies in that thing. Human jam, that's what you get – bolognese. If you want to get it out, you go down there!'

'You turn it off again first, you grit!' the woman snapped. 'Now get your ass down there and get that faggin' thing up here before somebody sees us!'

'And what if it's the switch that's faulty?' he retorted. 'I could get down there, it turns on, and suddenly I'm bolognese. I'm not doing it—'

Cleo shuffled further back from the edge . . . and the balcony creaked beneath her. Suddenly the shouting stopped. She pulled her head away from the edge, but it was too late.

'There's somebody up there!' she heard the woman bark.

'Damn it!' another voice spat. 'How long do you think they were there?'

'It doesn't matter. They saw us here, they'll be able to identify us when news breaks about the job. Split up – find them!'

Nothing more was said. Soft footsteps took off in either direction along the catwalk leading off the platform. Cleo crawled back into the corridor and stood up, her pulse throbbing through her body, her limbs trembling. She continued to stand there, frozen against the wall, while her mind tried to make sense of what was happening.

'Run,' she whispered to herself, willing herself to move. 'They're coming. Run!'

Almost as if she needed a push, she shoved herself off the wall and set off at a sprint. She had to assume that, whoever they were, they knew their way around. They would find a route up to her, and then . . . She didn't want to think about it. It didn't matter who they were. All that mattered was that they were after her, and they dumped bodies in sewage grinders.

Her footsteps were painfully loud, echoing down the narrow corridor, signalling to her hunters. She slowed down, softening her footfalls. The route along which she had come was too long and straight; if they had guns, they could shoot her from a hundred metres away. What she needed were some corners. Off one branch of the corridor, she spotted a ladder beside a guttering gas lamp. Hurrying up to it, she grabbed the rungs and started to climb. Stopping for a moment, she reached over and turned the valve on the lamp, switching it off. Maybe now they wouldn't see the ladder, and at least she could climb in darkness.

Running footsteps approached below, and she winced as the ladder squeaked with every rung she climbed. The footsteps slowed and advanced more carefully. All around her was pitch-darkness. To her right, she could feel the breeze from a ventilation duct. Cleo went completely still as somebody reached the bottom of the ladder. A torch was switched on and the beam played across the floor of the corridor below her, then found the foot of the ladder. It swept upwards, but stopped just short of her shoes. Then it shone away and down the corridor. In its glow she could see a white face, white hair and the dull shine of a grey gun barrel. The man began to move away, but then he sniffed at the air and turned back. He felt the body of the gas lamp, and pulled his hand away quickly. It was still hot. His torchlight came back up the ladder, and this time it found Cleo.

His gun came up, and as it did so, she jumped out into the darkness. The shot came as a dull thumping sound, not loud at all. The bullet hitting the ladder was louder, spitting sparks at her. Her knees scraped off the top of the ventilation duct and she nearly fell over the other side, but caught herself in time. Clambering along the top of the duct, every movement amplified by the hollow plastex, she tried to find another way out. The man was coming up the ladder behind her. She couldn't see a thing, and nearly fell again when the duct turned tightly to the right, and then left again. There was a ceiling a little more than a metre above her, holding the struts for the duct, but it was too low for her to stand up. She kept casting out with her hands on either side for some way off the vent, but there was nothing but empty space on either side. Then she hit a wall.

It was solid concrete. The duct went straight into it, without so much as a finger's width of a gap around it. There was no way to get into the vent; plastex was tough, made to last for centuries. She stifled a cry of despair. The man was coming along the duct after her. Reaching out into the darkness, she sought some kind of escape. But there was nothing. The sound of the man approaching grew louder, and she could see the torch strapped to his head, bobbing as he crawled. It was pointing down, so that he could see where he was putting his hands. Her mind grasped at something, a faint hope. With the torch pointing downwards, he couldn't see anything above him. She reached back quietly and felt the nearest struts that hung from the ceiling. There was a bar crossing between them. It was strong enough to hold her. With painstaking care, she silently lifted herself up onto the bar, getting her stomach up and over it. The man was getting closer. Gripping the struts on either side, she balanced herself on her stomach and straightened out her body, lifting her head and feet as high as she could. The pressure of the bar on her abdomen was almost unbearable.

The man's light came closer, closer, until he was crawling by underneath her. He saw the wall ahead of him and stopped. With his bigger body, he moved with difficulty along the duct and, when he turned to look behind him, he had to hold onto the edges to keep his balance. The bar dug into Cleo's stomach, and she held her breath until it felt like her lungs would burst.

The man was still looking down at the surface ahead of him. Taking one hand off the duct, he leaned back on his knees so that he could look up. For an instant their eyes met and Cleo did the only thing she could. She swung her legs down and kicked out at him with all her might.

One of her feet caught his head, and he toppled forward. His gun fell clattering into the darkness and, for a second, she thought he would follow it, but he caught the bottom of the strut and hung on, dangling below her. Her balance gone, she fell back onto the top of the vent. The man was starting to climb back up, with murder written on his face. Pulling the pepper spray from her pocket, she gave him a long blast in the eyes and he roared in pain, pulling his head away. She tore the torch from his head, and fell back on her side. In desperation, she kicked at his fingers, hammering at them with her feet until his grip failed and he fell with a scream into the gloom. Somewhere below, there was a muffled thud.

She listened for a while, but heard nothing more. He could be dead. If he was, she wasn't sure what to do. Her whole body was shaking, but she knew she mustn't lose her head now. There was still enough spray in the air to make her eyes water and her nose itch, but she was too wound up to care. Strapping the torch onto her head, she made her way carefully back along the duct, making as little noise as possible. There was no sign of anybody else. When she got close to the ladder, she turned off the torch and slid along on her belly. Waiting as long as she dared, she listened intently for any sound of the others, but there was nothing. Climbing out onto the rungs, she scaled up to a catwalk that was illuminated by electric lights. Sounds carried down it: voices in conversation, whirring flywheels, music and noise from computer games.

It was a pedal station. People. Normal, chatty, ordinary, unarmed people. Wiping her watering eyes, she sniffed back a running nose and smiled in relief as she walked into the hall where nearly three dozen people were sitting astride cycling machines, pedalling power into the city's system. Collapsing on a rest couch, she buried her face in her knees, comforted by the drab, dull familiarity of it all.

Sol was on a tram, making his way back to Ana's and pondering his next move. He knew a few of the places his father went gambling, but he was wary of visiting any of them if Gregor really had run up a big debt. If his father were in hiding, as it seemed, then giving the hoods who were hunting him his son as a hostage probably wouldn't be a smart move.

He thought back to that cop, Mercier, and wondered what he knew. But it was the other one who was in charge. Ponderosa, from the ISS. Sol decided that if these were the men investigating his father, he should find out what he could about them. The tram was stopping near a café, so he jumped off and went inside.

He bought a green tea and took the nearest available webscreen, where he did a search on Ponderosa. The only information on him was his list of awards; it was impressive. The single picture of him was one where he was shaking hands with Mayor Haddad as she presented him with a medal for Distinguished Service. There was nothing else recorded about him. That figured – the ISS probably kept their files locked up nice and tight. Your business was their business, but their business was their own.

Mercier scored a direct match, though. His past came up, displayed in text files and compressed images. There was nothing remarkable about him; his career had been mediocre, judging by the few medals and awards he had received. The detective had progressed through the ranks at a steady plod, and the file confirmed that he was now working at the Criminal Investigation Section. There was nothing more of interest. Sol decided to check his mail while he was online, and his father's too.

His inbox reflected his loner lifestyle. There was a single new message highlighted; he didn't recognize the address. It looked like a one-off send, the kind people used to remain anonymous. Opening it, he found a short note:

Sol. There are people looking for you – don't go back to the flat. Don't go out alone, stay among people. You mustn't try to find me, it's too dangerous, but I'm sending someone to

keep an eye on you. So you know who he is, he will be able
to tell you your mother's favourite song. You can trust him.
Gregor.

Solomon looked around warily. Memorizing the
address, just in case, he quickly deleted the message
and closed down the mailbox. He was standing up to
leave when the screen suddenly flashed white, and
words in large, black block capitals began to float into
view. At first he thought this was being aimed directly
at him, but all around the café people were giving
exclamations of surprise or disgust. The message was
appearing on every screen: THE MACHINE IS DYING, it
read. IT IS BEING EATEN FROM WITHIN. DO YOU CARE
ENOUGH TO ASK WHY?

Sol looked out of the windows of the café, and saw
that the same message was on the adscreens on the
street outside. That meant it must be all over the city.
Then, all at once, it flickered and was gone. Another
message appeared, this one a standard screen-card from
the Online Police with the city's crest; accompanied
by an authoritative voice, it informed everybody that
the city's web systems had just been subject to a virus
attack. Normal service would be resumed presently,
and the culprits would be tracked down and
prosecuted.

In a machine city co-ordinated by computers,
viruses were a big deal. Anybody caught writing or
sending them could expect a long stretch in prison.

96

The Online Police could shut down whole sections of the city in search of a suspect, if they needed to. It made the illegally posted message all the more intriguing. What did it mean, Sol thought: 'being eaten from within'? Hitching his bag onto his shoulder, he made for the tram stop.

Ana was in the apartment when he got back, making a lunch of spirulina pie and promeat. She had made enough for him, and he mumbled his thanks as he took the plate. Avoiding his over-attentive gaze, she coughed and sat down on the couch with her own food.

'The funeral for the two men in the crane accident is tomorrow,' she told him. 'I thought you and the others might want to go.'

Sol nodded. He didn't care much about the men who had been killed, and he had hated the Earth Centre ever since his mother's and sister's funeral; but he might be able to find out more about what had caused the accident to help put his mind at rest. The image of the smashed crane carriage was still fresh, and the incident niggled at him like a maths problem he couldn't work out, turning over and over in his brain without ever making any sense.

'The police were on too,' she added quietly. 'They want to speak to you again. Properly this time. I'll go with you. We can do it after the funeral.'

'Was it the CIS?' he asked.

'ISS. That man, Ponderosa.'

Solomon picked at his food, but he couldn't taste it. It was like sand in his mouth.

The funeral procession was long, stretching back along the street. One man had been Muslim, the other Unitarian, and so there had been two separate services, but the bodies were carried in the same procession through the streets to the Earth Centre. It was the tradition in Ash Harbour for those who died together to be recycled together.

Sol walked alongside Ana, careful to keep a discreet distance. His feelings for her had been getting steadily stronger since moving in with her, and sleeping just one room away from her was driving his imagination wild.

The open-topped hearse pulled up to the steps of the Earth Centre, and each coffin was taken on the shoulders of six men up the steps to the hall. At the end of the hall, past the rows of seats, was a conveyor belt leading through some curtains. Behind the curtain was a hatch. The hatch opened into the inner workings of the centre. The coffins were placed on the conveyor, and everyone took their seats. The lighting was in atmospheric spots, pitched perfectly for the sombre air of the place. The families were up at the front, and one widow was weeping inconsolably. In the high-roofed hall, her cries had a horrible, distant, hollow sound that made Sol think of a soul lost beyond reach.

The Earth Centre was made of concrete and soil. Placed in aesthetically pleasing formations along the reinforced concrete wall, clear plastex panels held large sections of deep brown earth; such a precious thing now that permafrost had rendered the soil in the outside world virtually lifeless. It was a reminder that bodies had always been given back to the earth; an attempt to make recycling more palatable. Corpses had to be recycled; nothing could be wasted in Ash Harbour.

The Master of Ceremonies said a few profound words that Solomon paid no attention to, and then the sound system started to play some piece of classical music – non-denominational, of course – and the coffins began to creep towards the curtain. They brushed through the parting and disappeared. The widow let out a long, sorrowful wail. Sol heard children crying in that helpless, confused way that they do around death. He got up and left before the crowd could begin making its way to the door. Behind the curtain, he knew, the bodies would be removed from the coffins. Those coffins would be used again before the day was out.

Out on the steps, he found Cleo sitting and smoking a joint of stem, holding it hidden in her cupped hand. She glanced back at him, licked her finger and thumb and hurriedly put it out, slipping it into her pocket.

'You're supposed to wait for the Master of Ceremonies to lead everyone out,' she told him. 'There's a piece of music they're supposed to play—'

'Don't like crowds,' he replied.

Cleo sniffed and nodded.

'Why aren't you inside?' he asked.

'Don't like funerals.'

He sat down beside her; she didn't seem to object.

'I can't get that day out of my head,' he said to her. 'I thought this would help.'

'Me too. Still couldn't go inside, though – it would do my head in. You think too much about where we are and where we're going, and the Dark-Day Fatalists start to make sense, y'know?'

Sol smiled, and then was struck by a memory of something his father had said once: *Sometimes, Sol, when things get really bad, I think they might have a point. They seem to have more peace than the rest of us. Maybe they really do have some of the answers.*

'Might be worth checking out,' he murmured to himself.

'What?' Cleo frowned at him.

'Nothing. Just talkin' to myself. Haven't been right in the head lately.'

'That'll be all the boxing.'

Sol's face darkened.

'You're one to talk, smokin' your brains out with that crap—'

Cleo held her hands up in defence.

'Sorry, sorry. Jeez, you take things seriously.'

Sol sighed. He had never been good about taking needling from girls. He didn't get much trouble from guys; not because he'd belt anyone who had a go – which he wouldn't, not since he'd left primary school – more because they respected the fact that he could.

'It's been a rough week,' he said apologetically. 'I'm a bit on edge. It just seems to be one thing after another . . .'

His sentence drifted to an end as he saw the Filipino man who was coming up the steps towards them. The Pinoy stopped in front of them and looked down at Sol. Sol immediately knew that this was a hard man. His shoulders bulged into his jacket, and his frame looked as if someone had packed a hundred kilos of muscle into a sixty-kilo body. The jacket looked baggy enough to hide weapons. Sol had been expecting someone like this to show up sooner or later. He thought of the gun sitting in his school bag, back in Ana's flat. It hadn't seemed right to bring it with him to the funeral. He self-consciously touched his broken nose.

'Solomon Wheat?' the man asked.

'Yes.'

'I'm looking for your old man.'

'Join the queue. I don't know where he is.'

'Word is that he's wanted for murder.'

'That's the word all right. Funny how it gets around.'

Sol was looking at the man's hands. The knuckles were misshapen with scars, but the man's face looked like it had never been touched. They were telling signs to a fighter. The man noticed how he was staring, and raised the backs of his open hands in front of Sol's face.

'He owes my boss money. He made a foolish wager, and now it is time for him to pay up. If I have to use you to get that money, I will. Do you understand? You do understand, don't you?'

Sol nodded, his mouth suddenly dry.

'Good. I'll find you again soon. Have a think, make a few calls if you like. Know where your father is before I find you again. Understand?'

Sol nodded again.

'Good.'

The man gave a stiff bow to Cleo and turned and walked back down the steps.

'How come he threatens me, and you get a faggin' bow?' Sol gasped, not realizing he had been holding his breath.

Cleo shrugged.

'Suppose even a debt collector can have manners.'

She had an expression of genuine sympathy on her face. There were enough people in her block in debt to gambling dens and moneylenders. Many of them lived in fear of a knock on the door late at night; there was nowhere to run in Ash Harbour if you owed money to the wrong people.

Section 8/24: Fugitives

Cleo sat in her local library, staring at the webscreen. After her close call in the lower levels the previous day, she had been watching the news for any reports of missing people in that area. She had not dared to tell anyone yet, in case the killers came looking for her. The one she had knocked off the ventilation duct could well have seen her face. Which would only be a problem if he were still alive. She didn't want to face the thought that he might not be.

There was nothing on the news reports about any murders. Feeling a little disappointed, she went to log off. But her search for news in that area had turned up one interesting snippet: BURST DRAINAGE TANK CAUSES FLOOD IN FILIPINO DISTRICT, the headline read. And then in smaller type below it: DRAINAGE WORKER MISSING — FEARED DROWNED.

Remembering the scummy water that had flowed down the streets the day before, she scanned down through the article. The flood had caused the electricity substation to shut down; that explained the power cuts she had experienced down there. There was little information on the female worker who was missing. The woman had been working in the area where the tank had burst. They were still clearing the flood debris, and a search was underway for her body.

Cleo finished reading and idly searched for more on the accident. What was it one of them had said before they all came after her? *They'll be able to identify us when news breaks about the job.* She wondered if the 'job' had had anything to do with the flood . . . or the woman going missing. She remembered too what Ube had said. If you messed with the Machine, the Clockworkers would come for you. There seemed to have been a lot of accidents happening recently. Maybe they weren't accidents at all. Putting her fingertips to the webscreen, she thought about the crane wreck. It was still giving her nightmares. Could these 'accidents' be the work of saboteurs? And did that mean that the Clockworkers were taking action? Stepping in to do away with those who interfered with the workings of the Machine?

Whoever they were, whatever was going on, it was way beyond her. She had homework to do and songs to write. Worrying about saboteurs and assassins was not on the school curriculum, and she had no wish to disappear. Cleo knew there were times when the wisest thing to do was to mind your own business. She logged off, and went to find her friends.

★　　★　　★

Sol regarded the body with a queasy feeling of nausea, and decided there and then that if he should ever consider suicide, jumping from a great height would not be the method he'd choose.

Standing with his father on the street, far below the DDF platform from which the man had fallen, he looked around at the crowd that was gathering. Everybody wanted to see the corpse. A fall from two hundred metres up was a pretty certain way of offing yourself, Solomon mused. But some vain part of him would object to what happened to his body when it hit. Pills were iffy – you could vomit them up and end up surviving, but then die slowly from liver damage. And hanging or drowning or slashing your wrists just sounded agonizing. But looking at this man's body, he definitely ruled out throwing himself from the top levels.

He knew from boxing how the skin could split under impact, that blood could splash as the flesh burst under pressure, but he'd never seen it on such a scale before. The man's body had been reduced to jelly by the impact, the bones completely shattered. The abdomen had exploded across the surface of the street, spewing organs and blood like the contents of a water balloon. Most of the organs were pulp, the intestines strung out like tangled spaghetti. Sol had had no idea there were so many colours in the human body; oranges and yellows, purples and blues. All now exposed to the sunlight, spread wide over the roadway.

'Look at the clothes . . . his hair,' Gregor said in a low voice. 'He was just a boy. It just got too much for him.'

They both looked up at the platform, high overhead.

Suicide was becoming increasingly common. Even the city's policy on birth control – only two children per family – had been suspended because of the sheer numbers of premature deaths over recent years. The DDF claimed it was all a symptom of the people's growing despair. They claimed that the authorities were in denial, that the Machine's days were numbered.

'Nutters,' Sol snorted. 'Stupid nutters.'

'No, don't think like that.' Gregor shook his head. 'Just because you don't understand somebody doesn't make them stupid. The Dark-Day Fatalists don't encourage suicide, they just attract a lot of chronically depressed people, folks who can't manage on their own. They think the DDF might have answers, but they're just like any religion: it's all about what you believe. And they believe the Machine is only going to carry us so far before it eventually fails. Either that suits what you think, or it doesn't.'

'But it doesn't suit what you think, right, Dad?'

'I think the world's what you make it, son. You're on your own, and you make the best of it. Sometimes, though, Solomon, when things get really bad, I think they might have a point. The ones who speak for the DDF, they seem to have more peace than the rest of us. Maybe they really do have some of the answers.'

They both gazed down at the ruptured body and listened to the wail of the approaching sirens. That would be the police to keep order, not the ambulance. Ambulances weren't called out for jumpers – the bodies were put straight into bags for autopsy. You couldn't resuscitate scattered body parts.

'Let's go home,' his father said. 'Your mother will have dinner on.'

Sol sat on the tram, the memories playing in his head. He should have been on his way to the police station with Ana, but he wanted to check something out first. If Gregor had harboured any ideas of joining the DDF, he wanted to know.

He didn't really have a plan. In fact, he wasn't even sure what the DDF were about; he knew that they believed the Machine would not last for ever, and that mankind had to find other ways, but as far as he knew they weren't offering any solutions. There seemed to be a quasi-religious aspect to their organization, but what form it took he couldn't begin to guess. Gregor was definitely not religious; Sol remembered the fierce and long-running argument between his mother and father about whether he should become a bar mitzvah. Nattie had been bat mitzvahed, but it had been a pretty low-key affair. Gregor had lost that particular argument. In the end Sol's ceremony had gone ahead too, because when it came to God, his mother was every bit as pig-headed as his father. It was only a few months later that Nattie and his mother boarded a tram to go shopping and never came home.

The chapter of the DDF cult nearest their apartment block was one of the biggest in the city. Known as 'sanctums', these meeting places were quiet, hidden buildings off the main streets. The tram took him to

107

within three blocks of the sanctum, and he walked the rest. His school bag was light on his back, carrying only enough books to hide the gun in the bottom of it. He had tried to carry the weapon in his waistband, like he'd seen in the films, but it wasn't comfortable, and kept slipping out, or down into his trousers. One encounter with the debt collector was enough to make an impression; he was not about to be caught unarmed again.

There was a sign over the door; it read:

THE DARK-DAY FATALISTS —
THIRD QUADRANT CHAPTER
'NATURE WILL ALWAYS BE THE VICTOR'

Over the sign was their symbol: three lines spiralling into nothing. It was meant to stand for the converging of life energies or some rubbish like that. Sol shrugged his bag further up onto his shoulder and rang the buzzer. The sound of a man in mourning answered.

'Yes?'

'My name's Solomon Wheat.' Sol spoke up. 'I'd like to ask you a few questions.'

'Have you come to discuss matters relating to your immortal soul?' the querulous voice asked.

'No.'

'Then come in,' said the man, sounding somewhat relieved.

The lock on the door clicked, and Solomon pushed

it open. The hallway inside was cool and dark, and the first thing that struck him was the smell of old paper. Straight down the hall, through a door at the end, he could see what looked like a library. Despite his cynicism, he found himself drawn towards the room, itching to see what they had. That room alone would have been enough to attract Gregor to this place.

'I'm afraid the library is off-limits to visitors,' a man said to him, coming out from a side door. 'You need to arrange permission in advance.'

'I . . . I was just curious,' Sol told him, pulling down his hood. 'It's not why I'm here.'

'I am Mr Hessel. I'm one of the clerics for this chapter. What can we do for you?'

The man was dressed in the simple black tunic and slacks of the DDF. His hair was long and dyed black, hanging loose over his pale, slightly spotty face. He could have been in his mid-twenties, but the long, hollow-cheeked look made him seem much older. This morose figure fitted well within these gloomy walls, the space enclosed by dark grey concrete and fake wood panelling.

'I'm looking for my father, Gregor Wheat,' Sol continued. 'He's about my height, stocky, dark hair. Looks like me, but older and more beaten up. I think he might have come here recently.'

'Was he an initiate?'

'I don't know what that means.'

'Did he join up?'

'No. Or, at least . . . I don't think so. But he may have been interested. He's gone missing and I just wanted to check all the places he might have been to in the last few weeks.'

'We have had nobody of that name here,' Mr Hessel told him. 'But then, people don't often tell us their real names – or even tell us their names at all. It's not required, you see. We are only interested in sharing a philosophy – beyond that, it's each to his own. What kind of man was your father?'

'Independent and stubborn,' Sol said bluntly. 'Look, if you haven't seen him, then you haven't seen him. I just—'

'People go missing in this city all the time, Mr Wheat. Some want to – some don't. I'm just trying to ascertain which category your father fell into.'

'What are you getting at?'

'There are times when individuals decide they want to remove themselves from the life they are leading – even from their families – and take a different route. This Machine that we live in is lubricated with the bodies of it victims. People who've got too caught up in the workings. Here in the Dark-Day Fatalist Order, we can offer help to such people. Among the officiates of our order we have experts in many fields—'

'My dad wouldn't kill himself. He was no victim!'

'I wasn't suggesting—'

'He's wanted for *murder*. He's on the faggin' run, okay? Did he come here or not?'

The cleric put his hands up opposite sleeves and regarded Sol with a patient expression.

'No. We've had no one stay here in the last few weeks other than our officiates. And our open meetings are held on the platforms. He might have been present at one of them, but I couldn't be sure. We get large numbers turning up these days.'

'Okay, thanks.' Sol pulled up his hood and started for the door.

'Mr Wheat?' Mr Hessel called after him.

'Yeah?' Sol turned back to look at him from under the edge of his hood.

'If your father hasn't told you where he is, perhaps it's because he doesn't *want* you to find him. Have you considered that?'

'Sure. But who says he's got the right to leave me in the lurch?' Sol replied.

'I mean, maybe he's trying to protect you, as well as himself.'

Sol thought about all that had happened over the last week.

'Well, then he's doing a crap job of it,' he grunted, and walked out.

When he emerged from the sanctum into the alley, he was feeling pent up and frustrated. Slipping his bag onto his back, he set off at an easy jog, eager for some exercise. He could go up a few levels and run along one of the walkways on the way back to Ana's apartment. He was late anyway. An elevator took him to a promenade level, where he ran past the couples out for a stroll, and the adscreens that relentlessly offered domestic servants, sun-shaft time, out-dome trips and any number of other things he didn't need. He ran to relax, to empty himself out, losing himself in the flow of adrenaline and the hypnotic rhythm of his feet on the walkway.

When he felt as if he had cleared his head out enough, he made for a nearby elevator. While he stood in front of the doors, waiting for the lift to arrive, he let his breathing return to normal, and his eyes fell on the webscreen on the wall next to the elevator doors. It was flickering, and the advert that had been looping as a screensaver disappeared, to be replaced by a message in heavy block capitals against a plain white background. It read:

WHO ARE THE CLOCKWORKERS? WHY DO WE FEAR THEM? DO YOU CARE ENOUGH TO FIND OUT?

Looking out over the railings at the city below, he could even see it on some of the giant screens in the main shopping streets. He shook his head in complete bewilderment.

'What's going on with this?'

'Where is he, Ms Kiroa?' Inspector Mercier asked.

'I don't know. He disappeared off after the funeral – he knew we were supposed to be talking to you.'

112

Ana folded her arms across her chest and stuck her chin out, unwilling to be intimidated by the inspector. He wasn't very threatening anyway; more tired and bureaucratic. They had caught up with her outside the school. She had been collecting some work from her room, and the officers did not realize Sol's class was having a weekend Monday.

'Where did you last see him?' Mercier was gazing patiently at her.

'At the Earth Centre. He went outside before the ceremony was over.'

Mercier looked to his sergeant, Baiev, and the other man nodded and moved away to speak into the commlink on his wrist. Mercier smoothed his little moustache and said nothing for a moment.

'Ms Kiroa, I believe Solomon is staying with you at the moment, is that correct?'

'Yes. His flat was broken into and he was attacked. And since you lot seem intent on ignoring his civil rights, I thought it would be safer if he stayed with me until his father was found. He doesn't have any other family.'

She felt suddenly uncomfortable, conscious of how it might look to a stranger for a young female teacher to have one of her male students staying in her flat.

'Quite.' Mercier put his hands behind his back. 'I wonder if we might go there now and have a look through his things. To see if there's anything which might help us find him.'

'No, we can't,' Ana snapped. 'You need a warrant

for that and you know it. He's barely been gone an hour. It's not like he's "absconded"—'

'Ms Kiroa, I'm afraid that that is exactly what he has done.' The inspector sighed. 'He knew he was to meet the police at a certain time, and he has wilfully avoided us. "Absconded" is the appropriate word. We can get a warrant if we have to; I was hoping you'd co-operate. The Industrial Security Section are still letting me handle this part of the investigation, you understand. If they take over completely, things are going to get a lot more complicated. And we are not the only people looking for Solomon. It would be better if we took him in before others did.'

'What are you talking about?' Ana frowned suspiciously.

'Before Gregor Wheat disappeared, he made some kind of bizarre wager with a man by the name of Cortez, a man who has some very violent people working for him. One of his enforcers was seen at the Earth Centre today. His name is Enrique Romanos.'

The policeman took a palmtop from his pocket and pulled up a display. He showed the picture to Ana. It was a head-and-shoulders shot of a man with a neck that was thicker than his head.

'He is known as "Necktie" Romanos, because of his favourite method of killing.'

'A necktie?'

'A garrotte, Ms Kiroa. Now, could we please see Solomon's things?'

★ ★ ★

Back at Ana's apartment, Sol stared at his face in the bathroom mirror. His nose was still a bit swollen, but the faint bruising around his eyes was going down, turning a sickly yellow. His dark hair was getting quite long, coming down over his ears, and he had the beginnings of a downy moustache that he had never got around to shaving. He looked pathetic. The teenage grit staring back at him had the face of a victim – the kind of kid who always got pummelled in the boxing ring.

On an impulse, he reached for his wash bag. He had brought his father's straight razor with him, and he took it out, unfolded it and scraped the edge down over part of the hair on his upper lip. The blade was well honed, and the hair came away clean. Without bothering to use any soap, he shaved away the rest of his adolescent moustache. The skin felt bare and tender underneath, but it made his face look better, cleaner. More intense too.

Continuing to stare at his reflection, his gaze wandered up to the tousled black hair on his head. There was a pair scissors in the cupboard behind the mirror, and he took them down. Holding tufts of hair out between two fingers, he started snipping. When he had cut it all close to the scalp, he turned on the tap and rubbed the bar of soap between his hands until he had enough lather to cover the top of his head. Pulling the razor over his scalp in slow, awkward strokes, he scraped one swathe of hair after another from his head. The blade cut his skin several times, and he winced as blood mixed with the soap and water, but he kept shaving. Slowly, he took all the hair off his head. He rinsed it clean until the water came away without blood in it, and then dried his bare scalp. Cleaning up the hair clippings, he wiped down the sink before studying himself in the mirror once more; he nodded with satisfaction. He definitely looked older now – harder too. Not like somebody you wanted to mess with.

Out in the living room, he opened the bag that held all the stuff he had brought from his apartment. The webscreen in the corner of the room was asleep, just showing the time: 4.28 p.m. He had missed his meeting with the ISS. Too bad, he decided. He pulled out a heavy jacket, the kind rarely worn in the upper levels of the city, and put it on. He needed big, baggy pockets. Taking the gun from his school bag, he slipped it into the jacket and tried drawing it quickly from the pocket several times. Good enough. He checked to see that he could take the safety catch off with his thumb without looking at it, and then put it away.

Solomon could feel the change in himself – a new sense of grit and determination. He knew the names of three different gambling dens that his father frequented. Two of them were in the Filipino District. He was going down there to find out what he could, and if anybody tried to get rough with him, he was going to shoot them.

★　　★　　★

116

When Ana got to her apartment with the two police officers, there was a man with a badly shaved head walking away down the corridor towards the exit on the other side of the building. She glanced at him again for a moment, then went to unlock her door. Mercier and Baiev paid him no attention.

Inside the apartment, the two men walked through to the living room. Ana showed them Sol's bag, and Baiev started going through it.

'I'll just use your toilet, if I may,' Mercier said to her, and she pointed him towards the bathroom.

The inspector seemed less interested in using the facilities than in perusing the finer points of the décor. He had left the door open, and Ana peered in to see what he was doing. She could feel moisture in the air and there was condensation on the mirror. Mercier ran his finger around the rim of the drain and looked at it.

'Baiev!' he shouted, pushing past Ana. 'That was him outside! He's shaved his head. He's definitely on the run – call for back-up!'

They charged out into the corridor with Ana chasing after them. A sense of outrage kept her on their heels; they were chasing Sol as if *he* were the criminal. Hissing through her teeth, she ran with the policemen as they crashed through the fire doors and into the side street. They split up, each taking a different direction, but there was no sign of Sol. Standing where she had come out, Ana took panting breaths.

The fact that Sol had escaped brought her a little gleam of satisfaction. The younger rebellious side of her enjoyed seeing the police evaded. Even if it was for the wrong reasons.

'An unfortunate turn of events.' Inspector Mercier sighed, walking back to her. 'If he's still in the vicinity, we should apprehend him. Otherwise our young Mr Wheat is on his own.'

Section 9/24: Fear

After leaving the building, Sol descended some steps to a lower street level, intent on catching a tram towards the city centre. He wasn't very familiar with the Filipino District and he wanted to take the main route in. It was after five p.m., and the streets on this level were clouded in shadow. Water was draining from a leaking pipe somewhere, the sound loud in these narrow, echoing spaces. Bats' droppings coated the ground beneath a low bridge. A homeless drunk was lying wrapped in a foil blanket, propped up in the doorway of a closed-down nightclub. There was graffiti on the walls; the usual complaints about life, as well as tags from the young hoods competing for territory.

A tram passed overhead and, somewhere nearby, a mechanical press was thumping in time with the shudder of a conveyor belt. He passed an open window and saw a factory floor where overalled workers were standing at benches, operating hand-cranked machines that broke down and recycled the soles of shoes. The men and women chatted as they worked; dirty jokes and petty small talk passed across the worktops over the whirring clank of the machines. People content to be busy.

Solomon should have been in training by now. Saggs would be wondering where he was; he rarely missed a session. Seeing the people at work, he was reminded of how many of the jobs in the twenty-first century had been taken over by machines. That had been changing back over the last two centuries. Muscle and bone were becoming valuable again, now that so much of what was made had to be salvaged from something else. He started to run at an easy pace, enjoying his strength, light on his feet. Jabbing the air with quick, loose fists, he mixed combinations, working on his breathing and his timing.

His mind was in the ring, sizing up his opponent, circling, doing the little dance like Muhammad Ali used to. He wished Ana would come to one of his fights, then she might see him as something more than a student. His imagination filled the hall, lit the floodlights, called his name from the speaker and sat Ana in the front row. That was why he didn't notice the car pulling up behind him, or see the two figures waiting under the shadow of a walkway arching over the street. The car swept past him and he looked up, surprised. He was walking past the two men at that moment, and one of them stepped out in front of him, swinging a punch at his face. Already psyched up, Sol blocked it and was about to counter when the other man slammed something hard and heavy against the back of his head. Lights exploded in his vision, and the world spun over on its side. His left arm went up to guard reflexively, much too late. But he wasn't out of it yet. His right hand went into his pocket even as he fell. One of the men bent down to hit him again, and he untangled the gun from his jacket and fired without aiming. His head was filled with dark confusion, his vision gone crazy. The gunshot was deafening, and the recoil kicked the weapon right out of his limp fingers. He heard a cry of pain, which he had time to note with satisfaction before something hit his head again and—

The first thing to register was the pain in his wrists. Then the pain in his head introduced itself as an old acquaintance who had returned to visit. His head was hanging forward on his chest and, when he lifted it, the pain raised its voice. As soon as he realized his position, he tried to support himself on his feet. He was hanging from his wrists, bound in what must be handcuffs. The metal bit into the flesh and bone, and he gripped the cuffs to try to ease the pressure. His toes pressed against the ground, taking some of the strain off his arms, but he was hanging too high to get his feet all the way down. He tried raising one foot to feel around, and discovered his ankles were chained to the floor. Sol opened heavy eyes, but saw nothing.

There was some kind of material over his face; he could feel it tied around his neck.

'Our little pugilist is awake,' a voice said.

Somebody untied the material around his throat and pulled it up over his mouth, leaving his eyes covered.

'Can you hear me all right, Mr Wheat?'

Sol struggled to regain his senses. He couldn't remember what had happened. He could vaguely remember being attacked . . . again. Nothing more. He didn't know where he was. He didn't recognize the voice. This wasn't the police station, he was quite sure of that. Somebody else had him. A hand smacked him across the head, arousing his headache's temper. He groaned.

'Can you hear me?'

'Yes,' he mumbled. 'What's going on?'

'You've been captured. We have taken you somewhere you won't be found, and you won't be getting out of here unless you give us the answers we're looking for.'

Solomon felt breath on the skin of his face, and smelled cheap aftershave.

'You were one of the guys who jumped me in the flat.'

'Hear that?' the man said to someone else. 'The kid's sharp! How's that nose by the way? Did I break it that time? Here, let me top that up for you.'

A fist struck him right on the bridge of the nose, and he cried out in pain. His eyes filled with tears as he struggled vainly against the handcuffs, but any movement caused him to lose purchase with his toes, increasing the strain on his wrists. It forced him to keep as still as possible.

'That only hurt you a little,' the man whispered menacingly. 'We're going to be doing much more than that. By the way,' he continued in a brighter voice, 'what's with the haircut? You look like you scalped yourself. You trying to start without us, or what?'

Another voice somewhere behind him gave a sardonic laugh. The sound told Sol something about the size of the room. It was small with a low ceiling. It probably had very solid walls.

'What do you want?' he gasped.

'We want to know who your father talked to last Wednesday.'

'I don't know,' Sol said, his voice trembling. 'I don't know where he is or anything.'

The hand pulled the material further up his face so that he could see down towards his feet. His gun was brought into view.

'Then where did you get this?' the man asked. 'This kind of hardware's not easy to get hold of. It wasn't in your flat when we searched it, and you weren't carrying it. So you've picked it up since then. Where'd you get it? You shot my pal here in the ear . . . shot his earlobe right off. Whole body to aim at and you shoot a man's earlobe – what are you, some kind of idiot? So, anyway, where'd you get the gun?'

Solomon was shivering, his throat tight, constricting his breathing. He didn't want to tell them about the note from his father. They wanted Gregor and he couldn't betray him, even if the little he knew wouldn't tell them anything.

'Who gave you the gun? You're not going to tell me you got it yourself? Not likely, kid. Who was your father in contact with? He has passed on information and you are going to tell us who to, or we're going to put you through a lot of pain. Do you understand me?'

Sol started shaking. He couldn't stop. The tension from trying to stay up on his toes was racking his body, and his calves were cramping up. Any time he let his legs relax, the cuffs bit into his wrists, and his shoulders began to ache. But now he was terrified too. He knew if he spoke, he would start crying.

'I want to show you something,' the man said to him. 'I'm not going to tell you what I'm going to do to you. I just want you to look at this and use your imagination.'

Through the tears in his eyes, Sol saw a pair of pliers being held up in front of him. He stifled a sob.

'That's not going to help you, so stop the blubbering right now. Just tell us what we want to know, and we'll make everything all right.'

'I don't know what you're talking about!' Sol screamed. 'I haven't seen my father since he disappeared! He left the gun with a note in the flat while I was asleep! I don't know where he is, or who he's been talking to – I don't know *anything*!'

'That's a start,' said the man. 'In a few minutes you'll be telling us everything you know. It's a good thing that you're loyal to your father. I'd expect the same from my own son, if he were in your position. But you'll break as soon as the pain starts, so why not just tell us now and save yourself the hassle, eh?'

Sol gaped in disbelief.

'That *is* all I know,' he protested. 'I swear to God! What else can I tell you? I don't know anything more!'

'There's always more, Mr Wheat.'

'This is stupid! I can't tell you anything more. I'd have to make it up, and then you'd hurt me for talking crap.' He arched his neck attempting to get a look at his tormentor, to try to make eye contact. 'What the hell can I do? I'd be lying if I tried to tell you where he is, or who he talked to. I don't know! I swear to God I don't know! What good is it if I lie to you? If you . . . if you hurt me, I'll end up telling you whatever you want to hear. But it won't be the truth, it'll just be anything I think will make you stop hurting me. What good . . . what good is that?'

His voice was frantic, high-pitched with terror.

'What's the point in that?' he whimpered. 'It's just stupid.'

'I think it's time to get started,' the man said.

Sol's face contorted in a sob, and he drew in a long breath.

Then came the sudden crash of the door being kicked in, followed by three silenced gunshots. Sol heard a body drop to the floor. There was fourth muffled shot, and another. A second body fell. Sol arched his head back, trying to see what was going on under the edge of the bag covering his head. He saw a man lying on the floor. Somebody was standing over him. The man had two bullet holes in his chest. The barrel of a pistol was aimed down at him, and a shot was fired into the centre of his forehead, spilling a bloody mess across the floor.

Sol's toes slipped from under him and he hung from his wrists, turning away from the scene as he tried to get his feet under him again. A strong arm wrapped under his armpit and around his chest, supporting his weight. There was a clicking sound, and one of the cuffs came loose. A chain slipped and he was lowered to the floor.

'Solomon? You're all right now. You're safe. Your mother's favourite song was "Dream a Little Dream of Me" by the Mamas and the Papas. My name is Maslow – I'm sorry I was late.'

The man named Maslow was a little taller than Sol, with wide, flat shoulders, and the burly build of a heavyweight. His once-black skin had the grey pall of someone who spent his life away from the sunlight of the dome. Deep lines described a hard life in his face. His frizzy salt-and-pepper hair was cut close to his scalp, and he had a perfectly black, tightly trimmed moustache that dripped around the corners of his mouth and down towards his chin. Sol sat shaking on a chair, his feet up on the seat, his arms wrapped around his knees. Maslow had pulled both of the dead men's bodies into the centre of the room, and was searching through the metal cupboards that lined one wall.

'Who are you?' Sol asked him.

'I'm a friend of your old man's – I mean, sort of. I owe him a debt.'

'I didn't know he knew anybody . . . like you.'

'You're lucky he did.' Maslow pulled a waterproof bag from one of the cupboards, one with an airtight zipper. 'Body bags. They were geared up for this. Looks like they get rid of bodies all the time.'

Sol stared hard at the bag. He could have ended up in one of those.

'How did you find me?' he asked. 'And how did you kill them, just like that? They seemed like real pros. I didn't stand a chance.'

Maslow glanced down at the bodies.

'I've had dealings with their type before. I've been following you since last week, and found out they were tailing you too. So I tailed *them*. They led me back here yesterday. When you were nabbed this afternoon, I was following on foot – I wasn't expecting the car. But I guessed where they'd take you.'

He laid out the body bags, one alongside each corpse, and unzipped them.

127

'Who were they?' Sol felt a chill run through him as he gazed down at the bodies.

'Professional killers and kidnappers; strong-arm men,' Maslow told him. 'But what you should be asking is who they were working for. I can't tell you that. Help me pack them up.'

Slipping down from his chair, Sol grabbed the feet of the nearest man and helped lift him onto the open bag. He pulled the bottom of the bag up around the feet and dragged the zipper up towards the waist. Maslow took it and finished closing it up. Sol had one last look at his torturer's face: a round, jovial-looking potato with light blue eyes, blond hair and grey skin. And a bullet hole through the forehead. They got the other man wrapped up – a bulkier, sharp-faced guy with wizened skin – and then Maslow went over to the aluminium sink in the corner of the room. Sol sat back down at the stainless-steel table and watched Maslow take cleaners and detergents from the cupboard under the sink.

'We can't hide everything,' the man told him. 'A good forensic crew will find some trace of us if they check this place out. So we have to get the bodies out of here and make it look like they just disappeared. The police have to have no reason to look here. We are going to scrub every centimetre of this floor, and wipe down every other surface. We can't leave a drop of blood anywhere. Got it?'

Sol nodded. Maslow cleaned the spattered blood off

the top of the table, and then he and Sol lifted the two bodies onto it, along with the four chairs. There was a mop in a utility room out in the corridor, and they carefully cleared all the blood from the floor, washing the red-stained water down the sink. For nearly half an hour they cleaned the entire room. Maslow took down the meat-hook that hung from a steel loop in the ceiling – the hook from which Sol had been hanging – and threw the cuffs and ankle-chains into a cupboard. When they were finished, there were only the two body bags left to suggest that there had been any violence.

Solomon's gun was lying on the table beside them, and he put on his jacket and pocketed the weapon.

'Next time, try to hit something more important,' Maslow said, without humour. 'Can you carry the smaller guy? There's a chute down to a fertilizer grinder back along the corridor. We can dump them down there.'

Sol remained thoroughly nauseous after mopping the gore off the floor, but he was otherwise feeling a lot stronger after the mundane work of cleaning up. Rubbing his raw wrists, he reached down, pulled the body towards him and hauled it onto his shoulder. It was incredibly heavy and awkwardly limp, like trying to lift a bag of stones. Maslow picked up the other one as if it weighed no more than a child and, turning to survey the room once more, nodded in satisfaction and then made for the door. Sol followed close behind, struggling beneath the weight.

The hatch to the chute was down two flights of stairs, in a row of chutes for garbage. Each one was labelled with the kinds of rubbish suitable: METAL, PLASTIC, DENCERAMIC, etc. All organic waste went into the fertilizer chute. Maslow lifted the hatch and shoved his body bag into it. He took Sol's load from him and despatched it with equal ease.

'By the time they come out of the bottom of the grinder, there'll be nothing to identify,' Maslow told him.

Reluctant to ask him how he was so sure, Sol just nodded. His stomach was getting ready to climb out through his throat, and there were some things he just didn't need to know right then. With no idea where he was, he let Maslow lead the way out. They were somewhere deep in the Machine, well below the main levels of the city. All around was the rumble of machinery and, from the cold edge to the air, they had to be in that chilly limbo underneath the muggy heat of the city's engines.

Here, in this part of the city, secret lives were led, and he was sure that this was where Maslow had spent a good deal of his life. Whoever this man was, he was like nobody Sol had ever met before. And despite the fact that he had just saved his life, Sol was loath to trust him. But this violent man was a means of protection against the nameless hoods who were trying to hurt Sol, and there was a strong chance that he knew where to find Gregor. For the moment, Sol had no choice but to follow him and do as he said.

Feeling suddenly frozen to the bone, he buttoned up his jacket and matched Maslow's stride along the echoing corridor and deep into the workings of the Machine.

Section 10/24: Glass

Sol sat watching a film called *First Blood* with Maslow. It was four days since he had first met the man, and they were sitting in a dingy deserted office on the edge of one of the vast underground fields of modified soybeans laid out on shelved racks that were spread under the edges of Ash Harbour. The room was cramped, with a decrepit desk and two sagging chairs, the shelves crammed with hoarded odds and ends. But the webscreen was working, so they sat watching the film. Outside the window, the lights came on and went off every eight hours, simulating a shortened day cycle that sped up the growth of the crops.

They had been on the move since the first day. Maslow said it wasn't safe to stop anywhere for long, but he seemed to be accustomed to life as a fugitive; there were places where he had food, clothes, tools and weapons stored – locked rooms and derelict offices and workshops tucked away in the hidden corners of the sub-levels. He wore gloves that he rarely took off, and was careful about clearing up any traces of his presence when they moved from place to place. Solomon knew he would have been reported missing and wondered who would be looking for him, and how long they'd keep up the search.

He had seen strange things down here; people with weird scars, and missing limbs capped with odd-shaped prosthetics. Through dust-covered windows he had seen glimpses of factory floors where human bodies seemed to have been bonded to industrial machinery; sights that made Sol question what his eyes were telling him. But Maslow never let him stop anywhere long enough to investigate, and these bizarre scenes remained a mystery.

Maslow jumped around on his seat, twitching like a kid on a games console every time the main character, Rambo, hit anyone, shot anyone, or jumped out of a bush and knifed anyone. Sol was finding the experience embarrassing, not to mention a little worrying.

His new guardian angel had taken him down to a cavern at one point, a place where construction had begun on a new tunnel, only to be postponed, leaving an incongruous mix of modern denceramic beams and supports standing in the untamed space of a million-year-old cave. Here, Maslow had taught him how to fire the gun. It had a built-in silencer, but it was worn out, so the shots were loud. After emptying two clips into a pile of sand, Sol was fairly confident he could aim straight. But then it had been a *big* pile of sand.

'Got 'im!' Maslow yelled, laughing as Rambo felled another inferior opponent. 'I love that bit!'

Sol turned to look at him with perplexed curiosity. This man, in whom he'd placed so much trust, was still a mystery to him. Sometimes he tried to act like a mentor, clumsily and insistently teaching; other times, he hardly acknowledged Sol's presence. His only pleasure seemed to be in these twentieth-century action films – cop shows, and war and spy movies – which he watched whenever they stopped in some refuge that had a working webscreen. Solomon thought it a strange taste for a man who did it for real.

They'd done some hand-to-hand stuff as well. Maslow knew techniques Sol had never seen: deadly things. Solomon had discovered that boxing was pretty limited when Maslow felled him several times without even using his hands.

But it was frustrating, all this action-man stuff. His new bodyguard hardly talked about what Solomon thought they actually ought to be doing: looking for Gregor.

Maslow had last seen him outside the depot on the day he'd disappeared. Gregor had given him the scarf, the note and the gun and had begged Maslow to protect his son. That was all Sol had managed to get out of this surly stranger. He didn't even know how the two had first met.

It was clear that Maslow didn't know where Gregor was now, and instead of trying to find him, he was intent on training Sol for something. And it was exciting, but Sol did not have time for it. He had asked the man a number of times how he had become indebted to Gregor, but Maslow wouldn't talk about it, and Sol got the impression that he was keeping something important from him. It was incredibly frustrating.

'Maslow?'

'Yeah?' The man kept his eyes on the screen.

'I'd like to check out some things. See if I can find Gregor. I want to . . . to retrace his steps the day he disappeared. Starting with the dome. Could we do that?'

Maslow grunted. His head tilted and he grimaced, as if he were unhappy with what he was thinking.

'Okay,' he said finally.

'Thanks.'

They sat watching the film for a while longer, neither speaking.

'Y'know, this guy – Stallone,' Sol piped up. 'He did a boxing film; it's much better than this. It's called *Rocky*. Have you seen that?'

'Ahhh, yeah. I started watching it once.' Maslow grunted. 'Arty crap. Too much goddamned talking.'

Solomon started to wonder if Maslow might be a bit simple.

It was Solomon's thirteenth birthday, and he was big enough to fit into a safesuit. Standing in the depot's changing room, he trembled with excitement as his father kitted him out. It was against company policy to take 'civilians' out onto the dome, but many of the daylighters did it. Some of the supervisors approved of their crews' tradition of showing their teenage sons and daughters life out on the glass – it built a closer-knit team, and helped to prime future recruits for a tough and badly paid career.

'Stay close to me at all times,' Gregor told him as he pulled the legs of the suit up around Sol's thighs and waist, and strapped close the harness built into the hips of the suit. 'There's no wind to speak of today, but gusts can hit at any time. The glass is clear, but that just makes it slippery, so keep the rope taut, and keep the slack behind you coiled, so you don't trip over it. Got it?'

Sol nodded. Gregor helped him get his arms into the suit, pushing the material up his forearms and then shoving on the big mittens that connected with an airtight seal into the sleeves. The three layers zipped and clipped up the front on different sides, and then Gregor pulled up the hood. He switched on the heater on the air intake and checked it was charged up. Before fitting the mask, he looked into his son's eyes.

'All the guys will be watching out for you; it'll be like having thirty big brothers and sisters out there.' He grinned. 'Some people get agoraphobic surrounded by all that open space, but you won't. You're like your old man. I remember my first time on the glass. It was the first time I'd seen the sky without a roof. It was . . .' He hesitated. 'Well, you'll see. I know you've been out on a tour on the pack ice, but this is different – you won't be in any vehicle this time, it's

136

just you and the elements. I don't want you to end up working out here, Sol, I want better things for you. But everybody should get to feel an empty sky over their head.'

He clipped the mask onto the rigid front of Sol's hood, checking the smart-lens lined up with his son's eyes. The outlets for Sol's breath fed through vents to the back of his hood, to stop the water vapour forming ice on the mask itself. Gregor gave him a thumbs-up, and Sol nodded and answered in kind. It took his father a fraction of the time to put his own suit on, and then he checked that Sol's safety harness was attached properly to his own before they walked towards the airlock. Sol's breath quickened as the internal door closed behind them.

The air temperature dropped suddenly around them; Sol couldn't feel it, but he watched it on the readout on the inside of his mask: 10° . . . -5° . . . -20° . . . -40° . . . -60° . . . It stopped at -73°. A soft alarm chimed, and the external door opened. Even with the tinting of the smart-lens, they walked out into a world of blinding white . . .

Sol awoke from his reverie as Maslow peered round the door and waved him inside. They were in a small maintenance depot on the west side of the wall, one Sol didn't know existed. Its entrance was about five hundred metres from the West Dome Depot, where Gregor worked. Inside was a rack of safesuits, some equipment rigs and a little-used airlock.

'The daylighters are done for the afternoon,' Maslow told him. 'They'll all be heading back in. We have maybe another hour of daylight, but after that the temperature's going to drop . . .'

Sol nodded. They would have to be quick. Finding a suit his size, he pulled it out and dismantled it, carefully fitting on each piece as his father had shown him. He had been out on the dome six times since then, but he still got the shivers now, as he got ready. Maslow was already half dressed, and Sol was surprised at the practised ease with which he fitted himself out. So he had been outside before too. He rigged a rope to Sol's harness, and then to his own.

'The open airlock will register on the dome-controller's board,' Maslow told him. 'But they probably won't pay it much attention. With the shifts finishing up, all the airlocks will be busy. Don't use the radio unless you absolutely have to. You know the hand signals, yeah? You ready?'

Sol clipped on the mask, and checked the lens readout to see if it showed any leaks. Picking up his plastic-coated ice-axe, he gave Maslow the thumbs-up. Maslow punched the access code into the airlock's oversized keypad, and the internal door slid open. On a bad day, snow would pile up against the external door, and they would have had to dig their way out, but not today.

Outside, they quickly scanned around for anybody who might still be out on the glass. In their fluorescent orange suits, they would be clearly visible to anybody this side of the dome's horizon. Moving ponderously in the heavy gear, they started out for the sector that Gregor had left in such a hurry – D63 in the Third Quadrant.

There had originally been machines to clear the dome's surface, but they had lasted about thirty years, gradually packing up as the means to reproduce their worn-out parts were lost in the city's hunger for dwindling resources. And so men had been sent up to take over the machines' jobs. Stairs and hand- and footgrips, piton points and rigging posts allowed the daylighters to climb across the dome when it was clear. Otherwise, they climbed over the snow and ice itself. Even with all the safety precautions, one or two died each year in avalanches and falls.

Looking up into the clear, darkening blue above him, Sol felt the exhilaration of being below such sheer emptiness. It was as if he could fall straight up into it, and it set his heart racing. A feathery frosting was already starting to coat the hexagonal slabs of diamond-hard concraglass, but Sol could see the city lights coming on beneath his feet. They climbed an arcing, denceramic stair up the curve of the dome, then branched off to one side, swinging from one piton ring to another and clinging to handholds. Sol braced the hardened rubber cleats of his boots against the slippery surface until his readout told him he was in the right place. He was already breathing hard, burdened by the weight of the suit, and his gasps were loud in his ears. Even with the variable tinting of the lens, the white was hard on his eyes. Behind him, he could feel Maslow's eyes on his back, watchful, protective.

All the daylighters' tools were made so as not to damage the concraglass's surface, but it still had a slight glaze of erosion because of its age. It was level enough here for Sol to release his handholds and kneel down. Scraping away at the surface coating of new ice with his ice-axe, he cupped his hands around his mask and put his face to the glass, squinting down at the city below.

Below him, most of Ash Harbour's people were going home. From this height, slightly distorted by the two half-metre-thick layers of glass, it was possible to observe the clockwise motion of the city; its streets, trams, moving bridges, its slanting escalators and counterweighted elevators all moving in a perfect cohesion that provided power – *life* – to the city. And in the middle, the triangular building that housed the three massive turbines of the Heart Engine, which continuously charged up all the other systems. But that was not what caught his attention. Directly below him, protruding into his view below the gantry grid, was the Third Quadrant tower crane. The crane he had been on the day his life had started to go down the toilet, where he and his class had watched Francis Walden and that other man, Falyadi, plunge to their deaths from the giant's arm.

'Well I'll be damned,' he muttered.

He pretended to keep looking, unsure if he wanted

Maslow to know what he'd found. Standing up again, he scanned around him, as if searching for clues. Beyond the edge of the dome and the precipice that dropped down the side of the mountain, there was only a white landscape, broken by the odd peak of what had once been nearby islands. Now the sea around Ash Harbour was covered in several metres of solid ice.

'Do you know what those turret things are, around the edges of the cliff?' Sol asked, pointing, his voice hollow behind the mask. 'They've always been covered in snow, every time I've been up here.'

'Gun emplacements,' Maslow answered. 'Back when this place was being built – before the weather finished off everybody outside – some of the people who didn't make the list tried to force their way in. Soldiers would cut them down from up here. I heard that once, somebody actually ran an oil tanker aground down there. After the attackers were dealt with, the ship got sliced up and recycled.'

'Do you think there's anybody else alive out there?' Sol wondered aloud.

'We lost contact with Cheyenne Mountain about twenty years ago,' Maslow said. 'The last reports said there was a famine. Everybody was fighting over what was left of the food. None of the other enclaves even lasted that long. I think we're all that's left.'

'Fighting over the food.' Sol sniffed. 'You'd think they'd want to put all their effort into growing more, wouldn't you?'

'That's not the way people think,' Maslow replied. 'The sun's going down. Let's get inside.'

They made their way back to the steps, and carefully descended towards the airlock, with Sol leading the way.

'Well that was a waste of time,' Sol moaned loudly. 'Maybe I've got the wrong end of the stick here. We know Dad owed someone money—'

'Cortez,' Maslow said. 'Necktie Romanos works for Cortez.'

'Right. Well, maybe we should talk to Cortez then.'

'That's looking for trouble, Sol.'

Sol turned to face him. 'That's what you're here for, isn't it? To keep me safe?'

'That's why we're not going near Cortez.'

'So I just have to wait until this guy, Necktie, finds me, yeah? 'Cos that is what these guys do. You got any money?'

Breath hissed from Maslow's valves.

'All right, we'll do it,' he snapped. 'But only because this is one problem we can solve with cash. If Cortez decides you're worth more as a hostage, we're going to be in it up to our necks.'

Section 11/24: Party

It was the weekend after Sol Wheat had gone missing, and Cleo was holding a party. Their class's high spirits were not a poor reflection on Solomon's popularity – in fact, his street-cred had taken a substantial leap upwards since his disappearance. Where once he had been a surly loner with no real friends, now he was a fugitive, on the run from the law. But the party, despite being named after him, was more for the benefit of his peers. Cleo took party themes seriously; she considered them a vital element in maintaining her sanity.

Living in a city surrounded by crater walls and roofed with a dome, teenagers faced a life that offered no wider horizons, no travel, no escape from life in the Machine. They all feared the onset of the dreary life of drudgery that would begin as soon as they left school – unless they happened to be among the lucky few who would get a few years' postponement in college. Cleo was certain that this was their most important time, before they were dragged into that abyss of work and routine. It was their only chance to be themselves with all their might.

Wild parties were a city-wide phenomenon, a natural reaction to a life where mankind's very survival depended on the bulk of their species getting up and going to work every day. But Cleo knew that even parties could become routine. If their celebrations every week were reduced to getting off their faces and falling home in a near stupor, they would cease to serve their therapeutic purpose. So she endeavoured to give each party an identity. This way, whenever they were telling their post-party stories, the event under discussion could be referred to by name; like when Faisal had accidentally scored with a transvestite at the 'Suicidal Student Teacher Party', or the time Amanda had thrown a full punchbowl over the head of that guy who had called her a tart at the 'Ten Days of Darkness Party'. Great times.

This was the 'Where's Sol? Party'. Everyone had to bring a means of finding Sol. People came with binoculars, or a magnifying glass, or a web-search list of ratting dens. Amanda had even brought a disc of late-twentieth-century boxing matches to see if Sol had somehow travelled back in time and was in the audience. With the rest of the Matsumura family away visiting relatives, Cleo had provided the venue – the roof of her apartment block – and some stem-soup with boxing-glove-shaped croutons. Enough of that, and anybody who really wanted to see Sol probably would. Most people brought gulp as well; the mixture of the two drugs could very well stop them from being able to see *anyone* ever again.

Having finished playing a good session with the rest of the band, Cleo and the other members of Freak Soup had handed over to another local group, and she had immersed herself in a very drunk conversation with Ubertino. Dressed in a singlet and baggy trousers, with her hair hanging loose and her feet bare, she was sitting with her legs dangling off the ledge of the roof, while he sat with his back to the dizzying view, huddled in the folds of his long khaki trenchcoat.

'. . . That's exactly right!' she declared over the music, jabbing his leg hard to make her point. 'That's exactly right! Exactly! Iced Breeze have never, ever had anything to say with their music. That's why the faggin' Internal . . . whassernames—'

'Climate,' Ube supplied.

'. . . faggin' Internal Climate want them. Because they're no *threat*. We're a threat. They're scared of us – of anyone with attitude! If Freak Soup got up on that stage, we'd wipe the . . . the . . . the—'

'Floor.'

'. . . the floor . . . we'd wipe the floor with those snot-nosed, boy-band drips. I mean, what do they even sing about? Love? Faggin' heartache songs? What do they know about heartache? They're faggin' fourteen! It's like a toddler moaning about puberty!'

145

Ube exploded into laughter just as he was going to take a sip of his drink. It splashed over his face, and he wiped it away with his sleeve, grinning. She stared at him with her hazel oriental eyes and giggled. She loved it when it was like this. If he wasn't more into boys, she'd have dragged Ube off to the dark end of the roof any number of times. But this was great, the way they were.

'That's right!' he nodded, turning serious. 'We sing about stuff that affects people. Real stuff. *That's* what we're about. About *life*.'

Cleo gulped back some drink. 'But that's what Internal . . . wotchmacallit—'

'Climate.'

'. . . what Internal Climate don't want. We're like a union, a people's union. But without all the union crap—'

'All that "Paragraph Three of Subsection B of the Back-Scratcher's Rules of Conflict Resolution" crap—'

'Right!' Cleo jabbed his leg again.

Ube was sure there would be a bruise on his thigh in the morning. He moved it a little further away, because she was only getting into her stride.

'All that malarkey. Without all that! We're a voice of the people! And if they don't want some faggin' conflict . . . well, they're goin' to get it! We pay them to provide us with a service, and then they sell us a line about how we should be grateful for them, and they try telling us how we're supposed to live our lives, just 'cos . . . 'cos . . . 'cos . . .'

'Just 'cos they *own* everything.'

'Right!' Cleo shouted, her voice raised well above the necessary volume to be heard over the music. 'This is a democracy! We vote . . . well, we don't vote yet, but in a year or so we will! And our government is supposed to be looking after us, not selling our city to the highest bidder. We pay taxes . . . well, we will be paying taxes when we're working . . . assuming we can find jobs . . . but . . . but . . . What was I saying?'

'This is a democracy.'

'Right! This is a democracy, and just 'cos they own everything in this whole faggin' city doesn't mean they can own people! And they sure as hell can't own *me*, right? And they can't tell me what to play or what not to sing, or . . . or . . . or . . . tell my band that we can't play at our own faggin' end-of-year ball! I'm not faggin' standin' for it!'

'That's it!' Ube yelled. 'You're absolutely bang on! So, what are we goin' to do about it?'

They gazed at each other for a few moments.

'I don't know,' Cleo said, feeling suddenly exhausted. 'I'm getting another drink. Want one?'

Cleo was on her knees, praying to the god of cold porcelain, and swearing that she would never drink again. As she threw up the last of the contents of her stomach and started dry retching, she tried to calm

147

down and lifted her head out of the toilet bowl. A sudden gag caught her by surprise, but there was nothing more coming out, so she closed the lid, flushed, and sat down wearily on the seat.

'Oh, God,' she muttered, for the fifth or sixth time.

It was after four in the morning, and she should have been comatose in bed, but she had been tormented by a nightmare about the man she had pushed off the ventilation duct, the one she had seen dumping the body. The mixture of guilt, drugs and alcohol had woken her from her sleep and sent her running to the toilet to be sick. As a result, she was suffering the initial offensive of her weekly hangover before she had enjoyed the benefit of a morning's sleep. Drinking just wasn't worth this. Bending forward, she groaned, but resisted the urge to pay tribute to the hangover god again. She stood up instead, and looked in the mirror. She was looking pale and haggard, and some vain part of her wondered what effect all this partying was going to have on her looks when she hit her mum's age. To hell with it, she decided. If you couldn't do parties, what was the point of looking good?

A sound in the darkness of the empty apartment beyond the bathroom door turned her head, and she stood silently, her keen ears searching where her eyes could not. A door squeaked quietly: the living-room door. Her mind was back in the gloom of the lower levels, being hunted by nameless armed men with guns.

Her breath caught in her chest, and she looked around quickly for some kind of weapon. Her pepper spray was in her bedroom. Casting her eyes over the contents of the bathroom, she found her father's straight razor. She would have preferred something with more reach, but it would have to do.

Opening the blade, she crept out of the bathroom and along the hallway towards the living room. The smart thing to do would have been to hide, and wait for them to go away – she was too hungover to be taking on intruders – but her instinct told her that they wouldn't be going away until they found her. Cleo gritted her teeth and kept walking, sure that it would be better to attack than be caught in a corner.

She passed the front door. It was still locked, and showed no signs of being forced. All their windows had bars that they closed at night. Whoever it was had no problem with locks. Holding the razor out in front of her in tightly gripped, trembling hands, she advanced towards the living-room door. There was no sound from the room, but the door was wide open. She jabbed around the door frame with the blade, and then jumped into the room, brandishing the weapon. But the place was empty.

An arm came from behind her and a hand clamped over her mouth. She let out a muffled scream and slashed at it with her blade. It cut through her attacker's sleeve and drew blood.

'Ahh! Damn it, Cleo!' the assailant yelped.

He let her go, and she spun round to see a skinhead youth with bruises around his eyes standing behind her. He had come in after her, obviously from one of the other rooms. Still gripping the weapon, she squinted in the gloom.

'Sol?'

'Yeah.' He winced, tenderly peeling back his sleeve and pressing his hand to the shallow wound. 'Sorry, I just didn't want you to scream, that's all.'

'Then why didn't you just say "Don't scream", you faggin' idiot?' she hissed at him. 'You scared the crap out of me! What the hell are you doing in my apartment in the middle of the night? How did you get in?'

'I'll fill you in on everything, all right? But I need to bind this up with something. And don't turn on any lights – they might be watching the front of the building.'

There was a first-aid kit in the kitchen, and Cleo, veteran of a thousand parties, was well used to patching up minor injuries. Studying her own handiwork – and the evident sharpness of the blade – she put a dressing on the wound and bound it with gauze. It was only a shallow cut, nothing serious.

Despite her burgeoning headache, she put on the stereo, but with the volume turned down. Her body did not function properly without musical accompaniment. While she worked, Sol told her what had happened to him the day of the funeral.

'Holy crap.' She shook her head. 'This . . . this is a

lot to take in. So where is this guy, Maslow, now?' she asked.

'He's the shy type, doesn't like showing his face much. Thinks I shouldn't have come here at all. I have to meet him back on the roof. That's the way we came in. I got right in your front door – he showed me how to work locks. You wouldn't believe how bad the locks are in these blocks, Cleo.'

'Whoa, I don't want to know how bad my locks are, all right? Not from a guy who jumped me in the dark. What's that all about, anyway? If some hoods kidnapped you and . . . and went to torture you, I mean, that's pretty illegal, right? Just go to the police.'

'Maslow says a lot of the police are in on it. It's not safe.'

'In on *what*? What's goin' on?' It was all fascinating stuff, but Cleo couldn't take her eyes off the top of Sol's head. 'You make it sound like there's a big conspiracy—'

'There *is* some kind of conspiracy. I just don't know what. Maslow doesn't talk much, but I know he's the one who gave me the gun—'

'What gun?'

He took it from his pocket and showed her.

'Jesus, Sol. That looks real!'

'It *is* real. Anyway . . .' He paused. 'What? Why do you keep looking at my head?'

'Well, it's your hair, honey. It's just not right. Did you do that yourself?'

She was trying not to smile.

'Yeah, what about it?' he snapped defensively.

She glanced at the razor on the kitchen counter.

'I think you better let me finish it off for you.'

His attempt to shave his head had not gone well, and nearly a week's growth had made it worse. Patches of stubble and fluff stuck out over the top and back of his head, where he couldn't see it from the front.

'You kind o' look like you have mange,' she told him.

'Ah, damn.' He sighed. 'I've been walking round like this for days.'

She led him into the bathroom and sat him on the toilet seat with his back to her. He soaped up his scalp, and then they continued to talk while she carefully shaved the rest of the hair from his head. She had been shaving her legs for a year, and was a lot better at using the razor than he was.

'Maslow said that Dad gave him the scarf and the note, and asked him to get me a gun. He hasn't seen Dad since, and hasn't been able to look for him because he's been keeping an eye on me. We've been down in the basement levels all week, but we haven't done much. He's showed me how to find my way around, and how to shoot, and how to open locks – you wouldn't believe how easy it is on some of these doors – and he's been telling me about the guys who caught me. But not a whole lot, really. He's not much of a talker – he goes off on his own all the time.

152

'Apparently, the guys who kidnapped me are part of some crimelord's operation that Dad crossed. He saw something, or heard something, Maslow isn't sure. But he says Dad didn't murder Tommy Hyung. He's sure of that.'

'Lean your head forward a bit,' Cleo told him. 'There. So, what are the police in on? What's the big plot?'

'Maslow's been trying to find out. He says the way they're after Dad, it sounds like something serious. I think it might have something to do with all the accidents that have been happening lately. Maybe even the crane wreck. It was the same day Dad disappeared . . .'

His voice drifted off, and Cleo wiped some soap off the blade with a cloth, then went back to doing the nape of his neck. He liked the feel of her fingers on his skin, and the way she directed the position of his head with gentle movements of her hands. Sometimes her hips touched against his back, and he closed his eyes and thought of Ana. After seeing his teacher at home – off duty, as it were – he had thought he would feel closer to her, but instead, it had just made him realize that she had a very full life out of school. It was funny to think of teachers that way. And the age gap was becoming more of a turn-off – she still talked to him more like a mother than a friend. Cleo's fingertips brushed against his neck and his skin tingled.

'It sounds like you're in way over your head,' Cleo

observed. 'And you're out there on your own with some guy you don't even know. Who says he's not on their side? Whoever they are. You need to go to the cops. Ms Kiroa could go with you – make it official.'

'Maslow's for real,' Solomon said coldly. 'He saved my life. And he's the only person who's doing anything about all this. I'd be dead now if he weren't the real thing. And I don't trust the police. You wouldn't either if you'd been in that interrogation room with them. I don't need their help now.'

'What you doing here then?' Cleo sniffed. 'I'm assuming you didn't just come to get your hair done.'

She brushed her fingertips over his cleanly shaven scalp; when she pushed them back the other way, it had a texture like very fine sandpaper. Sol turned and looked up at her as she rinsed off the blade and handed him a towel.

'As far as they're concerned, you're nobody special to me,' he said, drying his head. 'But we used to be pretty good friends, y'know? And . . . you're sound, and I think you've got more sense than most of the others in the class. And I reckon you've got the nerve to try something I need to get done – but I can't do it myself. Will you do me a real favour?'

She arched an eyebrow.

'If you'd seen the back of your head, you'd know I just did.'

Cleo was sitting in the school library during lunch hour, doing a search for Francis Walden. Sol had asked her to get in contact with the man's widow. She found the Waldens' contact details in the city register and, taking a deep breath, clicked the link to their home screen. The woman who answered the call was not the one she had seen weeping at the head of the funeral procession, but she resembled her enough to be a sister.

'Yes?' the woman asked.

'I'm looking for Mrs Walden?' Cleo enquired tentatively.

'What do you want?' The woman's blue-black face and stern voice gave the impression that Cleo was only one of a long line of people looking for Mrs Walden, and they were all plum out of luck.

'My name's Cleo Matsumura. I was one of the students in the crane car that passed her husband's before it . . . before he died. I was' – she cleared her throat – 'I was wondering if I could talk to Mrs Walden.'

'No. She doesn't like talking onscreen, and she's not taking visitors.'

'Please – I won't take up much of her time. I'd just like to talk to her for a few minutes.'

'Why?'

Cleo hesitated. The truth – that she had been asked to do this by a boy who wasn't really a friend of hers, and whom she didn't know very well, and who was on the run from the police and debt collectors, searching for his father who was also on the run, and trying to find out what his problems might have to do with a bunch of professional killers and their possible connection to the crane wreck – was probably not the best route to take.

'I wanted to find out a little about her husband,' she said finally. 'I suppose . . . Well, I saw him die, and I didn't know him at all. And I'd just like to know what kind of man he was. That's all.'

The woman stared at her for a moment, then her face softened.

'Hang on a second.'

A hold screen came up, and Cleo waited. A minute later, the woman was back.

'Helena isn't feeling up to taking visitors at the moment, but she said she'd see you. You can come round this evening, if you want. Say, about seven?'

'That'd be great, thanks.'

'See you then.'

The screen cut out and went back to the main menu. Cleo sighed and pushed back her chair. She should never have agreed to this; she was dreading meeting this grief-stricken woman. But something about being asked a favour by a hunted fugitive made her reluctant to refuse. Cleo had to admit that she'd been flattered by Sol's trust in her, and tantalized by the challenge to get involved in his adventure. Time would tell if she'd been monumentally stupid.

The rest of the school day dragged by as she wavered between anxiety and excitement at what was ahead of her. Getting on the tram at the junction outside the school, she grabbed an empty seat and rehearsed what she was going to say. Helena Walden lived out in the Easy Circle; the address was South Wall Villas, the large, spacious townhouses that nestled in the brightest quarter of town. Francis Walden had been an executive in the Schaeffer Corporation; a young man on his way up the corporate ladder, and already earning enough to live in one of the best areas in town.

When the tram had taken her as far as she could go, she got off and walked the rest of the way. It gave her a chance to ogle at how the other half lived. The houses were large, with expansive windows – some which even curved up into the roofs. Much of the architecture represented throwbacks to earlier centuries: the clean-cut, curving lines of the 1990s; the geometrical shapes of 1930s art deco; the intricate details of baroque décor. Nostalgia for times these people had never known. Cleo had played with the idea of being an interior decorator when she was younger, but she would never have the connections to make it into these circles, and they were the only ones who could pay. It took serious money to build something that was more than just functional.

People walked past her, and she could tell by their looks that her clothes weren't right. She always wore the latest street fashions, but in a place like this it was *who* made the clothes that counted. Their skin had more colour to it too; a brown, healthy glow. She felt pasty and white by comparison, despite her oriental complexion.

There were a lot of cars in this area, and many of them looked like old, expensive ones. Everything was clean and well maintained; most of the houses had window boxes, and some even had gardens. Cleo was amazed. Anybody who even left fake flowers out within reach in her area risked having them stolen. She stopped for a moment by a freshly mown lawn and breathed in the smell of cut grass. There wasn't even a wall round the garden. Looking round warily, she knelt and pressed her face into the green carpet. She could have stayed there for hours, savouring the surroundings. She stood up again, feeling embarrassed. There was a flowerbed to one side of the lawn and, as she passed it, she scanned about for any witnesses, and then plucked a bright yellow chrysanthemum from the bed, pressing it to her nose as she walked away. They wouldn't miss just one.

The Waldens' house was modestly small for the area, part of a terrace of identical buildings, all Georgian-imitation concrete moulding with glass-tiled roofs, all immaculately kept. The woman who answered the door was the same one who had answered the webcall.

'I'm Virginia, Helena's sister,' she said, introducing herself. 'You can't stay very long – she's been getting a lot of harassment and she just can't handle any more stress. Don't upset her, you hear me?'

Cleo nodded. Virginia led her down a clean, stylishly severe hallway into a back room with a window two storeys high that made the most of the dome light shining into the space. The décor, with its abstract metal wall hangings and clean-cut furniture, was a little cold for Cleo's tastes, but it had enough of a homely feel about it to keep it comfortable. This was obviously a room for entertaining guests. Helena Walden sat on a straight-backed chair, looking dignified but fragile. Virginia waved Cleo to a divan and took a seat next to her sister, holding her hand.

'Cleo; that's short for something, is it?' Helena said.

'Cleopatra,' Cleo told her. 'My parents thought the Egyptians were just wonderful.'

The offhand remark made the widow give a weak smile.

'Young people, you're always shortening things,' she said. 'I like things to have their proper names. Do you mind if I call you Cleopatra?'

'No, of course not,' Cleo replied, although she

thought it a bit stiff. But then it did suit the mood.

'What would you like to know about my husband?'

Cleo played nervously with her fingers. She had been hoping that the woman would have plenty to say about her dead spouse. She had this image of grieving people spilling tears and memories in massive quantities. All the questions that she had been running through her mind seemed trivial and intrusive now. She needed to hear about why he had been in the crane car that day, but decided to start with something safe.

'Some of us have had a hard time dealing with the accident,' she explained. 'I think it would help if we could . . . get a sense of the two men who died – a sense of who they were. What kind of man was Mr Walden? What did he do?'

'Francis was an excitable man.' Helena smiled at her. 'Full of energy. He couldn't sit down unless he was worn out, and it took a lot to do that. He'd wake up in the middle of the night and go for walks because his head was full of ideas. But the children could calm him down . . . he was so good with them—'

Her voice broke, and she stopped to compose herself. Cleo began to feel very awkward, painfully aware that she was imposing on this woman's grief under false pretences.

'Francis and I have two children – I don't know if you knew that. Francis Junior and Agnes. They were devastated. Agnes is still too young to understand, but she knows her daddy is gone . . .'

Cleo desperately wanted to leave now. She did not want to witness this woman breaking down in front of her. She hated grief – hated having to see people lose all composure and cry like hurt children. But she couldn't face failing in her mission either. She was here with a job to do.

'What did he do for a living?' she asked gently. 'Why was he up in the crane car?'

'He had just been made Executive Director, in charge of the personnel department. The executives used the carriages for moving around the complexes. He travelled in it every day; he said they were completely safe . . .' She took a handkerchief from her sleeve and dabbed her eyes.

'There had never been any crane accidents at his old job.'

'His old job?'

'He only moved to Schaeffer two months ago. Before that, he was with Internal Climate. They're Schaeffer's biggest rival, but Francis wasn't happy there—'

'Helena . . .' her sister said softly, a warning note in her voice.

'Oh, what does it matter to her, Virginia?' Helena snapped. 'She's just a schoolgirl, nobody's going to be asking her questions! Who else can I talk to now? I can't just become a hermit!'

Virginia sat back in her chair as Helena carried on.

'What was I saying? Yes, he wasn't very happy at

161

Internal Climate. His boss was Armand Ragnarsson – you know him?'

Cleo nodded. Everybody knew him. Apart from Internal Climate in the Third Quadrant, he also ran most of the Second Quadrant, producing the bulk of the city's food. Like the other executive giants – Takashi, who controlled much of the water filtration in the First Quadrant; Schaeffer, who dominated ventilation in the Third; and McGovern, who recycled the city's waste in the Fourth Quadrant – Ragnarsson was a famous figure. They were the Big Four. Nobody was sure who was the biggest but, even more than the mayor, they were the people who influenced life in Ash Harbour.

'Well, he worked them all very hard up at the office, and Francis especially so. Francis was responsible for dealing with accident claims. He was just the right man for that – he wouldn't give up on a problem until he'd found out everything he could about it, and he really cared about the people who worked under him. That was the kind of man he was, Cleopatra.

'And it was part of the reason he left Internal Climate and went to work for Schaeffer; he was finding that accidents weren't being reported. He couldn't do his job, because reports weren't being filed. If somebody had an accident, it was all hushed up. He only dealt with incidents that were reported, but he found people were being fired for speaking up. They had a union in the main complex, but even *they* didn't do a thing about it. There were even rumours of people going missing—'

'Helena,' Virginia hissed. 'You know what they said!'

'I know what they said!' Helena barked back. 'And I'll tell you what else I know. I know that if he'd left that damn company earlier and not asked so many questions, he'd still be alive, I know that!'

'I think you'd better go,' Virginia said to Cleo.

Cleo nodded, standing up as Helena broke into heaving sobs, with her sister's arms around her. Passing a polished side table in the hall, she paused and took the crumpled chrysanthemum from her pocket, setting it on the tabletop. She did not want any souvenirs from this visit. Walking to the front door, she let herself out.

The remains of the sun were gone from the street, and the glow from the dome just made the twilit surroundings darker. It was another gloomy grey evening and it suited her mood perfectly. She had more questions than answers, and now that she had seen that woman break down in front of her, she realized that she was no longer content to stand back and mind her own business. Cleo wanted to know what the hell was going on.

The ratting den smelled of hard alcohol, smoke, sweat, damp hair and blood. The mood was loud and boisterous, and Sol felt intimidated by the aggressive shouting and laughing of the men around him. The place was filled almost exclusively with men – women

163

did not often gamble on blood sports. As Maslow led him past one of the pits, Sol was jostled by moving bodies as they pushed against each other for a better view of the fight. Down within the ring wall, a pit bull terrier was engaged in a frenzied struggle with a horde of rats. Sol stopped to watch for a moment, transfixed by the violence. The floor of the ring was already spattered with blood, and several rats lay torn open under the feet of the combatants. The dog was tiring, wounded and half blind, but its ferocity was undiminished. Sol looked into the faces of the spectators and saw no sympathy for the animals, only a feverish lust for blood and winnings.

'Stay with me,' Maslow said from behind him. 'I don't want you being caught in here without me.'

They made their way through the crowd; the room with its low ceiling and bare concrete walls was in one of those lost, forgotten spaces between the engineering sections of the city. Hidden in the Filipino District, it was a place where men gathered to gamble on the fights, and drink and smoke their troubles away for a few stolen hours. The staff were all Southeast Asian, and the books were run with strict efficiency – the place had a reputation for being fair, but a man's life could still be ruined here with a few bad choices.

A bar had been constructed at one end, and four pits set up in what had once been reservoirs sunk into the floor. There was no proper ventilation, and the air was heavy and humid. At the bar, Maslow shoved in between two larger men and got the barman's attention.

'Tell Cortez I want to see him,' he shouted over the noise.

The barman didn't ask who he was, and Sol presumed that Maslow's face was known around here. The man waved to a boy at the other end of the bar and yelled something to him. The boy disappeared through a door at the back of the room.

'Cortez runs this place,' Maslow told him. 'He runs the whole district. If your father came here regularly, then Cortez will know him. If he owed money to a Filipino, then Cortez probably owns the debt.'

The barman got his attention and nodded his head towards the door in the back.

'Looks like we have our audience,' Maslow remarked.

They crossed the room to the door, and Sol was about to follow Maslow through when he spotted a tortoise making its painstaking way along the floor at the base of the wall. He reached down and picked it up.

'Somebody could stand on it,' he told Maslow.

'Nobody's going to stand on that thing,' Maslow chuckled. 'Not if they want to stay healthy.'

Down a narrow corridor, they were ushered into a small, dimly lit room away from the noise of the hall. Sol put the tortoise down in a corner, and the animal started for the door again in resigned disgust.

'That Mayon,' a voice grated. 'He was born under a wandering star and no mistake.'

Sitting in a simple chair at a table set for dinner was an old man. Standing by a door behind him was Necktie Romanos, the man who had threatened Sol on the steps of the Earth Centre.

'Maslow,' the old man nodded in greeting.

'Cortez,' Maslow replied respectfully.

'Who's the pup?'

'Gregor Wheat's son,' said Maslow.

'Ah.'

Cortez regarded Solomon with a piercing gaze. His round, benign face did not hide the coldness in his eyes. This was the look reserved for those who owed Cortez money, and Sol began to suffer a renewed fear for his father.

'How much?' Maslow asked.

Cortez turned his gaze on the younger man.

'Three hundred, plus a week's interest. Are you taking it on?'

Maslow took out a roll of plastic coins and threw three hundred and fifty credits on the table.

'That should more than clear him. I don't want to see Necktie or any of your other people near this boy again.'

Cortez didn't touch the money, letting it lie on the table. 'What's your part in this, Maslow?'

'I have a debt of my own to pay.'

Cortez nodded. He waved to the other seats around

the table. He had a cup of aromatic tea in front of him, and he gestured towards the teapot.

'You want something else too, I can tell. Have a seat, have some tea and let's talk like civilized people. Solomon . . . it is Solomon, isn't it? I bet you like to drink, a young man like you, eh? What would you like? We have everything.'

'I don't drink, thanks.'

'A careful young man.' Cortez smiled approvingly.

Maslow took a seat, and Sol sat down beside him.

'The boy's looking for his father,' Maslow said. 'You owe me a favour from that time before.'

'I don't know where he is. That was why Necktie came looking for his son.'

'We're trying to trace him.' Sol spoke up. 'Anything you could tell us would help. I don't know much about this . . . this side of his life. Who did he know? Who was he friends with? Three hundred credits was more than we could afford to gamble with. Why was he betting so much?'

'Easy! Slow down there, boy.' Cortez held his hands up. 'I'm an old man, and slow in my ways. One question at a time.'

He took a sip from his tea.

'My people built this city. They blasted out the crater, dug the foundations, hollowed the crater walls, riveted the steel and moulded the denceramic. And yet many of us are still forced to live beneath its feet, under the gutters and the machinery. But we retain our ingenuity,

Sol, and we can supply what others cannot. That is why people come down here from the higher, brighter levels. To satisfy their needs – for drink, for drugs, for cheap goods and cheap labour. We keep them sitting pretty in their comfortable lives. And I will always be happy to take their money.

'I didn't know your father well, he was just another face, eager to forget the terrible tedium of his life for a few hours. He knew many people here – this is a social place, and men talk easily when indulging forbidden appetites. The man he spent most time with is a local businessman named Tenzin Smith. He had some kind of bond with the man, I don't know what, but if you want to start talking to people, he should be the first. Smith has a workshop and office on Magellan Street, you'll find him there.'

'What about the bet?' Sol asked. 'It's not like him to risk that kind of money – I mean, I know he gambled on the fights, and on the animals, but never so much—'

'Oh, that.' Cortez gave a gurgling laugh. 'That was nothing to do with our business on the floor. That was a personal wager. Hah! Your father, he was struck with a temporary madness, I think. I thought he was having a joke, but everybody knows I never joke about money. He bet me three hundred credits that within two days there would be rainfall in Ash Harbour.'

Section 13/24: Death

They took a sub-city tram to Magellan Street. The carriage was nearly empty; at the far end, three pale, hungry-looking men in overalls were sitting in the half-trance brought on by the motion of the tram. Sol was thinking about the money Maslow had given to Cortez. He had handed it over like it was nothing to him, a sum that was two weeks' wages for his father.

'What do you actually *do* for a living, Maslow?' he asked.

The man glanced at him, expressionless.

'I solve problems for people. The kind of problems the law won't deal with.'

'What did you do for Cortez?'

'I warned him somebody was going to make an attempt on his life.'

'Did you kill them?'

'No, Solomon. I didn't kill them.'

'But it's part of what you do, isn't it?' Sol turned to stare into his face. 'You shot those men to save me.

And you've done it before, it's easy to see that. Do you go around saving hostages much, or do you shoot people for other reasons too?'

Maslow met his gaze.

'I do it when I have to. It's a different world, this low in the city – we work by different rules. You'll learn that when you've been living down here long enough.'

'Gregor said once that Cortez goes on all the time about his people being walked all over, but that he reckons people like Cortez do a lot of the walking.'

'Gregor should mind what he says,' Maslow grunted. 'That kind of talk can get you in trouble.'

'What, worse than betting more than you can afford on something that will never happen? What the hell was that all about? Why would Dad bet that it was going to rain in Ash Harbour?' Sol paused for a second as a terrifying thought occurred to him. 'Does Cortez kill people who don't pay up?'

'Cortez is a businessman. Dead people don't pay. But anybody who owes him and doesn't pay gets hurt. And the longer the debt is owed, the worse the hurt.'

Sol thought again about what Maslow did for a living.

'Why won't you tell me how you knew my dad?'

'I don't want to talk about it. Leave it alone.'

Magellan Street was a long, thin thoroughfare in an industrial area. Smith's workshop was halfway along, beneath the huge, swinging arm of a counterweight for a moving bridge that carried pedestrians from one level above the street to a higher one. A massive block of steel-reinforced concrete on a denceramic arm, it swung back and forth at slow but regular intervals as its platform transported the midday crowds up and down.

Its shadow swept backwards and forwards over the street as Sol and Maslow studied the entrance to the workshop from the concealment of an alleyway.

'I'm going to go in first, and check things out,' Maslow decided finally. 'It's not a safe place. No back exit – see the way it's backed up against the vacuum wall? The only other door is on the side, and it can be seen from the front. Let me go first and I'll wave you in if it's okay – got it?'

Sol nodded. Looking warily up and down the street, Maslow stepped from the mouth of the alley and strolled across, taking one more look around before knocking on the door. Sol watched him go inside and then leaned back against the wall, rubbing his hand over the stubble on his scalp. He was tired. This whole situation had left him scared and confused; who were these people who were after his father? What did Gregor know that had them so worried? And this new twist from Cortez had not helped. Why would his father make such a stupid bet?

He was roused from his musings by the appearance of a man in the alley at the corner of the workshop. He was peering round the corner as if he didn't want to be seen, but was looking casual about it. Sol stood up straighter and stared at him. At one point the man glanced across the road, and when Sol followed his eye-line he found a woman stopping to lean against a lamppost. She was looking casual too. Sol put his hand into his jacket pocket and found the handle of his gun, finding reassurance in its solid weight. His eyes flicked from the man to the woman and back again, studying them, watching to see what they would do. There were not many people on the street, and Sol was sure that both of them were watching the workshop door. Then the woman started across the road, walking so that her path would intercept a third person making his way towards the workshop along the pavement on the other side. She bumped into him just as he passed the corner of the alley, and he looked up in surprise. As he did, the man in the side passage grabbed him from behind and dragged him into the shadows. The woman struck him hard over the back of the neck with a short club as he stumbled backwards. All three disappeared from sight.

Solomon stood watching in shock, his heart pounding. Was this just a mugging, or was it something to do with him? The way they had assaulted the man brought back vivid memories of how he had been snatched from the street himself. His hand was sweaty on the gun's grip, but he was frozen to the spot, unsure of what to do. He had just seen a man viciously attacked, and he had the means to go and help. But

Maslow had told him that under no circumstances were they to draw attention to themselves. They were supposed to stay invisible.

Whether it was the bravado born of having a gun in his hand, or the days he had spent living as a fugitive with a trained killer, Sol found his resolve hardening. His father would have gone to help, he would not have hesitated. Running across the road, Sol ducked his head round the corner of the alley. The two assailants had their back to him, half hidden behind some large recycling bins. Their victim was obviously on the ground behind the dumpsters. Drawing the gun from his pocket, Sol walked quietly towards them, taking careful aim. He was within ten metres of them, but wanted to be sure that they could not dive for cover when he shouted. A quiet, insidious voice inside him hissed that he should just shoot . . . shoot now.

'Who else knows?' the woman was saying. 'Tell us now and this will be quick.'

'I don't know what you're talking about . . . I swear I don't know,' the man on the ground protested, just his hands visible, raised defensively. 'What do you want from me?'

Sol was close now; he knew he should call out, tell them to drop their weapons. Tell them to 'freeze'. He'd seen it so many times in films. But he just kept walking, gun held out in front of him like a torch probing a scary darkness. His voice was caught somewhere in his throat.

Suddenly, directly above him, there came a grating screech, and a shadow swept over him, slowing to a halt. The sound of a tremendous weight crashing down nearby made him stop. The ground trembled beneath their feet, and the shriek of grinding metal made all four of them look up. The huge counterweight had grated to a halt in mid-swing, hanging motionless above them.

Sol came back to his senses and lowered his gaze, to find the other three staring at him.

'Jesus,' said the woman. 'That's the—'

Sol still had the gun pointing at them. He swivelled to point it first at the man, then the woman. He swallowed a lump in his throat.

'Don't . . . freeze!' he barked.

The two would-be assassins burst out laughing helplessly. It was giddy, tension-breaking laughter, and Sol was shocked to see their victim smile despite being obviously terrified.

'"Don't freeze"?' the woman chortled. 'God, that's funny!'

'You're a card, kid,' the man exclaimed as he calmed down. 'Where the hell have you been? We've been looking for you everywhere! Give me that gun before you hurt someone. Come on, hand it over.'

He was reaching out, his hand almost touching the barrel of the gun. His other hand was sliding inside his jacket.

'Stop it!' Sol screamed, his throat tight with terror. 'Don't move!'

174

They weren't listening. People were supposed to listen when you pointed a gun at them. Solomon had expected to hold them at bay and get their victim out of there. Instead, it was as if they were willing him to shoot. Everything that happened next seemed helplessly slow and yet inevitable. The man's gun slid from his jacket. The woman already had her gun out and she was raising it. And then Maslow was behind her. He moved like a shadow. Some instinct must have alerted the woman, because she turned her head, but it was too late. He had one arm over her shoulder and under her chin, his other hand clasped the side of her head and, with one twist, her neck was broken, her body slumping limply against his.

Her partner was lifting his gun. Sol aimed, shutting his eyes as he fired. Only for an instant. His bullet took the man square in the face. The shot was loud in the narrow alley.

'We have to go . . . now!' Maslow said grimly. He turned on the man lying beside the dumpster. 'You're Smith, right? Tenzin Smith? You need to come with us.'

Smith didn't argue. Sol stared down at the man he had just killed. There was a small hole to the left side of his nose, and his eyes were still open. There was very little blood on his face, but a large splash of it on the wall behind where his head had been. Sol knew his life had just changed for ever, but part of him wasn't ready to accept it, as if it wanted to keep him at a distance from the gun in his trembling hand. Standing there in a daze, he shook his head. He had just shot somebody dead. He couldn't believe it.

'Solomon!' Maslow snapped.

Sol looked up and nodded. But his eyes fell again on the woman who lay at Maslow's feet, her head twisted at an impossible angle. Even more than the man he had shot, Sol found the sight of a woman killed like that profoundly unsettling.

Maslow grabbed Sol's shoulder and pushed him towards the mouth of the alley. All three of them hurried as casually as they could for the street, making themselves scarce before the gunshot attracted unwanted attention. Before long they had lost themselves in the warren of back alleys under the shadows of the upper streets.

Smith sat on a stack of concrete blocks, warily eyeing first Maslow and then Sol. They were on a derelict building site; a small bit of waste ground in the shadow of an electricity substation. Nearby, the glow of a light-well carrying daylight from the levels above was the only indication that it was still early afternoon. The gaslights around them flickered weakly, casting a frail, wobbling light. The power plant's hum throbbed out of sync with the ever-present rumble of the city, and the chill air had a grittiness to it; a smell of static and dust. Sol stood in front of Smith, with Maslow leaning against a wall to one side. Smith was short and stocky, with fair hair and a ruddy complexion, the broken-veined hue of a heavy drinker. His mouth drooped at the corners, and his eyes were a faded blue. He was trembling, still in shock from what had happened. Rolling a joint of stem with shaking fingers, spilling more than he rolled, he put it to his lips and pulled an ancient Zippo lighter from his pocket.

'I haven't seen your father in weeks,' he said again as he lit up. 'I'm sorry, I don't know what else I can tell you.'

'So why were those people about to do you in?' Sol asked.

''Cos, like you, they seem to think I know something I don't.'

'Do you have any idea where Gregor might be hiding?' Sol persisted. 'Anywhere he might go if he was in trouble? I have to find him. He's up to his neck in crap.'

'I think he might be aware of that, kid.'

'He's dropped me in it too – and you as well. You think he's aware of *that*?'

Smith glanced sourly at Maslow, then turned his gaze back on Sol.

'Look, Solomon. I'd help you find him if I could – honest.' Smith brushed his hair back, looking tired and under strain. 'I know this has got to be tough for you. But your dad's vanished off the face of the earth, and it's probably better he stays that way for the time being. If Gregor could help you, I'm sure he would. If he hasn't been in touch, it's because he can't, so cut him some slack.'

'What are you going to do now?' Sol asked him. 'They'll be looking for you too.'

'I've got some friends I can stay with for a while.' Smith sighed, rubbing his hands together. 'But long term? I don't know. You can't hide in this city for ever, there's just nowhere to go. If they really want to find me, they will eventually.' He looked up at Maslow again. 'Either I get myself some kind of protection, or—'

'Or you hold out until they find my dad themselves,' Sol finished for him.

'Yeah . . . yeah, and just hope for the best. Sorry, kid.'

'I wish you luck,' Solomon told him bitterly. He looked up at Maslow. 'Let's go. He's not going to be any use to us.'

'One thing, Solomon,' Smith called after him as they walked away. 'The guy they say Gregor killed? Hyung? Your dad had him pegged for an earhole. Maybe the grit had it comin', huh?'

Sol ground his teeth as he strode out of the building site and into a side street. He wasn't getting anywhere. Maslow followed close behind, leaving him to his thoughts and keeping watch around them for any sign of a threat. Sol could feel him at his back without having to look behind him; a reassuring shadow, his guardian angel.

'We're not getting anywhere,' Sol said at last. 'I need to talk to Cleo again, see what she's found out.'

'You mean go to her place?'

'Yeah. I've no other way of getting hold of her, seeing as we can't use the web.'

'I don't think that's a good idea, Sol,' Maslow cautioned him. 'Not this evening. We've just had a run-in with two Clockworkers; contacting Cleo would be a stupid thing to do right now.'

Sol stopped abruptly, turning on him.

'That's the first time you've called them that. "Clockworkers". You know more than you're telling me, don't you? Who the hell are they? What do they want with my dad?'

'I only know what they are, I don't know who's running them.' Maslow calmly met his gaze. 'Somebody with real pull, and I don't mean like Cortez; these guys want to affect the workings of the Machine itself. Over the years the system's grown much more . . . more complicated than it was supposed to be, and that makes it difficult to manage. The Clockworkers trim it – keep it hemmed in so it doesn't get out of control. Like I said, I've dealt with their types before. We've been lucky so far; we've crossed them twice and come out on top both times. But if we expose ourselves too much, then sooner or later they'll corner us.'

'Yeah? Well, I think Smith had it right,' Sol snapped. 'This city's too small to hide in for ever: they'll find us eventually. I think the only thing we can do is find out what's going on and get it out in the open. Get the police . . . the *real* police onto this whole thing and get it stopped. These grits are breaking the law – that's got to mean something! We just need to . . . to . . . show people what's up, y'know? Find out the truth and make it public.'

Maslow regarded him with what looked suspiciously like sympathy.

'Make it public?' he grunted. 'Who are you going to tell? Who do you think's going to care? You think anybody gives a damn about what goes on outside of their little lives? You want to risk your life to uncover some conspiracy and hope these people don't kill you when you start shouting about it? This is how this city works, Sol – you can't change that. This is real life, the hard stuff they don't teach you about in school.'

He put his hands on Sol's shoulders.

'You could uncover whatever operation has sent your dad into hiding, you might even get a reporter or a politician to listen to you, but that'll be it. This kind of thing goes on all the time – you think they're not aware of it? Of course they are! They're *part* of it – they're not going to do anything to help you 'cos it'll stir up too much crap. This whole damn city keeps working because people turn a blind eye to the likes of Cortez and the dirty deals and the strong-arm stuff. It wouldn't work without them.

'I promised Gregor I'd keep you safe, and I'll help you find him if we can; but you have to realize you're

180

in the underworld now. You won't be going back to school, you won't be going back to normal life; that's all over now, because if you get caught by these people, you're *dead*. You have to harden up and keep your head down, 'cos we're on our own here. Nobody's going to help us. Do you understand?'

Sol let out a ragged sigh. He had been hanging onto the hope that somehow, if he solved the mystery of Tommy Hyung's murder, everything else would work itself out. But he had seen enough to know that it wasn't true. The Clockworkers, whoever they were, seemed to be beyond the law. Even the police couldn't protect him for ever; not against these dark figures who haunted the city. His mind went back to the cold room where he'd hung from chains, where a man had shown him a pair of pliers. With a leaden, sinking feeling, he realized that by getting Cleo involved, he might have condemned her to the same fate.

'Solomon? Do you understand what I'm telling you?'

Sol nodded.

But what was left to him then? Was he condemned to spend the rest of his life on the run? And how was he going to find Gregor?

'I need to see Cleo again,' he said firmly. 'See if she's talked to Walden's widow.'

'Not today.'

'Why not?'

'Not today, Sol. Maybe tomorrow. Come on, we're too exposed out here. Let's get inside and find something to eat – I'm starving. We'll go and see Cleo tomorrow.'

Section 14/24: Demolition

Ana Kiroa sat on the grass with her eyes closed, Julio's arms around her, listening to the sounds of birds. A gentle breeze ruffled her soft hair, mixing with his warm breath on her neck and the side of her face. Leaning back against his chest, she drew in a long breath, relishing the mingled scents of fresh grass, pine and a dozen different flowers; some, like tulips and chrysanthemums, poppies and sunflowers, she knew from her walks in the conservation section of the hydroponic gardens; most she had never smelled before.

The sound of the wind in the trees brought a smile to her face and, keeping her eyes closed, she imagined herself on a wide, open hillside on the edge of a forest, looking out over a balmy, sunny landscape of untamed countryside. This was as far removed as she could possibly be from the utilitarian walls of the classroom. The sunlight was warm and bright on her eyelids. Wiggling her bare toes in the grass, she turned and kissed Julio long and hard on the mouth. A soft bell chimed, and he pulled his face back, smiling at her.

'Time's up, somebody else's turn now.' He gave an exaggerated frown.

'Drat.'

She opened her eyes and gazed resignedly around her at the screens that made up the walls and ceiling, showing the hillside as it had once been. They were in a private simulation chamber; hidden ventilation ducts blew the fake breeze across the room, the carefully regulated moisture and temperature levels mixed with manufactured scents to complete the illusion. Surround-sound speakers carried the sounds of the birds across the imaginary sky, along with the rustling sound of trees that had become extinct centuries before.

Even the grass was synthetic, a gently sloping bank three metres square; they'd had to leave their shoes at the door. She patted the creases out of the floral 'summer' dress she'd worn for the occasion. It was the most expensive thing she owned.

Time in one of these chambers did not come cheap either; she had never been in one before. But Julio worked for the owners, Internal Climate, and could get concessions. And he loved treating her. His square-jawed face and stocky body belied his somewhat nerdish lifestyle, revelling in the chaos mathematics of air currents and thermal patterns. Ana had never met anyone who could make ventilation sound so romantic.

'That was fantastic, thank you.' She hugged him as they walked over to the door. 'God, you can just imagine what it was like . . .'

Julio nodded.

'And to think you could just go out and do it,' he wondered wistfully. 'Sit on a hillside – a *real* one – for free!'

They sat on the seats provided, putting on their shoes. As soon as Ana had slipped on her wildly impractical stiletto pumps, she pushed Julio up against the wall for one last, passionate kiss as the images disappeared from the screens. When they broke apart, the scenes had changed; dark clouds, like swirls of ink in water, were looming over a mountainous region, with pulsing glows of lightning in their depths. The breeze had grown cold and damp. The next client obviously had a thing for storms.

'Jules,' Ana gasped as he followed her out the door, 'do you think they can do rain?'

'I *know* they can,' he said, grinning. 'But it costs extra. Maybe if we save for a month or two . . .'

Her mind lost in the wondrous possibilities of being caught in a rainstorm on a hillside with Julio, Ana let herself be led out of the facility.

'These things used to be open to the public, you know,' he said, almost to himself. 'The city ran them like the libraries. They thought it was vital for the children. Everything worked better back then too. A hundred years ago the dome had tropical temperatures

185

for half the year. I mean, the kinds of temperatures you had in the tropics before they froze over.'

Ana squeezed his arm.

'I suppose there was a better sense of community then,' he added. 'There were still other habitats out there; there might even have been a few people still alive outside the known enclaves. But the folks in Ash Harbour knew *they* stood the best chance of surviving. Nothing buoys up the spirits like knowing you're going to outlive the other guy.

'I don't think we appreciate what we've got now. This is a fantastic city, but nobody sees that any more, because they're not under threat. Sometimes I think what people need is a good scare to wake them up.'

'Don't go getting morbid on me.' Ana elbowed him. 'I'm out to have a good time tonight. You're supposed to be treating me like a princess.'

'Then command me, Your Majesty!' he exclaimed, with a grin.

They passed along a hall of private light-chambers, where people could pay to stand, soaking in the augmented daylight refracted through lenses and along mirrored channels; gloriously bright compared to the large, drab light-shafts found in public spaces around the rest of the city, and more secluded than the crowded sun-platforms beneath the dome. There were thermo-chambers, where people could get a genuine-looking tan – unlike the less salubrious ultra-violet orange that was available in beauty parlours in poorer parts of the city – and wind tunnels where adventurous souls could glide, paraglide and even skydive in the safety of voluminous padding.

And these were only a few of the tightly compacted activities that Internal Climate's Weather Centre could offer. For the right price. Ana and Julio strolled down the ramp that led from the grand entrance to the street, arms around each other, communicating their affection in tight squeezes and stolen kisses.

As they reached the brightly lit shopping promenade, turning to make for a nearby café, a dark red, muscular car rolled up, its powerful electric engine whirring with quiet arrogance over the sound of the music from the bars. The CIS inspector, Mercier, opened the passenger-side door and got out.

'Ms Kiroa. I wonder if you would come with us, if you don't mind?'

He opened the car's back door and waited for her to get in. He did not seem to consider the possibility that she might refuse.

'What's going on?' Julio demanded. 'What do you want with her?'

'It's all right.' Ana sighed. 'I know what it's about. We'd better go.'

As she made for the car, Julio went to follow, but Mercier held up his hand, stepping in front of him.

'Just the lady, sir. I'm afraid this doesn't concern you.'

'I'll decide what does and doesn't concern me.'

Julio's jaw muscles flexed, his body tensing at the challenge. 'I'm going with her.'

'No, you're not, sir,' Mercier replied firmly. 'Stand back, please, sir. Now.'

He was smaller than Julio, but his voice was loaded with authority. Julio's aggression faltered and he took a step back. His eyes followed Ana as she climbed into the car, and she felt a moment of pity for him as he stood helpless on the pavement. In an old-fashioned, protective way that she found hopelessly attractive, he prided himself on being 'her man'.

'Go home,' she called to him. 'I'll call over when I'm done here, okay?'

The car pulled away, and she gave him a reassuring wave, which he returned half-heartedly.

'So, what do you want now?' she snapped at the car full of policemen.

Beside her was the ISS inspector who had been interrogating Solomon when she had pulled him out of the police station. The ginger-haired driver had been there too, dressed like his boss in a dapper, wine-coloured uniform. The memory of that day gave her the shivers; three men intimidating a schoolboy as if he were a prisoner of war.

'Ms Kiroa,' the man beside her greeted her in a slightly reedy voice. 'We weren't properly introduced last time we met. My name is Inspector Ponderosa, ISS. We'd like to have a few words with you about Solomon Wheat.'

'I've already told him everything,' Ana said curtly, pointing at Mercier's back. 'Don't you guys ever talk?'

'The inspector has given me a full and comprehensive report,' Ponderosa informed her, his thin lips breaking into a warm smile. 'He excels at filing reports, don't you, Inspector? But I'm a social learner, I like to hear things from the horse's mouth, so to speak.'

'There's nothing else I can tell you. Sol's gone. I don't know where. Why don't you just leave him alone? He hasn't done anything wrong.'

'Yes.' Ponderosa looked out of the window at the passing street. They were in Roebling Hill, an affluent part of town not far from the city centre. As they travelled along the road, the shopping malls and office blocks were starting to give way to a well-heeled residential area. He talked while he watched the street, sounding almost as if he were talking to himself. 'Up until today, I would have agreed with you. But this afternoon, things . . . changed.'

He said very little else while they continued out towards the city wall, and Ana was left wondering where they were taking her. It wasn't to the ISS headquarters; that was in the other direction. Her brusque manner was all for show; an attempt to hide how nervous she felt. Every now and again Mercier would glance back at her from the passenger seat, and his face did not inspire confidence.

'Where the hell are we going?' she squawked, and then winced at how scared it made her sound.

'To the scene of a crime,' Ponderosa replied.

The neighbourhoods grew steadily worse out here; this was the Titan Banks, an industrial slum. The car swung left onto a wide main road, and glided out over a two-lane bridge that linked to the Outer Ring Road skirting the city wall itself. Near the middle of the span the driver pulled the car over, and Ponderosa asked Ana to step out. He followed her, gesturing towards the railing.

Below them was a helter-skelter of walkways, walls and pigeon-dropping-spattered rooftops. In the gaps between the criss-crossing roads and tram rails, Ana could see down three or four levels; it must have been a sixty-metre drop. The legs of the bridge joined the superstructures of buildings that housed businesses and workshops in the lower levels. Ponderosa put a hand on her shoulder and, for an irrational moment, she thought he was going to push her over the railing. But he simply pointed down at a group of people on a street two levels down. They were police officers; she could see their cars blocking off the lower street in both directions.

Ana realized she was looking at the scene of an accident – a big one. Lying on the street was what remained of a moving denceramic walkway, the type that swung people from one side of a divide to another, like a moving bridge. The entire structure had collapsed: she could see the remains of its arm sticking out from under the bridge she was standing on. Its steel-reinforced concrete counterweight dangled precariously from the other end of the arm, straining at its fulcrum.

'Three people killed, eleven injured,' Ponderosa said mildly. 'Lives ruined by the rot. There is a decay in this city, Ms Kiroa. We don't know if this was caused by inefficiency or outright sabotage, but we'll find out. There are people who want to bring this city to its knees; they are the rot, the cancer, eating their way from the bottom up. This destruction has brought three Machine districts to a complete stop by breaking the chain of movement and cutting the power flow; we've lost nearly half a million kilowatt hours since it happened. That's about four per cent of the city's daily power output – and the Machine's only working at sixty per cent capacity right now. There'll be a lot of people without lights tonight; water and electricity too. All because of a walkway collapse. The mayor is not happy . . . and neither am I.

'Anybody who messes with my city, Ms Kiroa, will end up dealing with me. I'll find the cancers that did this, and when I do I'm going to enjoy the surgery.'

Ana stared down at the ruined walkway, taking in the debris and splashes of blood picked out of the gloom by the newly rigged floodlights, the police officers walking around taking measurements and marking the positions of forensic evidence. Even from this distance it made her feel queasy. She turned away to see the ISS driver was standing by the railing, staring at her, expressionless. Mercier was still sitting in the passenger seat of the car, jotting something down in his notebook. He obviously had no role to play in Ponderosa's scene-setting.

'But what has this got to do with you?' Ponderosa asked suddenly. 'What are you doing here?'

He gave her a questioning stare, as if he expected her to have the answer. Then he pointed off to one side of the walkway's arm, below its counterweight.

'We don't know the connection yet, but you see that alley down there? You can't see into it now, it's too dark, but you see where it is?'

Ana regarded the dark rift between the buildings and gave a shrug. Ponderosa's expression hardened.

'That's where Solomon and another, unidentified man were involved in a double homicide. A man was shot through the face, and a woman had her neck broken. The alley is next to the workshop of a man named Tenzin Smith. We wanted to talk to him regarding Gregor Wheat's whereabouts. Mr Smith is now missing too.'

Ana felt her heart sink.

'How . . . how do you know—?'

'How do we know it was our young Mr Wheat? Because when he crossed the street on his way to the alley, he carelessly looked straight into the security camera Smith has over his workshop door. Moments later, the camera caught Solomon and two other men running from the scene.'

'Jesus.'

'It would seem he's keeping some very bad company, don't you think? And what about this man Mercier told you about, Necktie Romanos? Any idea why Solomon would have a debt collector after him? Is it to do with his father?'

'How should I know? You think kids talk to their teachers about this kind of stuff?'

Ponderosa leaned in close to her face.

'I want to know what the hell is going on,' he said softly. 'You are going to tell me everything you know about Solomon Wheat. I want to know who his friends are in school, what his hobbies are, what girls – or boys – he's into. I want to know who else knows anything about him. I. Want. To. Know. Everything.' He held up his hands, splaying his fingers either side of her head. 'You're a teacher. Educate me.'

Cleo was helping her younger sister with her homework; it was late, and Cleo badly needed a smoke, but Victoria was resisting her attempts to impart knowledge.

'But how can x be equal to twelve? It's a *letter*.'

'You're calling it x because you don't know what it is,' Cleo explained.

'But I know it's twelve!'

'Only because I've just told you. Imagine you don't know what it is, and you have to find out. To do the sum, you have to call it something, so you call it twelve . . . sorry, I mean x. Got it?'

'Kind of,' Vicky grunted, in a voice that said she remained unconvinced.

'Right. So you know y equals eight, yeah?'

'Yeeeaah.'

'So, if x minus y equals four, and you know y is eight, then what's x?'

Vicky lips moved as she did the simple arithmetic in her head. Cleo looked at her meaningfully. Vicky's eyes widened.

'Oh . . . twelve?'

'Exactly!'

They were in the living room, where the webscreen was playing pop music softly because Vicky couldn't study without it. Their parents were having one of their rare nights out, leaving Cleo to apply her feeble academic skills to her sister's first foray into algebra. Cleo hated algebra.

'Right, let's do this next one,' she breathed. 'If x plus y plus z equals sixteen, and x equals four and y equals seven—'

'It's "Devil's Jukebox"!' Vicky squealed as the first bars of her favourite song came over the webscreen's speakers.

Jumping to her feet, she dragged her sister out of the chair.

'You can dance to this any time!' Cleo protested, but she was smiling as she was hauled up to stand next to Vicky.

Together they spread their feet, raised their arms and started to do the new dance that was taking the city by storm. Bobbing their heads to the quick beat of 'Devil's Jukebox', they pranced from side to side, spinning on their heels and waving their arms up and down as they joined in with the singing.

'*I'mmm . . . picking my tune,*' Vicky sang at the top of her voice, '*from the Devil's Jukebox!*'

'*I'mmm . . . dancin' in nothing, but a pair of white socks!*' Cleo wailed into an imaginary microphone.

It was a silly, smutty song, and Cleo would have sneered at it if she had been with her friends. But Vicky never tolerated any pretensions from her. They danced around the small room, banging their shins on the furniture and finally falling entangled on the couch as the song ended.

'Okay, that's enough,' Cleo panted. 'You have homework to do. I'm going out for a bit.'

'Goin' for a smoke?' Vicky asked slyly.

'No.' Cleo glanced behind her at the door, in case their parents should walk in at that very moment.

'Can I come, then?'

'No – finish your homework. I'll be back in a while.'

'When are you going to let me smoke some stem?' Vicky persisted plaintively.

'When Dad says you're old enough to date boys,' Cleo told her.

'Damn it, Cleo! That won't be till I'm, like . . . forty, or something.'

Cleo picked up her jacket and left their apartment, making her way up the four flights of stairs to the roof. It was dark up there, her path lit only by the ethereal glow of the city, reflected off the bottoms of the sun platforms, the crane grid and the glass of the dome itself. Stepping over the vents and low walls of pipes that ran across the rooftop, she settled in her favourite place: in the shadow of an air-conditioner-plant housing that throbbed dully all through the night. The wall of the plant was always warm from the motors inside. Reaching up to a hollow under the lip of the plant's roof, she found the tin box that held her stash, and, taking it down, she sat on the ledge and looked out at the lights of Ash Harbour while she skinned up a joint.

Licking the feathery rice paper roll to seal it, she dried it with her lighter and then put it between her lips and fired it up. She drew in the smoke with a soft sigh, feeling its rough heat in her lungs. The gentle lifting sensation at the back of her skull brought a content smile to her face, and she rolled her head around to bring on that delicious dizziness. There was a sound of footsteps behind her, and she looked worriedly round the corner of the wall, a drug-induced paranoia rising within her. She became sure that somebody was watching her. Holding the joint hidden down by her leg, she peered across the dark roof, searching for the source of the sound.

A woman wearing a cap and dark overalls and

carrying a toolbox strode out from behind the structure that housed the winch for the elevator that hardly ever worked. Waving a small torch around, the stranger knelt down by one of the large pipes that snaked over the roof, turning the wheel on what looked like a valve of some kind. She moved on, bending down once more to do the same on a pipe further away. The woman disappeared from sight round the corner of the stairwell. Cleo let out a wheezy breath and stuck the joint back in her mouth.

As she sat there smoking, a faint sense of foreboding came over her. For some reason her mind went back to the day in the sub-levels, when she had seen the three people dumping the body. And the man she might have killed. His scream still came to her in quiet moments when she was in a funk.

She hardly ever saw work crews on the roof at night. In fact, her parents were always complaining about how hard it was to get anybody in to fix anything in the building. And when they did come up, they used bright lamps, not sneaky little torches. And they made a big fuss, so that everybody would see that they'd shown up. And they wore the maintenance contractors' light green overalls with the logo on the back. Cleo stubbed out the half-finished joint and put it in her jacket pocket, carefully replacing the tin box back in its hiding place. She headed for the door to the stairwell, wondering if the drug were playing with her mind.

Sauntering down the stairs, she was struck again by

the feeling that something was wrong. She stopped at the bottom of the flight, still two storeys up from their apartment. Stepping into the corridor, she stood there silently, trying to figure out what was disturbing her. The diode clusters that lit the corridor were dim, and some had failed completely, but that was quite normal. All around were the small noises of the building settling in the night – clicks and taps and creaks; again, all normal.

There was the soft, undercurrent hum of the air-conditioning system, which channelled 'fresh' air through the living quarters packed into the apartment block like the cells of a vast hive. Vents in the ceiling panels of the corridor showed where the duct ran along above, feeding the apartments on either side. People would have the vents in the apartments closed in the evening; the air fed in could be very chilly at night, and the recycled breeze tended to give everyone colds and coughs. The gas-fired heating system used different ducts.

There was the hint of a strange odour. Standing under the nearest vent, she sniffed the air. Two years of smoking stem had deadened her sense of smell, but she was definitely getting a whiff of something. Cleo walked further down the corridor, inhaling the air from another vent. The odour was stronger here, and her eyes opened wide with alarm as she recognized what it was. She knocked on the nearest door, and a sleepy-faced man looked out.

'There's a gas leak!' she told him. 'Call the . . . the caretakers, or somebody.'

He was about to retort, but instead he waved a hand in front of his face and drew a breath in through his nose. His expression changed to one of urgency.

'I'll make the call,' he told her. 'Let other people know, will you?'

Cleo started knocking on more doors, calling out to alert people. The smell was getting stronger in the corridor, but it still hadn't reached into the apartments. She came upon the sealed box that set off the fire alarm, and stared at it, hesitating. Was it that urgent? They'd had gas leaks before and there had been no evacuation. And the alarm system was electric; could it ignite the gas? To hell with it, she'd always wanted to do this; she smashed the face of the box with her elbow, and jumped as the alarm went off.

Suddenly she thought of her sister and started running. There had been too many false alarms in the block; people were moving too slowly. Nobody was taking it very seriously – there were even people complaining about the noise. The stink of gas filled the stairwell; it was definitely coming through the air-conditioning system. It could be filtering through the whole building, whisked on by the fans. She bounded down the steps, swinging round the rail as the stairs cornered, descending at a breakneck pace. Slamming through the door onto her floor, she raced down the corridor. Residents were milling around, wondering at the alarm. Some were already hurrying towards the stairs. They could smell the gas too.

We're two storeys down, Cleo thought to herself, and I can still smell it. It's right through the building. Victoria was leaning out of the apartment door, looking around in confusion. Cleo waved her arms at her sister.

'It's right through the—' she started to yell, and then there was a deafening boom, and a hot blast of air lifted her off her feet and sent her sprawling along the corridor floor.

The ceiling was exploding. Fire burst through the flimsy ceiling panels, exposing the utility rigging of wires and pipes above. In the aluminium air-conditioning ducts there was a rumbling, roaring sound as the ignited gas chased the oxygen along the metal channel, seeking out places to breathe as it burned up the air, searching for more food to feed the growing blaze. The ducting burst all the way down the corridor, releasing gouts of flame; people were screaming and running for the stairs.

Cleo felt a numb pounding in her ears, and scrambled to her feet as a breeze started to blow down the corridor. Smoke was already making it difficult to breathe, and she coughed, putting a hand over her nose and mouth to keep out the flecks of burned debris that filled the air. Vicky was lying in the doorway, blood staining her blonde hair. The blast must have thrown her against the jamb of the door. Cleo called for help, but everyone was rushing for the stairs. She gazed down the corridor in despair; flame was creeping down the walls, eating the paint, the fixtures; the ceiling panels, supposedly fireproof, were blazing in pieces across the floor. Smoke formed an impenetrable cloud that billowed towards her, driven by the fire's breath.

Grabbing her sister's arms, she pulled her into the apartment, kicking the door closed behind her. The explosion had burst through the duct in one wall, and the flames were creeping their way down the couch towards the floor. It was made of the same hardened lino as the ceiling panels. The floor shook as other explosions erupted through the building.

Dragging her sister across the smoky apartment to the living-room window, she quickly unlatched it. There was a fire escape outside. She was already exhausted, her lungs catching on the gritty fumes, making her cough and choke. As she opened the window, the draught of air gave new life to the blaze in the apartment, and it clawed across the ceiling. Cleo cried as she struggled to lift her sister's inert body through the window. Vicky flopped like an unfeasibly heavy rag doll, flimsy and awkward, but in a final heave Cleo fell backwards through the window, pulling her sister with her. They landed hard on the denceramic grille of the walkway.

From somewhere inside the building she heard a monster roar, and fire exploded through the windows two storeys above them, showering them with glass and burned fragments of people's homes. Cleo cowered over her sister's head and shoulders, screaming in terror. They were three storeys up, and the only way down from the fire escape was by a sloping series of ladders. Despite being more than three years younger, Vicky was almost the same size as her big sister. Cleo doubted she would be able to carry her down a ladder.

'Vicky!' she cried, gently slapping the younger girl's face. 'Vicky, you have to wake up! C'mon! Wake up!'

Vicky's eyes opened, but remained glazed over. She did not even lift her head. Cleo coughed and cursed, ducking down as flames came through their living-room window. Hauling her sister along the fire escape towards the ladder, she frantically tried to work out a way down. She was vaguely aware of sirens, but was enveloped by smoke. There was just her, Vicky, the fire escape and the blaze. Another explosion ripped through the building above her and she flinched, waiting for more glass, or even a wall to collapse over her. With no strength to carry Vicky down the ladder, Cleo climbed on herself, and pulled her sister's body after her. They fell heavily, but Cleo was able to hold on long enough to take the full force of Vicky's weight before she dropped onto the lower walkway. Vicky's left hand was bent back at an impossible angle: the fall had broken her wrist.

Cleo was breathing in heaving coughs – she had no more air left in her lungs. The world spun around her head as she crawled towards the next ladder, gripping her sister's other wrist. She gagged as she leaned over

the edge and, lifting herself onto her knees, she finally
blacked out, teetering forward over the three-metre
drop towards the ladder, and falling headfirst into the
arms of a fireman.

Ana Kiroa emerged from the ISS headquarters feeling cold and hollow. After three hours of being grilled by Inspector Ponderosa, she wanted to go home and have a shower, to clean the stain of this place from her body. It wasn't supposed to be like this. These men were enforcing the law; protecting innocent people from the criminals. Solomon and his father were wanted in connection with murders, but every name, every piece of information Ana had given to the police to help find the fugitives had felt like an act of betrayal. Held in a small room with Ponderosa and his bullying henchmen standing over her, asking the same questions over and over again, shouting at her, making vague threats; she had wanted to stand her ground, to show that they didn't intimidate her. But the only thing that stopped her breaking down in tears as she walked out was the desire to be clean, and to be wrapped up in Julio's warm embrace.

'Ms Kiroa?' a voice called after her, and she looked

round, fearful that they were going to call her back.

It was Mercier, walking up behind her, his overcoat folded over his arm. He had not taken part in the interrogation; Ponderosa had sent him on his way as if he were some lowly patrolman.

'Can I give you a lift home?'

She wanted to tell him to get lost, but it was a long tram ride back, and a car would get her there faster. She shrugged. He waved to a nearby car and it drew up; that sergeant, Baiev, sat behind the wheel. Ana let Mercier open the door for her.

'We'll have you back in no time,' he told her.

Ana was about to make an acidic remark about him being Ponderosa's delivery boy, but the cowed expression on his face as he spoke stopped her short. He climbed into the front, and Baiev pulled out into the traffic. The police radio crackled with abbreviated messages every few seconds.

'I'm sorry if Inspector Ponderosa seemed a bit hard on you back there,' Mercier said from the passenger seat, glancing round. 'He's a dogged investigator, one of the most respected men on the force; but his methods can be somewhat . . . insensitive, at times.'

'Aren't you capable of handling this case on your own?' Ana asked. 'How many inspectors do they need to run things?'

Mercier did not answer immediately, staring out at the road through the windscreen. She could see his doughy white hands resting on his knees, the nails neatly clipped. In his nondescript suit, with his officious manner, she was struck again with the image of the policeman as a bureaucrat, a career paper-shuffler. He looked back at her again, his flabby chin folding into wrinkles.

'The ISS have taken the lead role in this investigation. It's our job to help them where we can,' he said, but there was a petty tone in his voice. 'And we are happy to oblige. Isn't that right, Sergeant?'

Baiev nodded. Ana wondered if the man ever spoke at all.

'Might I ask' – Mercier looked back at her again – 'did the inspector put any questions to you about the crane accident at all?'

Ana frowned. With everything else that was going on, she'd almost forgotten about the horrific day of the school tour.

'No. Why would he ask me about that?'

'It's just that he's investigating that case as well. It's nothing, I was just curious. I'm sure your witness statement from the time had everything he needed.'

There was a peculiar orange glow against the dome's glass over to the south, and Ana raised her head to try to get a better view. She could hear sirens as they approached the Third Quadrant.

'What is that?' she asked hesitantly. 'What's going on?'

'There's a fire on Halske Street,' Mercier replied.

'Spartan Hall. There was a large gas explosion. Terrible business.'

'Spartan Hall!' Ana started. 'Some of my students live there! Take me there, please!'

'I'm sure there will be more than enough people obstructing the emergency services as it is, Ms Kiroa. I think it would be better if we just—'

'Please! I have to see if they're all right!'

Mercier gave a resigned sigh and nodded slightly to Baiev. They steered in the direction of the fire, and soon they could see a massive pillar of smoke, lit from beneath by the flames that were devouring the apartment block's insides. Ana leaned forward between the front seats, stunned by the scale of the inferno. As it rose into sight above the roofs of the other buildings, they could see that Spartan Hall had been devastated. Jets of water from the hoses of fire crews arced over the blaze, but there was little of the building left to save. The car drew up just short of Halske Street, prevented from getting any closer by the police cordon and the crowds of shell-shocked people staring aghast at the gutted remains of their home.

Solomon stood on the walkway above the piston well where Tommy Hyung had died, and watched Cleo's apartment block burn. Baffled by what he had learned from Cortez, he had gone back to tracing his father's last movements. Unsure of Gregor's route to this point, he had picked the shortest path from the depot to this walkway, searching all along the way for clues to his father's whereabouts. But he could find nothing. Gazing down at the eight pistons pumping, each one the length of a tram and almost as heavy, ramming down to within centimetres of the floor of the well, he imagined what would happen to a body that fell in there. The noise was rhythmic, harsh and overpowering.

He had not mentioned seeing the Third Quadrant crane to Maslow, unsure of its significance. He only had a hunch, and a weak one at that; Maslow's patience was already wearing thin, and Sol was acutely aware of his protector's warnings that he was putting them in danger. And now Cleo's home was on fire.

The pillar of dense, black smoke could be seen from all over the city, and Sol had soon located the source of it. He could only pray that Cleo had got out.

Fire was doubly hazardous in Ash Harbour, particularly one that produced such a massive column of smoke. With nowhere for the smoke to go, it had to be pumped out by the ventilators. And they weren't exactly at the top of their game at the moment. The smoke would stain the dome and settle on the city. It would clog the carbon-dioxide filters, and most of the toxic particles and fumes would stay in the air for days, the ash settling all over the area like thick dust. Long after the inferno was put out, it would still be affecting people's health.

At first he had asked himself if this could be his

fault. He had asked her to help, and the Clockworkers had set fire to her home to silence her. But it couldn't be; nobody would burn down an apartment block just to kill one schoolgirl – that would be insanity. And then he had started thinking about what Maslow had said earlier.

'You said "Not today"!' Sol shouted.

'What?'

Sol swivelled to glare over at the other man, who stood further along the walkway.

'"Not today", you said. As in "we can't go and see Cleo *today*. Maybe tomorrow". That's what you said.'

Maslow was leaning on the railing, sharpening a knife on a whetstone. He didn't look up.

'So?'

'So, why not today, Maslow? Have I been really faggin' blind, or what? You knew this was going to happen, didn't you?'

Maslow didn't reply; he just continued honing his knife.

'And you knew it was going to happen, because it was no accident, am I right? Somebody set this up. This is what the Clockworkers do, isn't it? They make accidents happen. This is how the city works, isn't it, huh? So how did you know that they were going to be doing it tonight? How did you know?' Sol stared across at him, irritated by his silence. 'Maslow . . . are you a Clockworker?'

The knife paused on the whetstone, and Maslow

finally met Sol's gaze. He came nearer to save himself from shouting over the noise of the pistons.

'Yeah, I'm a Clockworker. Or at least, I was. Now I'm out in the cold. As soon as they figure out it's me who's helping you, I'll be put on the wet list.'

He pointed with his knife at the distant blaze.

'That was to be our next operation. The two men who nabbed you off the street, the ones I saved you from, were my crew – or part of it. There are three others still out there. Come on, let's get away from this noise.'

'What about the other two, with Smith, in the alley?' Sol asked as they left the pounding machinery behind them.

'Another team. I didn't know them.'

'How many of you are there?'

'I don't know.' Maslow glided the stone in smooth swipes down the edge of the blade, cleaning off the burrs. 'A lot. None of the teams are supposed to know each other, although I've crossed paths with a few; we work in independent cells. Everything's secret.'

Solomon moved closer to him, his mind filled with questions, all remaining trust in this enigmatic, violent man shaken by what he was hearing.

'But . . . what's it all for? I mean, you destroy things . . . You *kill* people. What for?'

Maslow stopped to slide the knife back into its sheath on his ankle, and tucked the whetstone into a pocket.

'I started out as a cop, in a special tactics unit in

the ISS. But I didn't have the book smarts to be a detective, and I couldn't play the politics, so I was never going to get up through the ranks. About three years in, they did these psych evaluations on us . . . all kinds of weird crap. Anyway, I must have passed or whatever, because they said there was a position for me in a special unit, outside of normal police duties. It was covert, and they warned me that some of it would be on the wrong side of the law, and once I was in, I couldn't get out. But it would mean more action, and action was what I'd joined for.

'So I signed on. The only guy I knew above me was the captain who'd got me in, and the rest of my team. We were supplied with all the money and resources we needed. It was nothin' to do with police work – it was more like the old-style army special forces; back when there were armies. Sabotage, kidnapping, assassination, blackmail – hell, even forgery; faking signatures on contracts and whatnot. We did it all. Our job was to do whatever needed doing, any way we could. We lost a few people in actions over the years, and I eventually made it to Sergeant, took over the unit. Still, in twenty-two years I've met maybe twelve, thirteen guys outside of my team, but there's a lot more, and not all of them cops either. We were all operating for the same reason, though: to keep the city running like clockwork. Hardcore solutions for hardcore problems. We took out anybody who interfered with the Machine.'

Sol gaped in abject amazement.

'You didn't even know who you were working for? And you murdered people?'

'We were working for the *city*.'

'How do you *know*?' Sol shouted. 'You could have been working for the mob, or anybody, for God's sake! And you . . . you just . . . murdered people? Don't you . . . Can't you . . . Don't you have any problem with that?'

Maslow regarded him with equanimity, and even a slightly puzzled expression.

'Why are you getting all worked up?' he asked evenly. 'I told you, I was in it for the action. I was given a job to do and I did it. That's all there is to it.'

It was only then that Solomon saw Maslow for what he really was: a cold-blooded psychopath. Not one of the psychotic types he heard about on the news, the madmen who ran around killing indiscriminately; not the types who crouched giggling in padded cells, pulling the legs off spiders. Maslow just didn't care. Human beings meant nothing to him.

'Why are you helping me?' Solomon asked weakly. 'What happened to my dad?'

There was a long, hollow silence.

'The daylighters were forming a union, led by your dad's supervisor, Harley Wasserstein,' Maslow said at last. 'Gregor was against it – knew the damage a strike could cause. Leave the dome covered, and we lose all the power from the solar panels in the dome – over

212

the whole *city*, not to mention the emotional effect it would have on the people here. So he went to the police, turned informer. Somebody there put him onto us, and I became his control, his contact.

'But the daylighters found out. The day he disappeared, they were planning to kill him out on the dome, make it look like an accident.'

Solomon frowned at that. He had known some of these daylighters for years. He would have trusted them, and he was sure his father would too. Could he have been so wrong?

'Gregor got wise to them somehow, and escaped,' Maslow continued. 'But they went after him, and Tommy Hyung finally caught him out here on the walkway; they fought, and your father knocked him over the railing into the pistons.'

Sol felt cold shudder run through him. So Gregor had killed someone too. It must have been in self-defence – it had to be. His father was no murderer. At least, no more than Sol was.

'I saw it happen, got hold of Gregor and told him to lie low. He made me promise to look after you until he could get to you himself.

'And I had to do it. You see, Solomon, I was the one who blew his cover. He always said never to contact him at the depot; but I was impatient, and one day I came looking for him. Hyung overheard us. I screwed up, and Gregor got made. I nearly got him killed, so now I'm protecting you. I owe him that much.'

'But he was working for you.' Sol shook his head. 'Why are the Clockworkers after him?'

'He's been marked for a hit – he's no use any more, and he knows too much; but that's just the half of it.' Maslow smiled ruefully. 'We didn't know, y'see? Everything's on a need-to-know basis. Tommy Hyung was working undercover for another unit. He was a Clockworker too.'

Cleo sat by her sister's side in the hospital corridor. There were not enough beds for all the casualties from the fire, so anybody who wasn't critical had been laid out on trolleys in the hallways. Vicky had been semi-conscious when she was brought in, and then she had been put on oxygen and sedated before her arm was put in a cast. So now Cleo sat and waited for her to wake up. Their parents leaned listlessly against the wall by the end of the trolley, having given Cleo the only chair available. They were all exhausted; it was after four in the morning, and none of them had slept. For the moment, all their concerns were centred around Vicky; they were unable to face the fact that they had nowhere to go home to once she recovered. Ana Kiroa had shown up earlier to offer some comfort. Many of the students from their school had lived at Spartan Hall.

Vicky's eyes opened, crusted with sleep, and saw her big sister looking down at her. She smiled weakly, and Cleo beamed back, hugging her gently and kissing her cheek. Vicky wrapped floppy arms around her in return. They both started crying, and then they laughed as Vicky put on mock pout and said, 'You broke my wrist, you cow.'

'I wouldn't have needed to if you didn't weigh as much as a tram,' Cleo retorted.

They giggled and hugged again, and their mother and father crowded around them. They all embraced and cried with relief, their bottled-up emotions flooding out now that the worst was over. When Cleo felt she had made enough of a fuss of her sister, she left her in their parents' capable hands and told them she was going to get some air.

It was hard to find any privacy in the hospital: the pale green corridors were packed with patients on trolleys, staff hurrying back and forth, worried relatives wandering aimlessly, or sitting fretting. Cleo had heard rumours that there could be dozens dead, but nobody knew for sure – over a thousand had lived in the apartment block. She tried the roof first; it was still dark outside. But the rooftop had a crane pad, and the work of the ambulances was being supplemented by the cranes' emergency carriages, one of which was sitting on the pad, its paramedic crew sipping hot tea as they took advantage of the eventual lull. Cleo stepped back inside the stairwell and made her way down to the floor below.

She found a window that opened onto a fire escape, looking out over a deserted alley. Climbing out onto it, she shivered as its denceramic grillwork brought back the fury of the fire. She sat with her knees up against her chest, braving the cold air so that she could finally have what she so desperately needed. She took the crumpled remains of the joint from her jacket pocket and lit it, drawing in the smoke with an audible gasp of relief – and then coughed painfully as it scoured her raw lungs.

Someone landed on the walkway with a muffled jolt, and she gave a start, dropping the joint. It fell through the grille beneath her and she rolled onto her knees, pawing at it, but it was too late. She saw the little dot of fire drop through the walkway on the next floor before disappearing in a burst of sparks in the darkness.

'Goddamn it!' she hissed, then turned belatedly to see who had just lost her that last smoke. It was Solomon. 'You fagging grit! What the hell do you think you're doing, creeping up on me like that? You spigot!'

'Sorry,' Sol breathed. 'I was near the hospital, up on the roof over there, trying to find a way to talk to you. And then I saw you come out of this window . . .'

There was a figure standing in the shadows behind him, a hard-faced black man with a long moustache.

'Who's your friend?' she asked.

'This is Maslow, the guy I was telling you about,' Sol replied. He glanced down through the walkway's grille. 'I know it's no consolation, but if you knew what that stuff does to your lungs and arteries—'

'Guess how much I give a damn!'

Sol sat down beside her, unsure how to say what he needed to say. He had to know what she had found out from Walden's widow about the crane accident, but he didn't want to sound as if he was just using her. And seeing her like this, without her cool pretensions, reminded him of the girl he used to train with when they were young. It had been one of those friendships that only occurred in a certain time and place, but now he felt that closeness again. Except this time she was a budding young woman with all the right curves and an in-your-face attitude he was finding more attractive all the time. It made him feel all the worse for getting her caught up in this.

'Is your family all right?' he asked tentatively. 'Were any of them hurt?'

'My sister broke her wrist. Me and her nearly died.'

Sol nodded, stuck for something else to say. He never knew how to make small talk without sounding as if he was just making small talk.

'I'm glad you're okay,' he said. 'This wasn't an accident, you know? It was sabotage — the Clockworkers.'

'I think . . . I know.' She looked up at him. 'I saw one of them on the roof.'

She didn't think to ask Sol how he knew, it just seemed to fit in with his new occupation as wanted fugitive, and she was still recovering from her brush with death. A new suspicion was forming in her

217

mind. What if her connection with him was the reason the Clockworkers had come to her building? Would they really do all that to get at her? She couldn't believe it. But why else would they cause the fire? There was nothing special about that building – there were a hundred others like it. It must just have been a coincidence. And yet the suspicion would not go away.

'You wouldn't believe what they get up to, Cleo,' Sol continued. 'I mean, some people reckon they're a myth and yet they're going around pulling this stuff all the time. Sabotage, assassinations, kidnapping – and you think all this is to keep the Machine running smoothly? Like hell it is! Do things seem to be running smoothly to you? *They're* the ones *messing it up*, Cleo! And I can't even figure out why. Why would anyone do that?'

Cleo shrugged. She was hardly listening.

'You're here to find out what I picked up from Walden's widow, yeah?'

She looked round at him and he saw the exhaustion on her face.

'Yeah. Sorry.'

Cleo shifted her aching body into a more comfortable position and started telling Sol what she had learned from Helena Walden: about Francis Walden's investigations into accidents at Internal Climate, the company owned by Armand Ragnarsson; about how he claimed that accidents were going

218

unreported, and people were being silenced; and about his move to the Schaeffer Corporation.

'She didn't say it out loud,' Cleo added finally, 'but I think Helena reckons Walden was killed because he was going to blow the whistle on Internal Climate. People were getting hurt because the company didn't take safety seriously, and he wanted to do something about it.'

'The way things have been going lately, that would fit,' Sol muttered. 'Vincent Schaeffer was supposed to be in that carriage, but he got called away at the last moment. The Schaeffer Corporation controls even more ventilation than Internal Climate. Ragnarsson could off Walden and nail his biggest competitor into the bargain.'

'But there's an investigation, right? Won't the police figure this out?'

'Some of the police *are* Clockworkers. I'd say they know how to hide a crime.'

Cleo gave a humourless chuckle, shaking her head at the scale of it all. Here they were, still at school, and they were finding themselves up to their necks in murder and intrigue. She glanced up at Sol, seeing the same bemusement on his face.

'So, what are you going to do now?'

Sol thought about what Maslow had said. He was digging too deep into this system of sabotage and death squads that lay beneath the civilized skin of the city; it was too big a risk. And yet he knew his father was

219

caught up in it, and wherever Gregor was, he would be trying to dig himself out too. There seemed to be no way of finding his father without getting more involved in what was going on. As long as the Clockworkers operated freely in the city, his old life was over anyway. Sol glanced up at Maslow, who still stood apart from them, leaning on the railing in the shadows beyond the window's light. What else was there for him to do?

'I think I want to talk to Armand Ragnarsson,' he said.

Cleo walked slowly back through the hospital, lost in a daze. All around her the aftermath of the fire could be seen and heard, and smelled. The burns unit was filled with people, the ward heavy with the stink of charred meat, disinfectant and chemical salves. Patients moaned and screamed, children sobbed. There wasn't enough anaesthetic or antibiotics. Medicine was always in short supply in Ash Harbour; the plants and minerals from which drugs were derived quickly passing into extinction as the city's overstretched hydroponic farms struggled to meet the demand for food. In the operating theatres, surgeons worked frantically to save lives and limbs; hurried skin grafts, stitched arteries and amputations could be seen through the viewing windows. Surgery was being carried out in the emergency rooms, sometimes even on trolleys in the corridors themselves.

Cleo descended some stairs to the ground floor, and stopped as she entered the main waiting area. It was

221

thronging with people who still had to be treated. The mayor, Isabella Haddad, was working her way through the crowd, flanked by two advisers. Tall, dark-eyed and serene, she took people's hands, offering words of comfort, expressing her sympathy.

What are you going to do about this? Cleo found herself thinking. You stand there, making your sympathetic noises. What are you going to *do* about this? She wanted to shriek at these people intruding on this tragedy, but she hadn't the stomach to face the charismatic mayor.

Cleo found herself thinking more and more about what had happened to her – to them all. For the last few years she had believed herself to be a rebel, a voice of dissent against a society that forced young people into a box, condemning them to dreary lives of work and routine. She realized now that it was all talk, that it had all been about *her*; all she had wanted was the *image* of a righteous leader. It gave her music more credibility.

She hated herself for being so fatuous – so shallow.

Leaving the politicians behind, she walked on through to the emergency room. Muttered chatter and webscreen broadcasts melded with moans of pain and the beep and hum of medical equipment. Off to one side, Ana Kiroa was standing near a bed where doctors and nurses were trying to defibrillate a dying boy. Cleo stared in dull disbelief, hearing the whine of the flat-line.

'Clear!' one of the doctors yelled as he held the pads to the boy's chest.

There was a thump, and the body went violently rigid, jolting on the trolley. The whine continued. Ana was covering her face with her hands. Cleo got a glimpse of the boy's face. It was Faisal Twomey. It couldn't be Faisal. There was another thump. The whine continued. Ana looked up and saw her, and hurried over.

'Cleo, you shouldn't be here. Where's your family?'

'That's not Faisal, right?' Cleo said, blinking.

'It is, Cleo. I'm sorry.' Ana seemed almost to be trying to comfort herself. 'He breathed too much smoke. They did their best, they really did. Come on, let's get out of here.'

She went to take Cleo's elbow, but the girl did not budge, her entire body tensed like wire. Cleo turned to gaze at her, and Ana was struck by the intensity in her student's eyes. She knew that Cleo had always had a reactionary streak in her; a violent emotion that had yet to find an outlet.

'Somebody did this to us, miss,' Cleo rasped from smoke-choked lungs. 'I want to find out who it was. And why they did it.'

Ana's first urge was to try and placate the girl, take her back to her family and perhaps even get a doctor to sedate her so that she could sleep off the shock that was taking over her system. The fire had been an accident, that was all – there would be a proper investigation, but it was sure to turn up nothing suspicious. Like so many of the other accidents that had been plaguing the city. Ana chewed her lip; she could see something in Cleo's expression – a reflection of her own anger and frustration. She was thoroughly sick of the way their world seemed to be self-destructing, and she needed to do something about it.

'If somebody is responsible for this,' she told her student, 'we need to find out who benefited. Somebody, somewhere, is going to make money out of this. Let's find out who.'

Solomon sat in the passenger seat of a soon-to-be-stolen car, staring across the dimly lit street at the adscreen that dominated the wall of the elegantly tiered building opposite. The advert for cream cleanser had disappeared, to be replaced by the now-familiar blocky black type on its white background. Looming over them from the big screen, it read:

DO YOU KNOW ANYONE WHO HAS 'DISAPPEARED'? WHAT QUESTIONS WERE THEY ASKING BEFORE IT HAPPENED? DO YOU CARE ENOUGH TO REMEMBER?

Welcome to my life, Sol thought, snorting.
'What is all this?' He gestured at the screen in mild bemusement.
'Dunno,' Maslow grunted thoughtfully. 'Some upstart clench-holes, trying to buck the system; hopin'

224

to get people riled up. I don't know. They haven't a hope – people are sheep; they don't give a damn as long as their bellies are full and they've got screens to watch, stuff to smoke and drink. If these grits keep running viruses like that, though, it won't be long before they're found. They better hope the police get them before my lot does.'

It was six o'clock in the morning, and they were in a shopping promenade bordering Meridian Gardens, the most affluent residential area in the city. Armand Ragnarsson's address was not listed on the web, but somehow Maslow was able to get access to the unlisted database. He had also found out that Ragnarsson lived alone, protected by at least two bodyguards at all times. Now, sitting in the driver's seat of the car, Maslow watched a little screen on a device the size of a wallet scroll down through a long series of numbers, until it stopped at one. The car started and he deactivated the device and pocketed it, pulling the car away from the kerb and steering it towards the road that led down to Ragnarsson's plush home.

'I still think this is a bad idea,' he said to Sol. 'We're exposing ourselves when we don't need to.'

'*I* need to,' Sol replied quietly. 'Let's get on with it.'

He spoke to Maslow as little as possible now, uncomfortable with what the man was, but willing to use him for as long as he could. When he was growing up, Sol had always loved action films that featured elite special forces and expert assassins who, obviously, fought heroically for a noble cause. He understood how Maslow could have been drawn into it. But Sol realized now that you only became an expert through practice and training, and the kinds of organizations that required people to be killed on a regular basis were unlikely to be very noble.

Particularly in a city that had no foreign enemies.

Soldiers followed orders, they didn't get to pick their causes. Maslow and the other Clockworkers became elite killers by letting themselves be used, and after a while it probably didn't even matter to them what they were killing for. That was murder, plain and simple, and it seemed that Maslow was a natural. Solomon wondered how much of that he'd been born with, and how much was the result of hanging around with people who thought murder was just part of the job.

It was part of the reason why Solomon still found it hard to trust him. That, and the certainty he felt that Maslow had still not told him the whole truth about Tommy Hyung and his involvement with the daylighters. Sol found it hard to believe that Harley and the others could have planned to kill his father. They were a tough bunch, but he just couldn't see them as killers. Not like Maslow and his old crowd.

Maslow was dressed in a dark red ISS uniform, one of a dozen costumes he had in a wardrobe in one of his hideaways. Sol wondered if they were dead men's clothes. Probably not. The Clockworkers could no doubt get hold of whatever uniform or ID they needed.

Maslow had given him a standard patrolman's uniform that was too big for him, but the illusion would not have to last long – they just had to get into the house. Sol was sure that once Ragnarsson had a gun pointed in his face, he'd tell them everything they wanted to know.

The car glided through the streets, and Sol let his gaze wander over the lavish architecture. With such an emphasis on function in everything that was built in Ash Harbour, attractive but useless design features were a declaration of wealth. The buildings here had decorative details: casts of animals on the tops of pillars, columns framing the front doors, smoked glass. And there were dozens of other quirks and devices he had to struggle to remember the names of: crazy paving through gravel yards, fountains, coats of arms embossed on walls, floral designs sand-blasted onto glass.

So many things caught his eye. Lovingly crafted, they were made for one purpose and one purpose only: to please the eye. There was nothing like this where he lived. In an open square surrounded by shops that sold things which served no function, they passed a water feature, with four waterfalls flowing down shallow steps cut into a two-metre-high cube of marble. There were places in the city where you couldn't get a decent supply of drinking water, and here it was used for decoration.

Everything was clean and tidy, and it was the same with the people, sporting their expensive tans and immaculate, tailored clothes. They had a better diet too, and it showed. From the restaurants and cafés wafted the smells of fresh bread and pastry and something that might even be real meat. Probably grown in vats, but real all the same.

But it was the gardens that really struck him. He had rolled down the window to catch the odours, and now, as they sped past spacious houses, he could see grass. *Real* grass. And flowers, a bewildering array of sweet scents. The kinds of things he had only ever seen in the public hydroponic gardens, with their security cameras and proximity alarms.

Ragnarsson's house was surrounded by a genuine stone wall, fronted by an antique cast-iron gate hung on massive pillars. The gate was operated from the house by remote control. Maslow rolled down the window and leaned out, pressing the buzzer. A voice answered.

'Yes?'

'ISS to see Mr Armand Ragnarsson,' Maslow barked, holding a fake identification card in front of the scanner. Sol wondered how hard those were to make.

'Do you have an appointment?' the voice asked officiously, after the scanner had verified the false ID as genuine. A remote camera zoomed in on the car.

'Open the gate!' Maslow snapped back.

There was a pause while the security guard pondered over whether he wanted to argue with the ISS. Then the gate started to swing open.

Maslow winked at Sol.

'If you're going to bluff, you have to do it with attitude.'

The driveway was real gravel, and the gardens were professionally designed, the manicured lawn bordered with curving beds of flowers and banks of rockery. Flowers, trees and space said more about Ragnarsson's status than anything else. In Ash Harbour, wealth smelled of a garden in bloom. They drove up and stopped in front of the porch.

'Stay out of my way until I'm done with the security,' Maslow said, straightening his cap and the pair of dark sunglasses he was wearing – a popular look for menacing ISS officers.

A stout, square-shouldered man in a tracksuit answered the door – off his guard as he took in Maslow's uniform – and was hurled back down the hall when Maslow jammed an electrical stun-gun against his chest. The former Clockworker stepped inside, straddling the unconscious man and handcuffing his hands behind his back. A second bodyguard came striding briskly into the hall to investigate the noise and Maslow shot him with the stun-gun, the pins hitting his chest, the charge shooting out along the wires and sending his body into spasm. The man gasped and fell to the floor, twitching. His limp arms too were quickly cuffed.

Sol stood waiting in the hall as the Clockworker disappeared deeper into the huge house. Hands in his pockets, he gazed around at the luxuriant décor. Real wood furniture and wallpaper made from some kind of organic fabric. The floor was wood too. The second guard had hit his head against it when he fell, and blood was dripping from a cut above his ear. Sol wondered if it would leave a permanent stain on the wood.

He could see the attraction of this kind of work. Charging in to nail this hugely powerful businessman – this giant of industry. His influence and wealth couldn't protect him now. All it had taken was two committed people who were willing to do what needed to be done.

Maslow's voice came from the end of the hall.

'Sol!' he shouted.

Sol put on a pair of synth-fibre gloves and followed the sound. He was not prepared for the scene that awaited him.

Ragnarsson, a handsome man in his late forties, was in the large, well-equipped kitchen, where he had obviously been having breakfast. There was the smell of meat again, and a bowl of fresh fruit sat on the table: apples and oranges, pears and grapes. Worth more than a week's wages for most people. A woman in a traditional maid's outfit lay unconscious and bound on the floor.

Ragnarsson was in good shape, with a deep tan, corded muscle in his arms, a six-pack stomach and toned legs. Sol imagined that he would have been quite the sportsman in his youth. The expensive styling of his hair was still apparent despite the mess it was in now. Sol's stomach turned as he realized what Maslow was doing at his request. The industrialist was sitting on top of the cooker as the Clockworker bound him in place with electrical cord. He perched there, trembling, wearing nothing but his underpants, the rest of his clothes lying in a heap on the floor. A blindfold covered his eyes and he was looking around with his chin raised, trying fruitlessly to see under its edge. Maslow took off his cap and sunglasses, leaving his ever-present gloves on, and stood in front of their captive.

'Who are you? What do you want?' Ragnarsson asked in a controlled voice. 'Is it money? Just tell me what you want.'

'We have some questions for you,' Maslow told the industrialist. 'Answer them and we'll leave here without any more trouble. If you don't answer our questions, or if we think you're lying . . . I turn on this cooker. Do you understand?'

The man nodded; sweat was breaking out on his forehead, but otherwise he was keeping his composure. Sol glanced uneasily at Maslow. He moved closer. This wasn't what they had talked about. He had thought that they'd just question Ragnarsson at gunpoint, and get the answers that way. There had been no mention of cooking anybody. He fervently hoped that Maslow was just trying to scare the man, but by now he knew the Clockworker too well. Solomon had started this, he would just have to make sure Maslow didn't finish it.

'What do you know about the crane wreck last month?' he asked in a gruff voice he hoped did not sound like his own.

'The crane wreck?' Ragnarsson frowned. 'I . . . nothing. I don't know anything about it – other than what was reported.'

'You didn't know Francis Walden?'

'Yes,' Ragnarsson said hesitantly. 'He was a former employee of mine. He quit, transferred to Schaeffer.'

'Did you have him killed?' Sol asked.

'What? Of course not!' Ragnarsson responded indignantly.

Without warning, Maslow hit him hard on the nose. Sol jumped, taken aback by the suddenness of the blow.

'Did you have him killed?' The Clockworker repeated the question.

'Aaauggh . . .' Ragnarsson groaned, his mouth open, blood pouring from one nostril.

Solomon raised his fingers to the bridge of his nose, where he'd been hit so long ago.

'Did you have him killed?' Maslow raised his fist to punch the man again, but Sol caught his arm.

'*No!*' Ragnarsson yelled. 'No, I did not have him killed! What is this? Are you playing games with me? Who are you? Who sent you?'

'Who do you think we are?' Sol asked.

Ragnarsson scowled in his direction, but didn't answer.

'Who do you think we are?' Sol asked again.

The businessman raised his chin, his jaw set with determined defiance.

'Who do I think you are? I think you're Clockworkers who've just crossed the line, that's what I think. You've gone too far – way too far. Do *you* know who *I* am?'

'Who runs the Clockworkers?' Sol moved closer to him. 'Do they take their orders from you? Did you order the death of a man named Gregor Wheat?'

Ragnarsson cast his head around, as if trying to see through the blindfold. His expression had changed from controlled fear to one of puzzlement.

'Who the hell are you?' he demanded.

Maslow reached between his knees and turned the dial that switched on one of the rings on the cooker. Beneath Ragnarsson's bare thigh, the ring started to heat up.

'Did you order the death of Gregor Wheat?' Maslow repeated.

'*No!* Jesus, no! I've never heard of the guy.' Ragnarsson's composure slipped as he felt the heat under his leg. 'Please, God. Turn it off. Please!'

Maslow turned on another ring.

'I don't know who he is, I swear!' Ragnarsson was panicking, his teeth gritted as his leg started to burn. 'I'll give you anything, just please turn it off!'

'What about the fire in the apartment block?' Maslow persisted. 'Did you order that too? What other operations have you ordered? How many teams are there? Who else gives the orders? Is there anybody over you? This doesn't end until you start giving us some answers!'

Solomon watched in horror. Maslow was serious; he was going to burn the guy. His face was set in an implacable glare; he was not trying to help Sol now, he just wanted to break Ragnarsson. Something hissed, and their captive started screaming. Sol was frozen, his mind back in that small grey room with a man lifting the bag over his head to show him a pair of pliers.

He darted forward, pushing Maslow out of the way, and switched off the rings of the cooker. His stomach was heaving, but he kept the vomit down. He grabbed Maslow's arm and pulled him away. Maslow shook his head, staring at him in confusion. Sol bared his teeth and dragged the bigger man with him. When they got to the hallway, Sol turned on him with a tight, hysterical whisper.

'Are you faggin' insane?! We didn't come here to *torture* him!'

'Then why did we come here?' Maslow asked, looking genuinely puzzled.

Solomon stared at him helplessly, wishing he could explain: how seeing Ragnarsson tortured had sickened him, and he was afraid that if he saw enough torture, there might come a time when it didn't sicken him;

how it made them as bad as the killers who were after them; how it was unreliable, because anybody in pain would say anything to make the pain stop, anything at all. But he could see from Maslow's face that none of this would make any difference to him. To him it was just a job to be done.

'I've had enough,' Sol said at last. 'Let's get out of here.'

On the way to the library Cleo told Ana about Sol, swearing her to secrecy, but knowing that there was no way she could be sure the teacher wouldn't go straight to the police. Ana told Cleo about her interrogation by Ponderosa, and assured her student that as far as she was concerned, the police could go to hell. The library was nearly empty; three other people sat in front of webscreens, a fourth sat at a table reading a real book. The room was poorly lit, its cream and mauve décor worn and ageing, the furniture badly in need of recycling. Like most public services in the city, its maintenance budget had been cut to the bone. Cleo and Ana walked past the climate-controlled bookcases to the rows of web tables and sat down at a screen.

'Okay,' Ana began. 'If the fire wasn't an accident, then the purpose was to either kill a lot of people, or destroy the building. Let's assume for the moment that we're not dealing with mass-murdering psychopaths. So why would someone want the building out of the way?'

'To build something else on the site?' Cleo suggested. 'Solomon said he thinks it was the Clockworkers, and that they set up the crane accident too. And we think Ragnarsson ordered that.'

'Right, well, Sol's hunch notwithstanding, let's see who owned the building to start with – see if they've applied for planning permission or rezoning.'

The building was owned by Racine Developments. They sat, flicking through the city-planning website, searching to see if the company had made any suspicious applications.

'What's going on here?' Cleo murmured. 'Why are so many of these files locked? This stuff is supposed to be public.'

'Corporate privacy,' Ana told her. 'Corporations can keep their applications secret if they can prove it's important for their business. Which they always can. We need to go through each company's shareholder website. We can buy a single share in a company for next to nothing, then get access to their sites.'

Cleo could feel herself getting bored already. This was too much like schoolwork; she wanted to do something active. Sol was out there somewhere, prowling the under-city, gun in hand, taking extreme measures. It sounded so much more dramatic – and she had to admit to herself that she found this new, dangerous side to him something of a turn-on. But he had a professional hit man to help him, whereas she had . . . a teacher. She reminded herself that she had spent too long talking the talk and not walking the walk. It was time to knuckle down and make herself useful. She pulled her chair over to the screen next to Ana's and started searching for leads.

Section 17/24: Anger

Sol had arranged to catch up with Cleo on the fire escape at the hospital, but they weren't to meet until seven – after dark – and it was only four thirty. So Sol sat on the cluttered rooftop of a nearby salt refinery, the air warm and humid from the huge distillers beneath, which removed the much-needed salt from seawater pumped in from the frozen coast for drinking water. There was a growing sense of emptiness inside him; the feeling that he was never going to see his father again. After the episode at Ragnarsson's, it seemed as if he had run out of options. There was nothing left for him to do.

'I thought you were ready for that,' Maslow said from behind him. 'You have that edge, I know you have – you just need to forget all the sentimental rubbish you've picked up in your old life. In the alley, when you shot that man, I *knew* you had it in you to do that. But I knew you'd hesitate with the woman. That's why I took her first and left the man to you.'

Sol was barely listening. He had been having nightmares about the killings in the alley; more about the woman with her twisted neck, but also of the man with the hole in his face. The thought sent a shiver through him. But he could reconcile himself to that; it had been self-defence, them or him. Not with Ragnarsson. At his instigation, they had broken into the man's house and tortured him. Even now, Sol knew there would be people who would have no problem with that. The end justified the means, it was how these things played out. It was what being hard was all about. But always there was the figure of his father, shaking his head, disgusted at what his son was becoming. Gregor, who was hard without being cruel, whose strength was tempered by decency. He needed to remember who he was doing this for.

Sol missed his dad. It had not really hit home until now how much he needed him. Ever since his mother and Nattie had died, Gregor had been his rock. He realized that he had never shown enough appreciation of his father. Everything had been warmer, more fun, when Nattie was there to banter with, and Mum would hug him or tousle his hair as if he were still a little kid; Mum, who always got emotional about silly little things. It used to bug him until she died, and then he found that it was what he missed most about her. But in his grief he had closed up and stopped feeling much affection for his father. They had just got on with life. He supposed that Gregor knew his son loved him. But it had been a long time since Sol had shown it.

'It's not enough to be a fighter,' Maslow went on. 'It's about doing whatever it takes, having the nerve to do what other people won't. You know what I mean? Maybe you don't yet, but after you've lived this life for a while—'

'This *life*?!' Sol spat, turning to glare at him. 'What life? My father's missing – I'm starting to think he might even be dead. I'm hiding all the time, sneaking around like some . . . some rat; the police are after me . . . I'm afraid to go anywhere without you – a professional murderer – to babysit me, in case the people you used to work with find me and kill me. I helped torture a man . . . I'm supposed to be training for the boxing trials! I'm supposed to be taking exams; I'm supposed to be leaving school next year! I can't sleep, I can barely eat, I'm so scared sometimes . . . Nothing's ever going to be normal again . . . This isn't a *life*.'

He stared wearily at Maslow.

'I'm not like you. I can't live like this, and I can't . . . hurt people like you do. I just can't.'

Maslow regarded him in stony-faced silence.

'What choice have you got?' he asked.

Sol was saved from having to answer by the appearance of Cleo and Ana down on the street. They were striding briskly towards the hospital entrance. Sol and Maslow clambered to a corner of the refinery roof that looked over the drive up to the hospital door, just in time to see the teacher and her student walk in.

'Looked like they were moving with a purpose, didn't they?' Sol muttered. 'Wonder what they found out.'

Cleo and Ana emerged from the hospital at the head of the angry crowd. Cleo's teeth were grinding as she walked, her thoughts a mass of indignation and frustration; a burning rage bursting to be expressed. They had spent hours in the library, untangling the web of corporate entities that hid those responsible for the fire.

There were thousands of companies in Ash Harbour, but most of the major business ones were parts of the different commercial empires run by the Big Four: Ragnarsson, Takashi, McGovern and Schaeffer. Their interests overlapped, and there was a constant struggle between them for domination of the city, but for the most part Ragnarsson controlled food production, Takashi the water supply, McGovern managed the waste and Schaeffer controlled the air. Between them, they owned seventy-five per cent of the city's property. It was disturbing, how little of the city was owned by ordinary people. Much of the rest of Ash Harbour's interests were divided between lesser industrialists like the mayor, Haddad, and back-street businessmen like Cortez. But it was the Big Four who really ran the show.

Racine Developments, which owned Cleo's apartment block, was itself owned by Lodestone

Housing, which was owned by Carter & Chen Properties . . .

Behind her, people flooded out of the hospital entrance; exclamations of rage, of disgust and disbelief bubbled like a simmering volcano on the verge of erupting. Word spread to those who had already left the hospital; those who had gone to find places to stay, to sleep, now that their homes were gone. The crowd swelled with those who rushed to join them.

Carter & Chen Properties was owned by Ash Harbour Bank, which was a subsidiary of the Renaissance Banking Corporation . . .

Forty-six people had died in the apartment-block fire – mercifully few in a block that housed over a thousand people – and there were still victims who would not make it through the night; there were many more who would be maimed or scarred for life. Pain and grief had driven people to look for someone to blame, a focus for their need to make sense of their tragedy. And Cleo and Ana had provided one.

The Renaissance Banking Corporation was owned by Occidental Financial Holdings, which was owned by the Schaeffer Corporation. And the previous year, the Schaeffer Corporation had put forward a plan to build a state-of-the-art leisure centre on the site of the apartment block. A petition from all the people in the area had stopped them, the inhabitants of the block stating their firm objection to having their homes bulldozed to make room for a gymnasium, a weather centre and some tanning salons. Today, the very day after the fire, the Schaeffer Corporation had made their application again.

Cleo and Ana had been unsure of what to do when they had discovered this. They had looked for other instances where the Schaeffer Corporation had benefited from accidents. And once they really started searching, there seemed to be no end to what they found. It seemed impossible that nobody could have noticed this before.

But then they had begun calling around the news agencies. As soon as they mentioned Schaeffer, the journalists made their excuses and hung up. Not a single reporter expressed an interest in their story; some even sounded scared. One woman, who had actually lowered her voice to talk to them, told them that her webnews organization was owned by Schaeffer. Most of them were, and those that weren't wouldn't go up against him. Cleo and Ana had started to feel afraid. They called the police and were put through to the Industrial Security Section, who informed them that the fire was being treated as an accident. Did they have any material proof of arson? Cleo could not say for sure that the pipe on the roof that she'd seen the worker tampering with was a gas pipe, or that it wasn't a routine maintenance check. Ana had asked if gathering proof wasn't the job of the police. The policeman had said they should be careful about making accusations they couldn't back up.

Feeling frightened and powerless, Cleo and Ana had returned to the hospital and told anyone who would listen about what they had found. And this time, people paid attention. The crowd marching down Bessemer Street towards the headquarters of the Schaeffer Corporation was now six hundred strong . . . and growing.

Sol and Maslow followed the crowd, trailing through the understreets and over rooftops. They watched as more and more people joined the march, and what it lacked in organization, it made up for with momentum. And it was not passing unnoticed by the authorities. As the crowd grew, so did the number of police cars and vans shadowing them in the surrounding streets. It was illegal to travel in such large groups; massing in crowds such as this was only permitted in certain static areas of the city, where the concentrated weight would not interfere with the motion of the Machine.

'Where are they going?' Sol wondered aloud as he and Maslow scaled a ladder that would take them over the pigeon-painted roof of a food-processing plant. 'Ragnarsson's headquarters are the other way.'

'It's not Ragnarsson they're after,' Maslow replied, pointing overhead. 'We're heading right into the centre of the Third Quadrant.'

Sol glanced up, and there, high above them, was the giant tower crane. The Schaeffer Corporation's tower crane. Where two men had died when one of its carriages had fallen from its arm. Vincent Schaeffer's carriage.

'They're fools,' Maslow grunted as he pulled himself up onto the roof. 'No organization; the police will break them up in no time. And now your friends down there are going to be marked. You start something like this, you're messing with the Machine.'

Sol followed him over the ledge and hurried through the rows of huge, tilted solar panels that made the roof look like the deck of an ancient sailing ship, to the far side, where he could look out on the street below. He wanted to be down there with them; there was a visceral anger in that crowd that touched something in him. All the fear and pain and frustration he had felt over the last few weeks boiled up inside him, wanting to be shared with others like him.

The crowd marched on into the heart of the Third Quadrant, coming to the majestic, monolithic headquarters of the Schaeffer Corporation. And waiting there in orderly rows in front of its steps were two squadrons of a hundred and twenty red-clad ISS troopers in full riot gear. From a crane carriage suspended overhead, senior officers were observing the scene.

The building was a minimalist, sloping slab of ferro-concrete twenty storeys high, filling the end of the street. Its dark-tinted windows bulged like a hundred insects' eyes, and, on either side of the street,

245

matching buildings rose like canyon walls. As the crowd shuffled to a halt in front of the riot troops, a silence descended on the street. A menacing sense of impending violence hung in the air, the police officers' transparent shields raised in a barricade, their gas masks hiding any show of emotion. For just a moment there was perfect calm in which all that could be heard was the perpetual rumble of the city's works in motion.

Then Ana spoke up.

'Bring out Schaeffer!' she cried. 'This company burned down these people's homes! We want some answers! Bring out Schaeffer!'

Other voices took up the call. 'Bring out Schaeffer!' they demanded in increasingly louder roars. There was no plan, no idea of what they would do if he emerged. This crowd of individuals had become a single entity, a massive animal in pain, crying out in its anguish for comfort and for revenge.

'Disperse and return to your homes!' a voice ordered over a loud-hailer from the crane carriage overhead. 'You are in contravention of Section Eight of the Illegal Gatherings Act. Disperse immediately! Disperse and return to your homes!'

The police officer's choice of words could not have been worse.

'*What homes?*' a voice screamed out. 'They've burned our homes to the ground!'

Shouts echoed the cry, and the massive creature

246

surged forward, the people on its leading edge stumbling ahead of the crowd to be pressed hard against the first row of shields, the nervous police officers roughly shoving them back. Ana and Cleo found themselves being shunted backwards by the glasstic shield of the trooper in front of them. They were being crushed, and the crowd was becoming dangerously aggressive; Ana called out for calm. Other voices joined in and the crush eased. Word started to filter through that there were more troops behind them. They were surrounded. Fear welled up; people began to grow uneasy . . . defensive. The enormous conglomerate behind Ana flexed with emotion, and she suddenly realized how close they were to calamity.

'This is your final warning!' the loud-hailer declared. 'We will not allow you to endanger the city. Disperse immediately!'

Nobody budged. It wasn't clear if what happened next was a deliberate act, or a panicked move by some frightened riot trooper, but there came a popping sound, and something arced lazily overhead, trailing a tail of smoke. The tear-gas canister landed right in the centre of the crowd, and suddenly there was mayhem. For the second time in as many days, people found themselves coughing and choking, unable to breathe in poisonous fumes. Blinded by the chemical smoke, those in the centre pushed outwards, and the creature that was the crowd swelled, its edges crashing against the shields that barricaded both ends of the street. The police staggered backwards against the weight of the people, only to find themselves pushed forward again by their comrades behind them. More tear gas was fired into the crowd, and the cloud of eye-stinging smoke spread quickly over the street.

'What are you doing?!' Ana shrieked at the officer who was jamming his shield up against her. She stood protectively in front of Cleo, holding her back. 'We just want some goddamn justice!'

The air was thick with fumes, and she squeezed her eyes shut as they started to burn; it was as if somebody was squirting boiling water in them. She screamed until her chest was so constricted by the crush of bodies against her that she had no breath. Her nose and throat felt full of thorns and she gagged, her empty stomach pushing bile up into her mouth. She spat on the shield pressing against her face, opening her swollen, tear-filled eyes to look into the gas-masked face of the trooper in front of her. The edge of his shield was pulled down, and he raised his heavy baton over his head. Her arms were pinned against her chest; she couldn't even raise them to defend herself.

'You're supposed to *protect* us!' she screamed. 'You're supposed to protect *us*!'

The baton came down hard on her skull, crashing into her consciousness in an explosion of pain. Light burst in front of her eyes. Her head felt as if it would shatter. Through blurring vision, she saw the man raise his baton again, and then there was only the shock of impact, fading into nothingness.

Section 18/24: Unity

Either it was an hallucination, or a feverish dream, or it was real; Ana wasn't sure which. She was lying stretched out on a grassy slope under an empty blue sky. Soft bundles of cloud drifted over a higgledy-piggledy patchwork of farmland below, but not up here. If she could have smelled the clouds, she knew she would have got a definite hint of onion, or perhaps pepper, off them.

Sol and Cleo sat a short distance away, wearing flesh-coloured gas masks and wide-brimmed straw hats. Ana tried to get up and move closer to them, but she found she couldn't. That was all right; she was happy right where she was. God, it was so good to finally get out of the city for a while! From somewhere nearby she could hear a dull ringing that was quite irritating, but it wasn't so loud that she couldn't hear what her two students were saying.

'. . . so how did you get her out?' Sol was asking.

'When the cops waded in and started bludgeoning

everybody, they left gaps,' Cleo replied, her voice rubbery behind her mask, and quite hoarse. 'I could barely see, and I was choking so badly . . . but somebody helped me drag her clear. The doctor said she's got something called a compression. The skull, or the blood or something's pressing in on the brain. They have to operate, but there's so many people hurt. That clench-hole hit her really hard . . . *three times*. Doc says she's lucky to be alive. They don't know if she's going to have brain damage, or what. Jesus, it was horrible . . .'

I'm fine, Ana called to them, when she realized they were talking about her. *Hunky-dory, really. There's no need to worry.* They didn't seem to hear her.

'You should have waited to talk to me,' Sol said sullenly. 'We could have done something more productive. Maslow said it was a waste of time the moment he saw you come out. He said even if you guys didn't start it off, they'd plant agitators . . .'

Who's Maslow? Ana enquired, but they didn't reply.

'They had a right to know!' Cleo snapped. 'Those were their homes that burned down, not yours. And anyway, you were off playing the Spanish Inquisition with Ragnarsson. And what did you find out? Zilch. What would you have done, if I'd gone to you? Paid a "visit" to Schaeffer too?'

What does she mean, Sol? Ana frowned.

'I wouldn't have got hundreds of people tear-gassed, that's for sure,' Sol snarled back, the valves of his gas mask fluttering. 'If Schaeffer's running the Clockworkers, then he's the one I want.'

Birds appeared in the sky overhead; peacocks with impossibly long tails, arcing over like slow, languid missiles. Ana felt as if she were pressed against a pane of glass, as if she were watching Sol and Cleo through a window; she felt short of breath, her chest constricted.

'So you going to set your hit man on Schaeffer now? The two of you going to knock him around a bit? Kill him, maybe? That'll solve a lot, won't it?'

Cleo's voice was starting to break with emotion. Ana sympathized – it had been a hard day for all of them. She couldn't quite remember why.

'If I have to,' Sol replied. 'What choice have I got? I can't . . . I can't think of what else to do. They've wrecked everything. There are people who want me dead – I don't know what they look like, or how many of them there are . . . they can go anywhere. They could be anyone. It's like having ghosts after you.'

That's why you need all the help you can get, Sol! Ana exclaimed wheezily.

'That's why we need all the help we can get,' Cleo argued. 'The police can't all be in on it. Most of them are normal slobs like us. We just need as many people involved as possible, if we could somehow let everybody know what's going on—'

Exactly, Ana affirmed. *Listen to her, Sol.*

'The riot didn't even make the *news*,' Sol hissed. 'It's

this city – it's— It just uses you up and spits you out. You can't change the whole system, and they'll kill you for trying. We're cogs; we don't count for squat – all you can do is look out for yourself.'

'Then you might as well just kill yourself now, if that's what you think,' Cleo grunted hoarsely, her voice wavering. ''Cos what hope have you got? You're as bad as those goddamned DDF. As long as we let the Clockworkers run this city, they'll get you eventually. But they can't stop all of us. 'Cos *yes*, we're cogs in a machine – but it's *our* machine. It won't work without us. All those grits sneaking around wrecking things, all the small-minded giants in their swanky offices . . . they *need* us – more than we need them.'

Damn straight, Ana shouted, punching the air. *Don't fight with each other! Get out there! Raise some hell!*

'Did you just see her fingers move?' Sol said, looking over.

'I think so . . . Do you think she can hear us?' Cleo's face was unreadable under the gas mask.

'My coach always told us that hearing's the last sense you lose when you're knocked out.'

'Did he get knocked out a lot?'

'He's a better coach than he was a boxer.'

'We should tell somebody she's here,' Cleo mused. 'Doesn't she have a boyfriend?'

'Yeah, Jude or something,' Sol muttered.

Julio, Ana laughed. *Julio. You'll love him, Cleo; he's a sweetie. I wish he were here. Would you call him for me?*

Another man suddenly appeared on the hillside.

'Sol? We need to go.'

Who's this? Ana asked.

He looked like that detective, Mercier. Except he was more rugged now, less like a paper-shuffler.

'I'll walk up to the roof with you,' Cleo said. 'I need some air; my throat's still killing me.'

And then they were gone. The hillside was very empty without them, and Ana felt herself sliding down the hill, as if the grass were steep and wet, sliding down into the onion-smelling clouds, and she was terribly lonely . . .

Leaving their comatose teacher with the four other patients in the cramped hospital room, Sol and Cleo walked out into the corridor. Maslow was already striding towards the stairwell. Cleo cast a lingering glance back at Ana, lying motionless in the bed. An oriental woman dressed in doctor's scrubs crossed the hallway from one of the other rooms, intent on the medical palmtop in her hand. She gave them a perfunctory smile and brushed past into the room.

Cleo watched her check Ana's chart, and then gauge her pupil response with a pen torch. The doctor shook her head gently and took out a syringe. Cleo saw the set expression on the woman's pale face and found little hope there. Turning away, she hurried to catch up with Sol and Maslow. She had a nagging feeling that she knew the doctor from somewhere, but she couldn't place where.

Sol and Cleo followed Maslow towards the stairwell. He opened the door, and froze. Carefully closing the door, he motioned them towards the elevators.

'Someone's coming up the stairs. Three people, in a hurry.'

He had his hand in his jacket pocket, and Cleo glanced at Sol to see he had done the same. Did they spend their whole day expecting a gunfight? How could anybody live like this? As if they could be shot dead at any moment.

And then Cleo remembered where she had seen the doctor's face before. It was on the day she had gone to the Filipino District to buy some guitar strings from Cortez, when she had seen the three people disposing of a body in the sewage-treatment works. The pale-faced Oriental woman had been the one in charge.

'Sol, wait!' she cried, pulling on his sleeve.

'We can't wait,' he said. 'We have to get out of here. Now.'

The elevators were at the T-junction at the other end of the magnolia corridor; two sets of doors, flanked by fake giant rubber plants. As they reached them, Sol pressed the 'up' button and watched the displays to see which was going to be first to arrive. Maslow had his eyes trained on the door to the stairs.

'No, listen!' she insisted frantically. 'We have to go back. That doctor's a goddamned Clockworker! Sol!' She started to drag him back. 'She was doing something to Ana!'

Sol's face dropped. He hesitated, frozen by indecision. The left elevator opened with a chiming sound, just as the door to the stairs swung open. Maslow's gun was out of his pocket, coming level as the first person out of the stairwell saw him and started to raise his own gun.

Maslow's silenced shot took him in the shoulder and he fell back against the woman behind him. Cleo let out a shrieking gasp and swivelled to leap into the lift for cover. She stopped short when she saw the face of the white-haired man in front of her; an instant of recognition passed between them. It was the man who had chased her in the sub-levels, after she had seen them dumping the body. One of the Clockworkers. For one absurd moment she felt relief that he was alive, but that was erased by fright.

Sol, his hands stuck in the pockets of his jacket, saw the expression on her face and turned in time to face a punch curling towards his head. With no time to block it, he met the fist with his forehead, the pale man's knuckles cracking against it with a satisfying crunch. Sol's reflexes took over; pulling his hands free, he laid into the man with two hooks and a cross, sending the Clockworker crashing back into the lift. The other two men in there were drawing their weapons. Sol's right hand was back in his pocket but, as he pulled out the gun, one of the other men grabbed his wrist and dragged him into the elevator. Sol squeezed off a shot but it went straight into the wall.

The gun was knocked from his hand, and a fist hit him across the face. But the small space put him at an advantage – they couldn't all get at him. He ducked his head down and spun up with a barrage of jabs, elbows and knees. It gave him the split second he needed to get back out through the door, slapping the CLOSE button on his way out.

Cleo seized Sol's fallen gun, and fired three shots into the ceiling of the elevator, flinching with each report. It was enough to keep the Clockworkers' heads down. Maslow put four more bullets through the stairs door, which was jammed open on the fallen man's body. Then he spun and fired two more into the elevator before the doors slid closed.

'Get out of here!' he bellowed as he took up a position on the corner of the corridor, gun aimed at the stairs door.

Grabbing Cleo's arm, Sol sprinted away from the stairs along the perpendicular hallway.

'We have to help Ana!' she cried.

He didn't reply, but his face was set in stony resolve. 'Sol!'

'We can't!' he gasped, with despair in his voice. 'Don't you think I want to? They'll kill us if we go back.'

They turned another corner, slamming through a set of double doors.

'Where's the fire escape?' he barked at her. He and Maslow had come in from the roof.

'Over . . . the other side,' she panted. 'Left, and left.'

Barging past an orderly pushing a trolley of laundry, they heard more muffled shots behind them. The corridor branched off to the left, and they careered down it, Sol still holding onto Cleo's arm. Racing past a row of recycling chutes, they dodged round some kind of wheeled medical apparatus left standing in the hallway, and took another left. The corridor ended in a solid wall. Cleo stared at it in disbelief.

'I came out from a different floor,' she wheezed. 'I thought they were all the same . . .'

Sol swore under his breath, looking round for another way out. They didn't dare go back the way they'd come. Stepping cautiously out into the previous corridor, he quickly checked one door after another. Rooms without windows; dialysis machines, ultrasound scanners. Surprised patients looking up from their beds, nurses asking his business, windows with no fire escapes. His gun was back in his pocket, his palm sweaty against the grip.

'Sol.' Cleo put a hand on his arm. 'We can use this.' She was indicating the six recycling chutes in the corridor wall. 'The one for fabric, it's big enough.'

'It's a long drop into a locked bin.' He shook his head, his eyes warily watching the end of the corridor. They heard the dull thumps of five more shots.

'Not to go down. To go up,' she prompted him.

She went first. The chute was less than a metre

square but, by climbing in backwards, she was able to stand on the lip of the hatch, push her back against the far wall, and wedge her hands and then her feet against the opposite corners. Jammed in like this, she worked her way up the vertical shaft, her body straining with the tension. She had once been a keen gymnast, but she'd quit a couple of years back – she was too busy being cool to be competitive – and Cleo wondered if she'd bitten off more than she could chew here. She guessed it must be at least three metres up to the next hatch . . . assuming the floor above had one.

Sol climbed in behind her and, as he took his feet off the lip, the hatch swung shut, cutting off the light. But Sol had anticipated this, and strapped to his head was a bright but tiny torch. Cleo was reminded of the man who had come after her along the ventilation duct in the sub-levels – the man who had just shown up in the elevator. He had used exactly the same kind of light. Sol had started to act like a Clockworker, and now it seemed he was equipped like one too – she wondered where the transformation would stop.

She was careful not to look down. There was just enough of the chute visible below her to send her heart into her throat, and Sol's light dazzled her eyes. Instead, she edged her way slowly upwards, conscious that if she relaxed her hold, it was a long fall, and she would take Solomon with her. They could only hope that they didn't get hit by a bundle of bedsheets or a load of soiled underwear on its way down to the laundry room. Her breathing was loud in the plastex chute, and she imagined the Clockworkers passing the hatches and hearing their breathing, the scraping of their hands and feet against the corridor wall. Her calves started to cramp, and her shoulders and neck ached with tension.

'Can't you go any faster?' Sol whispered up to her through gritted teeth.

The tops of her thighs started to knot up now as well. Cleo's fingers touched the edge of the next floor's hatch just as her legs began to shake uncontrollably. Thankfully, the hospital did not have latches on their hatches and she pushed it open, peering out. The way was clear; straightening her legs to shove herself out of the chute, she moaned and crumpled to the floor as the cramps screamed pain at her. Lying there, she tried to stretch out her knotting muscles. Moments later, Sol followed, his face twisted in discomfort, but he was still able to stand up once he was out. Cleo swore that if she lived through this, she was going to stay in better shape. She swallowed her pride and let him help her to her feet.

They turned to find a stunned doctor gazing at them with his mouth open.

'Hi,' Cleo told him as she wiped sweat from her forehead. 'Just . . . just, eh, checking for blockages.'

This floor had access to the fire escape. Once up

on the roof, Sol led her across a utility frame full of cables and pipes to the roof of the salt refinery. From there, there were numerous routes of escape across the rooftops.

'How will you find Maslow?' she asked him.

'If he makes it out, there's a place we arranged to meet if we got separated,' he replied. 'But that won't be until tomorrow. We need to find somewhere to hide out until then.'

'That woman was giving Ana an injection of something. What do you think it was?'

'I don't know,' Sol said, shaking his head.

He didn't want to think about it – there was nothing they could do now anyway. He felt empty, hollowed out. They had failed Ana and lost Maslow. But there was no time for recriminations. For now, he had to concentrate on keeping them alive.

Cleo looked out across the tops of the buildings before them. So the Clockworkers had come for Ana. And now they would be looking for her too. The city had taken on a different air; stretching out in front of them, it was a crazed warren of mechanical works, architecture and anonymous faces, a million dark paths and shadowy corners. Too many places to conceal watching eyes, or waiting killers. She shivered in the chilly evening air.

Sol grinned sheepishly at her.

'Welcome to the other side.'

★　　★　　★

261

Solomon led Cleo across the deserted floor of a textiles mill. Rolls of patterned fabric were stacked up all around them; huge sheets hung on racks, their dyes drying, or on machines, waiting to be printed or embroidered. There was a stale, chemistry-set smell from the dyes and, from a bin at the end of the design workshop, the scent of rotting vegetable matter, used to make some of the colours.

'I need to call my parents,' Cleo was saying. Her jacket was too thin for this environment, and hunger was making her colder.

'They'll expect that,' he responded, shaking his head. 'If you call the hospital, they'll trace the call. The same goes if you contact anybody who's known to be friends with you or your parents.'

'I can't just disappear on them! They have to know I'm okay.'

'We'll get a message to them somehow . . . but later, all right?'

He stopped at a grate in the floor and pulled it open. Underneath, metal rungs set into the ferro-concrete formed a ladder that led down a dark vertical shaft. He strapped on the torch and led the way down.

'Pull the grate closed after you,' he said, from beneath her feet.

Sol had explained to her that Maslow had been a Clockworker, that he knew what they could do. He had shown her how she had to avoid streets with surveillance cameras, stay clear of public places, and how to read the grid system that allowed them to find their way through the sub-levels, far from the more inhabited parts of the city.

In the under-city, among the enormous engineering works that supported Ash Harbour's structure, most of the space was taken up by factories, or the cheapest, most cramped tenement housing. Grey-skinned homeless and some delirious drunks huddled under blankets, hoping for handouts. The noise of the city was louder, more thunderous down here, carried through the walls and along the twisting streets and narrow alleyways. They passed factories where human bodies laboured over clanking machines, oblivious to the time of day, struggling to make quotas and finish their long, punishing shifts.

This place gave Cleo the creeps; every face she saw was an imagined assassin, or an informant who would wait for them to pass and then report them. But Sol was savouring his new role as guide and mentor. On his own, he would have been nervous down here without Maslow; having to look after Cleo, though, gave him a renewed confidence. He felt more at home, now that he didn't have Maslow babysitting him.

At the bottom of the shaft, beneath the textiles mill, there was a huge room being used for storage; it had two other exits, which he knew led out to a sewer on one side and a utility tunnel on the other. With three escape routes, it was a good place to hide. During the day the factory staff only ever came down to dump reject rolls of material for storage until they were recycled. He climbed up a stack of rolls and walked along the top to a grille in a ventilation duct. Cleo watched as he pulled out the grille, reached in and dragged out a holdall. In it were two blankets, some packs of food and a large flask of water.

'Maslow has a few stashes like this around,' he said softly. 'We can hole up here until morning; the factory's shift starts at nine. They can't see us here from down on the floor anyway.'

Cleo was trembling with the cold, and she quickly took one of the blankets and wrapped it around her.

'What've you got to eat?' she asked.

'Dried stuff,' Sol said. 'Not sure what it is. It's supposed to be full of vitamins and all that. Tastes like salted carpet.'

'It'll do.' Cleo grabbed a packet and unwrapped the waxed rice paper.

Munching into it, she made a face, but persevered.

'Told you.' He shrugged as he sat down beside her.

Cleo watched him as she ate. She could see he was enjoying this . . . this adventure. All she could think about was that her family would be going out of their minds with worry. She was uncomfortable and cold; Sol was hardly a fountain of entertaining conversation and she had no music and, most importantly, no stem. The craving for a smoke was made worse by anxiety and boredom. And she needed something to help get her mind off Ana, and what might have happened to her. Cleo's thoughts went back to the hospital, to her family and all the other people she had left behind. She remembered the doctors' vain attempts to resuscitate Faisal and she felt a dull pain in her chest. The food was little comfort: it quelled her hunger, but left her thirsty. Taking a drink from the flask of water, she began to contrive ways of getting hold of some stem.

'I could really do with talking to Ube,' she said. 'He could help us – his uncle's a cop. Maybe find out who we can trust in the police—'

'You're here because I got you mixed up in this,' Sol replied. 'You want to do the same to Ube?'

'We need help . . . What about going to Cortez? He's this Pinoy mob boss—'

'I know who he is. He won't do anything for free, and we don't have any money. He might even be working with them.'

'I don't think he'd turn us in,' Cleo tried again. 'He . . . he likes me.'

'How do you know him?'

'I get my guitar strings from him. And stem, sometimes.'

'Ah.' Sol finished his food and took a swig of water.

'What's that supposed to mean?'

'Nothing.'

'It's not nothing. You were saying something with that "Ah".'

'I was just saying "Ah", that's all.' Sol rolled his eyes.

'Don't read into it. I'm turning off the torch – the light could attract attention.'

'Don't,' she said quickly. 'There's no windows, and nobody's in the factory, right? I don't want to be in the dark.'

Sol left it on. The diodes ran off electricity drawn from his own body, and would not run down. They huddled under the blankets, neither speaking for a time.

'We need help,' Cleo said again. 'What if they killed Maslow?'

'They didn't.'

'How do you know?'

Solomon didn't answer, staying quiet for a time. Then: 'So what kind of a name is Cleopatra Matsumura, anyway?'

'Cleopatra's Egyptian, like the pyramids. You know – the big triangular stone things we learned about in history? Matsumura is Japanese Asian. Samurai warriors. Karaoke.'

'Oh.'

'So what kind of a name is Solomon Wheat?'

'Solomon was an old Jewish king. Famous for being really smart. Wheat . . . That's not our original name, it used to be Wiescowski, or Wiekovski or something. Eastern European Jews weren't too popular when everybody started moving south in the big freeze, so my great-great-great-great-something-something grandfather changed it to "Wheat" so he could get work. It's from a place called the Ukraine. Cossacks.

That Chernobyl disaster. It was one of the first places to freeze over.'

'Oh.'

Cleo looked down at the patterns of leaves and flowers on the fabric beneath them. It was rough to the touch, and there was little give in the barrel-sized rolls, but she snuggled in the furrow between two of them, tucking her arm under her head as a pillow. She was exhausted, and in no time at all she was asleep.

Cleo awoke, cold to the bone, in pitch-blackness. Her befuddled brain was still recovering from a nightmare about faceless figures with syringes and it took her some moments to remember where she was. Her hands explored the strange, humped shapes around her.

'Sol?' she whispered. 'Solomon? Are you there?'

'Yeah,' he muttered back, from less than a metre away.

'Can't you sleep?'

'One of us needs to stay awake while the other sleeps,' he said. 'To keep watch.'

She crawled over to him, shivering. Throwing her blanket over him, she crept in under his, huddling close to him. He tensed at first, but then relaxed, shifting his body slightly to accommodate her. His skin felt much warmer than hers. Putting her arm over his chest, she pushed her face into the crook of his neck. Her body gradually stopped shivering, and she wriggled up closer to make the most of his warmth, letting him slip his arm under her head.

'Don't get the wrong idea here,' she murmured in his ear. 'You're not my type. But I'm cold, I'm scared and I'm strung out. I just need something to get me through the night.'

Her lips started on his neck, kissing him under his ear, and then on his jaw, and his cheek, before finally opening over his mouth. Sol pulled the blankets over them and wrapped her in his arms. It had been so long since he had held anyone close, and opening up to her thrilled and frightened him in equal measure. He was no longer on his own . . . and he no longer had just himself to worry about.

Section 19/24: Hunted

Sol woke with a jolt. He had not meant to fall asleep – at least not until he was sure Cleo was awake to keep watch. A faint light filtered down from the shaft above. Cleo had a wristwatch, charged from the static on her skin. He checked it: half-past eight. They'd slept longer than he'd intended, but seeing as they weren't dead, or being dragged off to some secret sub-level prison, he had to assume they had not been discovered.

Cleo moved under the blanket beside him, and he cradled her head against his shoulder. He turned onto his side and stroked her face.

'Hey, we have to get up.'

She opened her eyes and blinked.

'It's still dark,' she muttered sleepily.

'It doesn't get any brighter down here.'

She groaned, and tucked herself into him.

'Tch. Don't wanna go,' she moped in a baby's voice.

'We have to meet Maslow,' he told her.

'Honey, there are boys who'd kill to be where you are now.' She rolled over and looked at him.

I know, he thought, peering through the gloom at imagined faces in the patterns of the musty fabric. I have. 'Come on. Get up, we have to get going.'

Sol had been glad to have Cleo with him yesterday – to have someone to share the danger – but now it made him uncomfortable. You couldn't take the same kinds of chances when you had to look after somebody else.

With the torch switched off, Sol climbed the ladder to the top of the shaft, reached up and carefully lifted the grate slowly, raising it just high enough for him to peek out. The factory's high windows let in enough of a glow from the gas lamps outside for him to see. A foot landed right in front of him, another swinging over his head, and he nearly dropped the grate. The feet strode away past him, making for a door in the near wall. A man, moving stealthily, switched on a torch and shone it into the adjacent room. Sol risked a glance in the other direction. Another man was shining a beam of light in among the mill's machinery.

His breath caught in his throat, Sol eased the grate back into place again, looked at Cleo and put a finger to his lips. He pointed frantically downwards, and she immediately started descending the rungs. Following close behind, Sol kept lifting his eyes to check above him. In his haste to climb down, he stood on Cleo's fingers, and she stifled a yelp, drawing in a hissing breath. Footsteps sounded above them. Cleo scrambled down to the bottom of the ladder and ducked away out of sight. Torchlight shone down through the grate, catching Sol in its beam.

'They're down here!' a voice yelled.

Sol dropped the last two metres to the floor of the storeroom, just as the grate was pulled aside. He saw a gun drawn and heard the thud of a silenced shot, but the bullet went wide, sparking off the floor near his feet. He was out of sight in the darkness now, and he had a light to aim at. Pulling his pistol from his pocket, he flicked the safety off, leaned out under the shaft and fired two shots straight up at the torch-beam. There was a cry and the torch fell, trailing a streak of light down the shaft until it smashed on the floor at Sol's feet.

'Let's go!' he said breathlessly.

They took the door to the utility tunnel, which led them out into a high-walled courtyard illuminated by gaslight; flames flickering in the glass tops of tall poles. There were doorways in every wall, and an open ceiling which looked out onto the level above. Sol chose the door opposite them, slamming his shoulder into it and charging up the stairs on the other side.

The stairs led out onto a walkway around a light-well, some seven or eight metres wide. A scream from above made them look up, just in time to see a young woman plummet past them, her screech dopplering down around the walls of the well. The bungee cord attached to her feet pulled taut and stretched, then yanked her back up towards them, bouncing her off the wall. She wailed and then laughed hysterically. Far above them, voices whooped with encouragement, people grouped around the rim of the well. Thrill-seekers, looking for an illegal rush. Cleo and Sol hurried along the walkway, round the light-well to the tunnel on the other side.

This tunnel took them through to a section of the hydroponic gardens. Rows upon rows of deep-walled trays held myriad plants, an exotic array of strange-shaped leaves and insanely colourful flowers. This was no farm, this was one of the conservation gardens, tended by botanists who one day hoped to repopulate the planet's eco-system. They heard footsteps running on the light-well walkway behind them, and they set off again, rushing through the foliage, the air filled with wild, scintillating smells. There was an elevator at the far end. They had reached the wall of the city; the lift would take them up through the gardens on the crater wall.

Sol slapped the button to call the elevator and turned with his back to the doors, aiming his gun at the door they had just left. Cleo got a terrible sense of déjà vu and, as the doors opened, she fully expected to see one of the Clockworkers standing there, ready for them.

The lift was empty. She pulled Sol in and hit the button for the highest floor.

A tall man with greying hair burst into the garden

at the far end just as the doors were closing again. The elevator started to move.

'Well,' Cleo panted. 'We're getting . . . to see . . . a lot of the city.'

Sol found a purple flower with prickly leaves caught in the collar of his jacket and offered it to her, still struggling to get his breath back.

'Oh, how sweet.' She smiled. 'Nobody's ever given me a thistle before.'

Her eyes watched the floor-counter anxiously as she pulled the flower off its stem and held it to her nose.

'How did they find us?' she wondered aloud.

'I don't know. Some security camera we missed – maybe somebody saw us.' Sol checked his ammunition. He had reloaded with ammo from Maslow's holdall; there were eleven rounds left in the gun, and thirteen in a spare clip. It gave him little reassurance – the Clockworkers were much better with guns then he was.

'This is going to keep happening, isn't it?' Cleo said quietly.

Sol spared her a grim glance before turning to glare at the floor-counter.

'Why did they make these things so *slow*?' he muttered.

A bell pinged and the doors slid open. Sol raised his pistol, and an old woman standing waiting to enter let out a piercing shriek as she found a gun pointed at her face.

273

'Sorry, sorry.' Sol held up a hand apologetically as they rushed out.

They ran on. Solomon shoved the gun back in his jacket pocket and searched desperately for somewhere they could take refuge.

'Where are we going?' Cleo called through heaving breaths.

Sol didn't answer. They weren't far from the West Dome Depot. Wasserstein and the daylighters would help him, he was sure of it. But who there could he really trust? There was no way to be sure. Apart from Cleo and Ana, there was no one in the city he trusted now.

'I've got to . . . stop,' Cleo said from behind him. She was getting a stitch, her hand clutching her side. 'Look, we don't even know . . . where we're going. Sol! Stop for a minute.'

They stumbled to a halt, leaning on the railing of the promenade floor. Cleo coughed several times, and drew in long, laboured breaths. Sol grimaced.

'That's the smo—'

'Don't!' she snapped. 'Not another word!'

There were people walking past them, out for a stroll, or avoiding the crowds on the start of the work cycle. Cleo clutched Sol's arm. There, coming from the direction of the elevator, was the man with the greying hair. Dressed in a dark-coloured casual suit, he had a hawkish, drawn face and the same pallor as Maslow; a black man who did not spend enough time in the light. His hand was inside his jacket, his eyes fixed on them, shouldering past people walking the other way.

She and Sol turned to run, and saw a policeman coming from the opposite direction. Sol looked over the railing, frantically seeking a way down. There was nothing, just a hundred-metre drop to a wider balcony floor stretching out beneath them. The cop was making his way over to them. The Clockworker on the other side was slowing down, hesitating.

'There's enough room to get round,' Sol said from the side of his mouth. 'We could rush the cop, maybe get past—'

'Maybe we should ask him for help.'

'He'll take us in, Cleo. They'll know where we are. It'll only be a matter of time—'

'Excuse me, folks,' the policeman hailed them, coming over, 'but I'm going to have to ask you your business up here. Could I see some identification, please? Nothing personal, y'understand. It's just with all the suicides we've had jumping from here over the last year, we need to check everybody out.'

Sol and Cleo looked back towards the Clockworker. He was hovering a few metres away, pretending to enjoy the view of the city.

'Hello?' the patrolman prompted them. 'Some ID, please? Now?'

They made a show of rummaging through their pockets.

'People your age are at particular risk, y'understand.

All those issues to be resolved. Disputes with your parents, bad skin, exams, dating . . . All those hormones getting you worked up and confused – I know it's tough being a teenager. We were all there once, y'know.'

There was no one else around now, just the cop, the Clockworker and them.

'I don't seem to have my card on me, sir,' Sol replied. 'My name's Lennox Liston. My dad's a daylighter. He works up here. I'm not suicidal – things are going great.'

'I'm Aretha Franklin,' Cleo added. 'I'm with him. We're very happy.'

'That may well be,' the patrolman said, 'but I'm just going to have to check you out. If you'll come with me, we just need a webscreen – there's one along here.'

Sol and Cleo exchanged looks. This wasn't working out. But the Clockworker did not seem to want to act while they were with the policeman, and neither of them was ready to give up this temporary safety. They followed the patrolman to the webscreen on the wall nearby. He punched in a code, and spoke into the microphone:

'Officer Meredov: Identity Search. Liston, Lennox, and Franklin, Aretha.'

'Searching . . .' a toneless voice replied.

The screen flashed and flickered abruptly, then blanked out to a featureless white. Heavy, square type faded in, growing to fill the screen.

'Oh, for God's sake!' the cop exclaimed. He sighed in exasperation. 'This is getting beyond a joke!'

The type spelled out a message in the now-familiar format:

WHY WERE THERE NO REPORTS ON THE NEWS
ABOUT THE RIOT AT THE SCHAEFFER CORPORATION'S
HQ? DO YOU CARE ENOUGH TO WONDER?

Both Cleo and Sol were distracted for only a moment, but that was all it took. Suddenly the Clockworker was behind them, bringing a cosh down on the back of the patrolman's head. The cop slumped to the ground, unconscious, a trickle of blood running from his split scalp.

'Don't run, don't shout out, or I'll kill you,' the attacker growled, his gun steady in his other hand. 'Where's Maslow?'

Neither of them answered, momentarily paralysed by the assault on the policeman.

'Where's Maslow?' the Clockworker repeated. 'What's his game? Why did he turn?'

'I can take you to him,' Sol told him hesitantly. 'But only if you let us go once you've got him.'

'Sure,' the man grunted. 'Don't try anything funny, though. You'll get it first, yeah? You've got a piece – give it to me.'

Sol reluctantly pulled the gun from his pocket by its trigger guard and handed it to him.

'Right, let's take a walk.'

Cleo threw Sol a questioning glance. The look she

received in return did not inspire any confidence. They were under no illusion that the man would let them go once he'd found Maslow.

With his gun in his jacket pocket, the Clockworker followed them as Sol led the way along the wide balcony to the corridor into the daylighter's depot.

'Where is he? Where are we going?' the man demanded.

'We arranged to meet up, if we got separated,' Sol told him. 'He said to wait in a certain place and he'd find me.'

The Clockworker wasn't satisfied, but he continued to follow them.

'No tricks, you get me?'

'Yeah,' Cleo replied. 'We heard you the first time.'

They crossed the workshop floor, ignoring the people around them at the machines, recycling tools. After a furtive peek into the canteen and the monitor room, Sol took a left, praying that he was in time. The shift change was at half nine.

He was. They climbed the stairs to the exit floor and emerged into the changing room. Thirty men and women were in the middle of getting into their safesuits. Those from another shift were changing out, having just finished their shift on the dome.

'Hang on a second,' the Clockworker said suspiciously.

But Sol kept walking. At the far end of the room, Harley Wasserstein was pulling on a suit over his huge frame. Solomon was hoping that he wasn't wrong about his father's old friend. He prayed that Maslow had been lying about the daylighters. Harley looked up, and a broad smile spread under his white-blond beard as he saw Solomon.

'Sol, lad!' he exclaimed. 'We thought you'd disappeared! What the hell are you doing here?'

His smile faded as he saw the expression on Sol's face. God, I'm sorry for this, Sol thought to himself. He stared hard at Wasserstein, whose eyes went cold as they moved from Sol and Cleo to the man standing behind them.

'Hi,' Sol stuttered to Wasserstein. 'Is he here?'

'No,' Wasserstein responded, standing up, a full head taller than the other man. 'No, he's not. There's been no sign of him.'

The Clockworker stepped forward, glaring at the daylighter, and then looked around in confusion. Fifty-nine heads turned to see what was going on.

'What are you playin' at, kid?' He swivelled uneasily, trying to keep all the daylighters in sight.

'This guy says we owe him,' Sol went on, holding Wasserstein in his gaze. 'He's here to collect.'

'All right.' Wasserstein regarded the Clockworker with the kind of expression he reserved for something he'd scraped off his boot. 'How much are you into him for? What's it going to take to get rid of you?'

'What?' The Clockworker screwed up his face, his hand still gripping the gun in his jacket pocket.

'How much is it going to take to pay off the debt?'

The other daylighters were sidling closer, some picking up tools from the benches. This man was obviously a debt collector who had come looking for Gregor Wheat. Nobody liked debt collectors, and no lowlife heavy was going to mess with the daylighters in their own depot. Sol took Cleo's hand and started to edge away.

The Clockworker saw them move, and for a moment his attention was divided between them and Wasserstein. His hand was already drawing the gun from his pocket. Wasserstein spotted the movement and lunged forward, enclosing the Clockworker's entire hand in his huge fist, crushing it into his chest so that he couldn't fire the gun. The Clockworker wriggled to get his hand free.

'Run!' the daylighter roared to Sol as others closed in on the hit man with wrenches and ice-hammers.

Cleo was already making for the door, with Sol close on her heels. There came the sound of silenced gunshots, and two people started screaming. Then three. As they hurled themselves through the door and bounded down the stairs, a bullet struck the wall above their heads. The Clockworker was coming after them again.

At the bottom of the stairs Sol turned left, heading for the utility corridors that ran around the edge of the depot. They offered more corners and cover.

'He can call others,' Cleo panted. 'They could cut us off.'

As they took another turn, they came upon a low, heavily built denceramic door, and Sol skidded to a stop. There was a readout displayed beside the door: air pressure and temperature. A light glowed green beside the readings.

'We can go through here,' he said, hitting the lock release. 'It'll take us out of the depot.'

The door slid open. It was nearly forty centimetres thick. Cleo didn't realize where it led until he had closed it behind them, and she had a chance to look around.

'Oh, Jesus,' she gasped.

'They must be doing some maintenance,' Sol told her, watching through the slab of glass that made up the door's small window. The Clockworker ran past, gun drawn. 'We may not have that long.'

They were between the two layers of concraglass that made up the dome. Sloping up from their feet, a vast glass hill interspaced with a grid of denceramic beams stretched into a false perspective as it curved away from them. A symmetric forest of spring-loaded struts separated and supported the two layers, creating a space between them about one and a half metres high, each layer of concraglass nearly half a metre thick. It did not lessen the sense of vertigo they got as they looked down through their feet at the city below. Sol and Cleo were almost able to stand upright, their heads and shoulders hunched.

Ash Harbour had been built into a mountain, the

centre hollowed out like the crater of a volcano, but all resemblance to nature stopped there. The entire city had been built inside a vacuum insulation system, the crater walls hollowed out and reinforced with denceramic, the hollowed sections hermetically sealed and the air evacuated. This was the secret to the city's capacity for retaining the heat created by the Machine – the people of Ash Harbour effectively lived in a gigantic vacuum flask.

The section of dome in which Cleo and Sol now stood should have been devoid of all air or gases. Somewhere nearby, a work crew must be carrying out maintenance.

'There are doors every hundred and fifty metres or so,' Sol told her. 'We can get out at the next one along – it'll bring us out beyond the depot.'

Their breath was emerging in plumes of vapour; the space was cold, and getting colder. And yet Cleo could feel the warmth of the glass through the soles of her shoes. Putting her hand up to the glass above her, she found it was freezing cold. Flakes of snow were already falling on its upper surface. Gold-coloured strips of solar cells – invisible from the streets – were attached to its lower surface, to make the most of the daylight. Walking along the glass ledge that followed the circumference of the dome was unnerving, with nothing between the glass and the city streets hundreds of metres below.

Something buzzed past her ear, and blood spattered

the strut that Sol was passing – he flinched, crying out, his hand to his neck. Cleo turned and ducked down as the Clockworker took another shot. He was about sixty metres behind them, far enough back on the curve for his aim to be spoiled by the dome's jungle of struts. Cleo was crouched down and running now, overtaking Sol on the ledge and grabbing his arm. His other hand clutched the left side of his neck, blood seeping through his fingers. Another shot skated off the ledge near her feet and ricocheted up and down ahead of them. Hard as diamond, concraglass was made to withstand centuries of cataclysmic weather. Ricochets made every bullet twice as dangerous.

Sol was loping unsteadily behind her and was having trouble keeping up. Cleo heard the Clockworker's running feet echoing around them. A third shot clipped the sleeve of her jacket, making her lose her footing, and she fell sideways onto the sloping glass, Sol tripped over her feet and landed heavily, crying out in pain. Cleo looked back as she scrambled up; the man was less than thirty metres behind them – he had a clear shot now – but he was sprinting full tilt towards them. Sol was back up, and they ran together. The door was there ahead of them; by some miracle it was still open behind the departing crew.

A siren started to sound through the dome. Sol looked about anxiously, his glance into her eyes all she needed to tell her what it meant. They were evacuating the section. In minutes, the whole place would be as airless as outer space. Sol started to roar as he put every ounce of effort into his race for the door, but his movements were becoming less co-ordinated, and he was struggling to maintain his balance. The wound in his neck was making him dizzy. He collapsed just metres short of the door, shaking his head and crawling on. Cleo leaped over him and seized his shoulders. Dragging him backwards towards the door, she looked up to see the Clockworker slowing down to take aim . . .

A jet of water shot past her, spraying the slope of glass, finding its way down to the Clockworker and blasting him off his feet. She looked behind her as two men stepped out, directing the nozzle of a fire-hose at the gunman. The siren was loud in her ears, and the sound of the water reverberated off the glass floor and ceiling with a soft bellow. She helped Sol stagger out through the door, and the two would-be firemen gave the Clockworker one last blast before hurrying back out, closing and sealing the opening behind them.

'Don't watch, girl,' one of them said solemnly. 'It won't be pretty.'

But she did watch. The Clockworker reached the door, hammering on it, but the pumps had started, the safety locks had kicked in. He fired three shots at the lock and the glass, but the bullets just bounced off, making him jump back. Dropping the gun, he slammed his fists against the glass, screaming desperately, but apart from barely audible thuds, the sound did not carry through the door. Cleo could not take her eyes off his face.

As the section of dome decompressed, he appeared to gag, gradually losing the ability to breathe; his face went red, and veins stood out under his skin. He stumbled backwards, curling up against the sloping glass. His body went into spasm as his blood began to boil, his arms and legs thrashing. Cleo stared in fascinated horror right up until the point where his eyes burst, and then she fell to the ground, crying.

Harley Wasserstein was striding up the corridor, his left hand pressing a dressing to his face. As he stopped, he took the bandage away to look at it and they could see a straight line scored up the side of his face, oozing blood. Below it, the blond hair of his beard was a matted red. He pressed the dressing back into place and looked down at them.

'We're going to get you to some friends of ours – they'll be able to help.'

'What about him?' Cleo gestured towards the door.

'You were never here,' the daylighter said. 'This never happened. We'll open the place up again, clean it out. We'll take the body up top and dump it over the edge. Nobody'll ever find it.'

Section 20/24: Sanctum

The sign over the door read:

THE DARK-DAY FATALISTS —
SECOND QUADRANT CHAPTER
'NATURE WILL ALWAYS BE THE VICTOR'

A symbol above it showed three lines spiralling towards a common centre.

'Great,' Sol snorted.

His hood was up to hide the bandage on the side of his neck. The bullet had missed the major veins and arteries, grazing some muscle. Messy, but superficial. He and Cleo stood with three daylighters in a gloomy alley, looking at the battered door. It had a spy-lens, and they had no doubt they were being studied from within. The door swung open, and a short, dumpy Pinoy man with grey, wispy hair, wearing a plain black suit and spectacles, waved them in.

'We've been expecting you,' he said.

The daylighters wished them goodbye and hurried back up the alley.

Inside, there was the smell of real books and the murmur of voices. They were led down the painted concrete hallway of the sanctum to a large, open, hexagonal room, lit by gaslight. Here, a collection of some twenty black-clad figures waited. Some were sitting in easy chairs, books in hand, others were standing as if deep in conversation. All of them turned to stare as the two teenagers were ushered into the room. The walls were lined with bookshelves, the concrete-beamed ceiling a hexagonal cone that rose to a rounded point, and the flickering light gave the place a warm, informal feel.

'My name is Mr Ibrahim,' the man with the glasses said from behind them. 'Welcome to our chapter. Please, sit down. You are safe here, at least for the moment. We have some food and drink on the way, but in the meantime if you could indulge us, we would like to hear your story. How is it that you have come to be hunted by the Clockworkers?'

Sol scanned the room suspiciously. He was not at ease here, but Cleo seemed to relax somewhat, and flopped down on a couch. Starting with the day of the crane wreck and Gregor's disappearance, she explained the whole thing. He had told her everything, so let her do the talking as he continued to stand, eyeing the faces around him. His gaze fell on a fair-haired man with a drooping mouth and broken veins in his nose and cheeks. Tenzin Smith, his father's friend from the ratting dens. So this was where he had come to hide out. Smith nodded to him, and Sol looked away. But it helped put his mind at rest; if Smith was safe, then chances were that the Clockworkers would not look for them here.

He sat down on the synth-fibre couch beside Cleo and listened to her tell their story. It seemed incredible to him now to hear it told by someone else. The crane wreck, being captured and nearly tortured before he was saved by Maslow. It was relaxing to hear her relating all the events that had brought them to this point, and see the men and women around them listening intently. He should have felt uncomfortable among all these people, but a feeling welled up inside him that he couldn't fathom; some strange, disarming warmth. It took him a few minutes to put a name to it. It was a sense of normality. The sheer ordinariness of sitting among people and talking . . . or at least, listening to someone talking.

'Sorry,' he said abruptly. 'I need to use the toilet.'

'Out to the hall, second door on your right,' Mr Ibrahim told him.

He hurried into the men's room, pushing through the door of a cubicle and bolting it behind him. Sitting on the toilet seat, he drew in several shuddering breaths, pressing his fists against his eyes. He wasn't going to cry, but the tightness in his chest would not go away until he had let out a series of gasping sobs. Putting one hand up to the bandage on his neck, he breathed long and deep, calming himself. He was just letting things get on top of him. He couldn't let that happen – not yet. Not until they were really safe and he had found his father could he let his defences down.

When he came back into the library, Cleo was just concluding her narrative. He sat down next to her, and she shot him a glance, putting a hand on his knee.

'. . . So, after watching that guy burst in the vacuum, I'd had about as much as I could take. When Mr Wasserstein told us he knew of somewhere we could hide out, it was a real godsend. We're really grateful for your help. I don't suppose any of you smoke, by any chance?'

A few of them exchanged looks, but nobody confessed.

'We need to find out about what happened to Ana too,' Sol said quietly. 'We have to know . . . if we could contact somebody at the hospital or—'

'Yeah,' Cleo added, ashamed that she had been thinking about the stem before Ana. 'We just need to know if she's okay.'

'That hospital is in a state of chaos at the moment, but we'll try,' Mr Ibrahim told her. 'There's strength in numbers, Miss Matsumura. And I believe we may have a common cause. Why don't you and Mr Wheat try to relax; we'll have some food along any minute, and then we can talk about where we go from here.'

A few of the other people in the room started to fire questions at her:

'How many people came after you in total? Roughly?'

'Did . . . did they seem to you to have had any police training?'

'Did this Maslow have any other weapons stockpiled?' a feeble old man with a goatee piped up. 'Any heavy munitions? Explosives?'

Cleo looked hesitantly at Sol.

'We cannot achieve meaningful change through force of arms!' a stern-faced, black-haired Pinoy woman retorted.

'There won't be any change at all if they shoot us every time we try anything.' The elderly man waved his puny fist in the air. 'We need some firepower!'

'Violence is not the answer!' chided a young black man, who looked like a student. 'You don't win an argument by starting a fight. We must use reason and rational debate.'

'Fat lot of good that'll do you against semi-automatic rifles!' the old man exclaimed, his head extending on a chicken-like neck.

'Jonah is right!' another voice spoke up. 'They control all the media. Nobody will hear our arguments. We need to make some bombs or something!'

'We've been over this before,' Mr Ibrahim began. 'There's no point—'

'How do we know unless we try!' somebody pleaded, cutting him off.

'We need to engage the mayor in a vigorous debate!'

'We need to *bomb* the mayor!'

'We can't risk causing any more damage to the Machine!'

'Tell that to the Clockworkers!'

'Perhaps we could unite the city in prayer?'

'Oh, shut up!'

Sol and Cleo sat bemused by the dispute that was building around them. Tenzin Smith came over and perched on the couch opposite them.

'They can go on like this for hours,' he said, with a wry grin. 'Want to get out of here?'

Cleo and Sol nodded eagerly.

There was more than one way in and out of the Dark-Day Fatalists' building.

'They're a well-meaning crowd,' Smith said as he led them down a long spiral staircase, 'but they can't agree on squat . . . except that the Machine is on its last legs, of course. Half of them are academics: mathematicians, historians – big thinkers. Lots of long-term plans. Some of the others are engineers, tradesmen . . . even cops. You name it, we have 'em here. Makes for a lot of arguments.' He winked at Cleo. 'They're stingy with their stem too. I've a devil of a time getting hold of any.'

At the bottom of the staircase was a heavy steel door. Sol guessed they must be on the second or third sub-level. The door opened onto a rubbish-strewn laneway; they were greeted by the sound of rats scurrying away at their emergence. Around them were the roots of buildings, foundations and enormous pillars for bridges and supports for engineering works. The only light was from the street above them; cars and mopeds passed by overhead, sending dust sifting down. The most surprising thing was the graffiti art. Every vertical surface was covered with it: gangland tags, band logos, funky cartoon characters, semi-realistic paintings of extinct animals in Ash Harbour settings; angry, obscene declarations of protest, illuminated song lyrics.

'Trying to make sense of their world.' Smith waved his hand around him. 'Sometimes you just have to spew out all the crap that's going on in your head.'

They walked on down the lane; Sol and Cleo wary, now that they were outside their new refuge, but Smith seemed unconcerned. They passed under three huge drive-shafts, coming to a large building that was emitting steam from vents in its walls. Smith walked up the steps to the door. He opened it without knocking. Sol held back, but Cleo turned to him, nodding. She trusted Smith.

Inside, some stairs led up to a balcony that looked out over a nightmarish combination of a gymnasium and some industrial disaster. Heavy machinery pumped, whirred, spun and slammed in some incomprehensible manufacturing process. It took Sol a couple of minutes to make sense of it, because he could not take his eyes off the humans tangled in the works.

'Recycling fixtures,' Smith told them. 'Nuts and bolts, washers . . . ordinary things.'

The workers were bound into the clanking machinery, some pedalling, rowing, cranking, others pumping handles or lifting what must once have been robotic arms. Conveyor belts, lathes, grinding wheels, presses, drills – everything was being powered by the movement of the people in the room. In some machines there were people who were missing limbs, the prosthetics worn to replace them engineered to fit into their place in this human-driven engine. The air was thick with the smell of sweat and oil and hot metal. A furnace at the far end of the factory floor had its bellows pumped on either side by two men with no legs, their corded, perspiration-soaked upper bodies bare to the waist. They had obviously been chosen because, without legs, they could fit into the niches that had once been occupied by machines.

'There are factories like this all over the city,' Smith informed the two teenagers. 'The work is poorly paid or, if you're doing time for a felony, there's no pay at all. I'm an engineer. Do you know what I do for a living? I make customized prosthetics. Somebody loses their hand, or their arm or their leg in an industrial accident, I fix them up something so that they can go back to work in the same job. It's that or they and their families starve. There's no help for them – the companies don't care who gets hurt.'

He turned his back on the factory, leaning against the railing to look at Sol and Cleo.

'The city's dying, a little bit at a time. Metal, plastic, denceramic . . . it all wears down, and it can all be recycled. But every time, we lose some. Resources are dwindling. This whole place used to be fully mechanized, but bit by bit machines have failed, and they've had to replace them with humans. Humans fitting into roles designed for machines.

'I can't tell you how many accidents I've seen; some caused by carelessness, bad management, cutting corners – being cheap. And some caused by sabotage, to remove some small, independent competitor that threatened big company profits. Or because the bosses needed to get some of their property out of the way, and the city council wouldn't let them.' He looked at Cleo. 'Like an apartment block. Or sometimes the sabotage would be to remove somebody who was causing trouble. Like staging a crane accident.'

'You know Francis Walden was murdered?' Sol asked. 'And the other guy, Falyadi?'

Smith nodded.

'Walden was a safety officer, Falyadi was an accountant. They came to us because they'd discovered that Schaeffer was running the Clockworkers. They said they could get proof. We originally thought that Schaeffer was making a bid to gain complete control of the Machine. We didn't have a clue; he's been in control for years. Haddad and the other politicians are just puppets for these industrialists, but Schaeffer's the most powerful of the lot. Walden and Falyadi had accounts that showed Clockworker funds, and we were going to release them over the web. Schaeffer got to them first.

'The myth is that the Clockworkers exist to protect the Machine. But it's exactly that − a myth. They've been around in one form or another since Ash Harbour was built, and they have one job: not to protect the Machine, but to maintain the *status quo*. They make sure the control of the Machine stays in the hands of a small and powerful elite. It's as simple as that. People like Schaeffer think they have the God-given right to run our world and they'll use any means to keep it that way.

'The crazy thing is, they're destroying the very thing they're trying to control. With the way things are wearing out, this city *might* last another hundred years. Meteorologists say the ice age could last another six centuries . . . maybe much more.

'You know we used to have engines, oil-driven machines, for restarting the Heart Engine if it stopped? For saving us from *extinction*! The only things that could have jump-started our city if its heart failed. The city council used up all the oil, and broke up the machines for parts.

'And every accident the Clockworkers create brings the Machine closer to grinding to a halt, and us all freezing to death. Schaeffer and his cronies, they're fighting over who gets to steer the ship . . . while it's sinking.'

He ground his teeth.

'Even if everything could be fixed up properly, the Machine won't last for ever. The DDF are dedicated to finding other ways to survive.'

Cleo and Sol continued to stare at the macabre scene below them.

'My God,' Sol muttered. 'No wonder you're all suicidal.'

Sol gripped the edge of the work table he was sitting on and gritted his teeth. Smith pushed the needle into the edge of the wound in his neck, pulled it through and drew the thread out. He pushed the point into the other side of the small gash, making Sol whimper.

'I'm sorry we've no anaesthetic,' Smith said. 'Even the hospitals can't get hold of enough these days. Try not to tense up too much, it pulls it open.'

Sol drew a sharp breath in as the needle went in again, his knuckles white as his grip tightened on the table. Smith wasn't a doctor, but he apparently had some experience in dealing with wounds. Sol's had to be stitched, or he would keep losing blood. He was close to passing out from the pain. Cleo was away in some other part of the building, talking revolution, making new friends and searching for stem.

'Are they hiding my dad here somewhere too?' Sol asked the engineer.

'No. Sorry.'

'Would you tell me if they were?'

'Not unless he said I could, no.' Smith dabbed away some blood with a dressing. 'But like I said last time, I don't know where he is.'

'You wouldn't tell me about all this back then.'

'Because of Maslow. I didn't know who he was, but I could guess *what* he was. I've seen him around; him and his kind.'

The needle drove in again, and Sol screwed up his face, his whole body tensing. He could feel the thread being pulled through the edge of the scored tear left by the bullet. To try to take his mind off the pain, he looked around at the room they were in: an office with a desk, a worktable covered in electrical odds and ends, and some cupboards. It had a hidden entrance in the library wall, behind a bookcase. Not exactly original, but it worked. One wall of the secret room was lined with small shelves holding thousands of data cards. The other three walls were covered in printouts of photos – accident scenes: dead faces, factory floors, offices, city streets, even a few of the daylighters' depots.

'What's with all the photos?' he asked.

'We carry out investigations of accidents,' Smith replied, his attention focused on his stitching. 'It's part of what we do. We also advise unions, find whistle-blowers, provide information for the media. But we try to keep a low profile; it's not a good idea to be seen as a threat. As I'm sure you know.'

Sol winced as Smith gently pulled the thread tight, closing the edges of the wound and tying a neat knot.

'That's you done and dusted,' Smith said as he taped a fresh dressing into place over the injury. 'Try and take it easy – don't move your head too much.'

Solomon was hardly listening. He was staring at a photo of the workshop in his father's depot. Some of the daylighters were standing over a lathe; blood was visible on the controls. His father was in the picture, in the forefront, the only man in his crew who did not wear a beard.

'One of your dad's mates lost two fingers when the tool-post on the lathe broke,' Smith informed him. 'Metal fatigue. They'd warned the company about it. Nothing was done.'

'When was this taken?' Sol asked, staring at one of the faces.

Maybe Smith hadn't noticed; the man looked different with a bushy beard.

'About two months ago. Why?'

Sol swung the door open and walked out.

'Sol? What is it?'

'Thanks for the stitches,' Sol muttered. 'I'll be back in a few hours.'

'You can't go out!' Smith called after him.

'I won't be long.'

Sol was striding quickly away. Cleo, who was in one of the adjacent rooms, heard their voices and hurried out.

'Where are you going?' she asked.

'I have to meet Maslow.'

'I'll come with you,' she told him.

'No. I'd prefer it if you stayed here.'

'No, listen. You know all those black and white messages we've been seeing on the screens? Somebody here was doing that – they write the viruses and post them on the web. I've had an idea—'

Sol shook his head in disdain. Posting messages on the web. They were good people, and they'd already begun to earn his trust. But was that really the best they could do?

'I want to talk to Maslow about it,' she persisted.

'That might be a problem,' Sol said as he reached the door to the spiral staircase.

'Why?'

Sol slammed the door in her face. She heard his footsteps descending the stairs, and then he was gone.

Section 21/24: Heroism

The hideout where Sol had arranged to meet Maslow if they got split up was a short walk from the Dark-Day Fatalists' building, but it took him nearly an hour to reach it without being seen. He wondered if he would ever again be able to go outside without constantly looking over his shoulder. Tucked away in the attic of a deserted sewage-treatment facility, it was a back room with a small window that looked out on the roofs beyond. The unused sewage works below still pervaded the air with a faint but perpetual reek; as he picked the lock and slipped inside the building, Sol could see the end of a row of tanks, where workers had once sieved the foul gunk. There was a lot they could make from sewage: fertilizer, health products . . . It was even processed and made into a nutritious food. Since the city's inception, the poorer people in Ash Harbour had been eating the city's crap.

The room was at the top of a rickety, neglected staircase. He locked the door behind him. Behind a loose panel in the wall of the small room was another of Maslow's stashes. Along with a bag of emergency supplies, there were four weapons wrapped in burlap: an automatic pistol, a revolver, a stubby sub-machine gun and a short-barrelled pump-action shotgun. Sol rolled out the bundle, slipping the automatic and some spare clips into his jacket pocket. Then he took the shotgun out, loading it with ten shells. It would make bigger holes. He pumped it, chambering a shell, and sat down on an empty crate. He sat with one knee up, supporting the shotgun's stock, which he kept aimed at the door.

Time passed, slowly. He waited with determined patience.

After nearly three hours he heard soft, uneven steps on the creaking staircase, and then the gentle scraping of a metal pick in the old tumbler lock. The door opened cautiously, and Maslow shuffled in, clutching his hip. The left leg of his trousers was soaked in blood. Supporting himself by using a short scaffolding pole as a crutch, he looked even paler than usual. Sol levelled the shotgun at him. Maslow looked dismayed, but not surprised.

'You're holding that all wrong,' he grated.

Solomon's aim did not waver. Maslow met his eyes and held them.

'I saw a picture of my dad's crew today,' Sol told him. 'There was only one face I didn't know – or at least, I didn't know it up until recently. You were wearing a beard in this photo, but I knew it was you.'

He kept the gun trained on Maslow as the Clockworker closed the door, put his back to the wall and sat down heavily on the floor, groaning with pain.

'And what did you make of that?' Maslow asked wearily.

'Remember how you said that Gregor had turned informant, and that his crew planned to murder him?' Sol said in a shaky voice. 'Did you really think I'd believe that? Dad would never shop his friends, and as for them murdering him . . . that's just . . . People just don't kill that easily. Not everybody's like *you*.'

Maslow continued to stare. Sol glared back.

'You worked on the crew, you knew my dad, but I didn't know you. You were the last one to see Gregor alive. You're Tommy Hyung, aren't you? Aren't you, Maslow? Dad was a crane operator before he lost his job. He saw somebody messing with the crane from where he was working on the dome . . . He realized what it was, and he tried to warn somebody, am I right? And Tommy Hyung saw him go, and went to stop him. But it wasn't Hyung who was killed in the piston well. You changed the dental records to protect your identity, right?'

Maslow let his chin sink down to his chest, but didn't answer.

'You said you were good at forgery – that was one of the things you did. Could you forge my dad's handwriting? You sent those messages, didn't you? So whose ... whose remains did they pull from the bottom of the piston well?' Sol uttered the words through gritted teeth. 'Who was thrown in, Maslow?'

Maslow heaved a tired, painful sigh and raised his head, his gaze meeting Sol's.

'Good work, son. You finally figured it out. I killed your dad.'

'DON'T CALL ME "SON", YOU BASTARD!' Sol screamed.

'Keep your voice down.'

Sol's finger tightened on the trigger. He didn't care who heard them now. There was a pounding in his ears, and his teeth were clenched, his hands shaking.

'I was just doing my job,' Maslow wheezed. 'But something changed the day I fought your father.'

He winced, and lifted his jacket and tunic to look underneath. Sol saw a dressing taped to his hip. It was leaking blood.

'When I was your age,' Maslow continued, 'I wanted to be a hero. Like in the films and comics: a good old-fashioned war hero, or a superhero, fighting crime. I wanted people's respect, to have kids look up to me, streets named after me. I wanted statues of me erected in the city squares.

'As I got older, I realized life just wasn't like that. There are no real heroes like in the films. But there was plenty of action to be had, if I wanted it. They put me to good use in the police, and then I went to work with the Clockworkers and that was like being a secret agent. I loved it. But I was getting old, Sol, and I couldn't see a . . . a good end, y'know? Nobody knew what I'd done; there was nobody outside the circle I could tell . . . I mean, not unless I killed them afterwards.

'I joined the daylighters to break up this union they were forming. I got to know your dad, and I liked him. But when I spotted him taking off after looking down at the crane, I knew he'd seen too much. Imagine what was going through his mind, Sol. Above everything, he knew you would be taking a ride on that crane the following day. He must have been frantic to warn somebody. So I went after him. I lost track of him in the depot for a couple of minutes. Time enough to make a webcall—'

'Which he did, didn't he?' Sol cut him off. 'He called Cortez. Dad knew he could end up disappearing, so he made a mad, stupid bet, because he couldn't trust anybody, not even the police. But he knew Cortez would look for him . . . for the money. He was that desperate.'

Maslow nodded.

'I caught sight of him when he left the depot, and I chased him as far as the piston well; he was in good shape – I knew he was going to outrun me. I shouted after him – I yelled that I only had to make one call, and the Clockworkers would come for his son.'

Maslow stopped and winced as pain stabbed up his side from his hip.

'So Gregor turned back. It was beautiful, Sol, you should've seen it – one on one. I had to kill him to silence him; he had to kill me to protect you. To protect *you*. A righteous battle. He knew what I was, and he still fought me, and goddamn it he was tough. But he failed you in the end. He just wasn't good enough, not against someone like me.

'And as I watched him fall, I realized that he was the hero I'd never been. It sickened me to think that. And that was when I decided I'd take his place. I'd be a hero for you.'

Sol stared at him, aghast.

'You're insane,' he rasped.

'It doesn't matter what you think,' Maslow replied. 'It's what I've achieved that's important.'

'But you knew I'd find out eventually . . . You *helped* me find out!'

'It was only right that you did. And self-sacrifice, well, that's what being a hero is all about.'

'You're faggin' nuts!'

Sol still had the shotgun aimed at Maslow's chest. It would be an easy thing for him to squeeze the trigger and finish it all here and now.

'Don't hold it back against your side like that,' Maslow told him. 'The kick'll break your ribs.'

'What happened to your hip?'

'I got out of the hospital after you and Cleo took off, but a couple of them caught up with me. I nailed them, but not before they put a bullet in me. Broke my pelvis – lost a lot of blood. Walking's a bitch. So you gonna kill me, or what?'

Sol's finger was still tense against the trigger. Moving the butt of the shotgun away from his ribs, he braced it better with his arm. He remembered the crane wreck, the broken corpses of the dead men. He remembered the two men, dead and recycled now, who would have tortured him in that little grey room. He remembered seeing Maslow break a woman's neck, as he himself blindly put a bullet through a man's face. He remembered the fire in the apartment block, and the riot. Ana Kiroa being bludgeoned into a coma and possibly killed at the hospital. Himself and Cleo being hunted by the Clockworkers, and saved by the daylighters. The perforated remains of the man in the dome's vacuum. He remembered Smith's room full of accident reports . . . and he remembered something Cleo had said. The only thing he couldn't remember any more was what it felt like to be a normal sixteen-year-old.

'No,' he said at last, looking at the pitiful man in front of him. 'I'm not going to kill you. I'm going to make you a real hero.'

It was late, and Cleo was sharing a meal of promeat and veggie-soy stir-fry and rice with Tenzin Smith. They ate in the DDF's kitchen, the lights low, the only sound the omnipresent, sub-sonic rumble of the city. Cleo was worried about Solomon, and did not feel much like talking. Smith, on the other hand, was pleased to have somebody new to talk to. A social man at heart, he was a reformed alcoholic who needed constant distractions. He was doing enough talking for both of them.

'. . . Now, Natasha, my third wife? She was a terrible cook – she could burn water. Finally left me after I threw one of her meals out of the window. Mind you, she was always a bit of a snob. Came from one of the First Families, didn't she? Thought she was better than the rest of us . . .'

Cleo had been unable to score any stem. Now it was all she could think about, and Smith's nattering was beginning to get on her nerves. Her own food had gone cold too, and she pushed the remains of the rice around the plate, lost in her craving for smoke. They had plenty of books here, and a whole museum given over to the Golden Age, the beginning of the twenty-first century, before they knew the ice was coming. Stupid, useless things like satellite dishes for television, umbrellas, clocks with different time zones, bottles of sunscreen . . . even stuffed animals. But no stem. She frowned as her mind wandered back to the one-sided conversation.

'. . . Embeth, my fifth wife, she could cook up a storm. But she had a tongue that could cut through steel—'

'What did you mean,' she cut in, 'your . . . Natasha was one of the "First Families"? We did something on that in history, I think.'

Smith paused, smiling.

'You don't pay much attention at school, do you?' he said, chuckling.

'I can't really concentrate properly without music, and they won't let me play my stereo in class. I asked.'

'Ash Harbour took decades to build,' he told her, shaking his head at what she assumed were the declining standards of education. 'It was only one of over twenty refuges that went into construction once mankind realized what was' – he waved a hand over their heads – 'what was coming. An ice age like the world had never seen. Our lush, green, succulent planet was fast becoming uninhabitable. Some people said we'd done it to ourselves – that our industry had created this catastrophic climate change. Others said it was coming anyway.

'None of that mattered. All that mattered was that by the end of the twenty-first century, we had to have defences built against this apocalypse. So governments started constructing shelters. Some of them were laughable. Deep holes in the ground, badly ventilated, with inadequate heating. Slipshod engineering, poorly reinforced. Half of them weren't even prepared for growing their own *food*. They thought they could live off tinned grub!' He laughed. 'Frozen fish and powdered eggs! It was like they thought they just had to hide out until the storm blew over in a few years. Like it was a nuclear war or something. But this thing was going to last *centuries*. Most people couldn't even get their heads around the enormity of it.

'But enough did. There were only a few places left where it was still possible to build on this scale. You know Ash Harbour is only a few hundred kilometres from a fault line? It was going to have to withstand earthquakes, on top of everything else. But it was the only one with a dome this size, and there was nothing like the Machine anywhere else in the world. It took years to design it, and the construction was on a scale that nobody had ever attempted before. Millions of people were involved. Millions. For a city that would only be able to support a few hundred thousand. Imagine that.

'So when the time came to get people into these shelters and seal them up, war broke out. As everybody knew it would. There were certain people who were essential for running and maintaining the Machine. They and their families were the first people to be given places inside. Then there were some politicians, and scientists and military guys . . . You know, the ones who'd been in on it from the beginning. And all of these people made up what became known as the First Families. They had to be trained first. Every aspect of their lives had to be directed towards getting the Machine working, and keeping it working. Then they would have to train the rest. Imagine that: nearly three hundred thousand people would have to learn to live their lives as vital components of the most complicated mechanical device ever built. It was unprecedented.

'After the First Families, the rest of the places in

the city were decided by a lottery. There was chaos, of course, and you'd better believe that corruption ran through the whole process, so plenty of people lost their rightful places. But eventually the hordes were fought off, and the city was sealed. And everybody outside was left to die. The same thing happened at all the other refuges, all over the world: MacDonnell in Australia; Mandela City in Pretoria; Brazil; Armenia . . . Hell, somebody even attacked Cheyenne Mountain in Colorado with nuclear missiles trying to get in! Can you believe that? It had started life as a goddamned nuclear shelter, so that didn't work.'

Cleo sat, listening quietly. Other people's problems seemed more real to her, now that she had so many of her own.

'And they just locked them out?' she asked. 'They left them to die?'

'They had to.' He nodded. 'Or everybody was finished.'

He put the last forkful of food into his mouth and pulled Cleo's unfinished plate over.

'Anyway, most of them are gone now; the other shelters. Could be that we've just lost contact with some, but it's unlikely. Hell, the whole damn lot of them could be gone for all we know. We thought we were so smart. This place ran without a hitch for over a hundred years, before we realized how many things we were running out of—'

Smith's monologue was interrupted by a hammering on the front door of the building.

'Police!' a voice bellowed. 'Open up!'

Smith lunged to his feet, grabbed Cleo by the arm and rushed her out of the kitchen and down the hallway to the library. Mr Ibrahim was coming the other way.

'I'll give you as long as I can!' he told them in a hoarse whisper.

'Open up, or we break down the door!' the voice came again.

Cleo was on Smith's heels as he belted through the library and down the passage to the rear door. He stopped as he heard voices on the other side of the door. Turning, they ran back and opened the door to the spiral staircase. Footsteps were hurrying up towards them.

'Goddamn it!' Smith muttered through bared teeth.

He led her back into the library and swung open the bookcase that hid the secret room. From the door, they could hear Mr Ibrahim enquiring what the problem was.

'We have a warrant to search these premises,' somebody told him in an officious tone. 'We're looking for one Solomon Wheat, who's wanted in connection with two murders. Is he here?'

'No,' Mr Ibrahim replied truthfully.

'Well, we'll just check for ourselves, sir, and see what there is to see, eh?'

Smith closed the bookcase and locked it, leaving the room's light off. He switched on a screen, tapped in a command, and an array of screenshots opened up, showing different views of the sanctum. Police officers were filing into the hall and breaking into groups, starting to search each room in turn. Cleo had not noticed any cameras; they must have been well hidden.

'This is a safe room,' Smith whispered from the darkness. 'The walls are lined with lead – their scanners won't find us.'

'What about the others?' Cleo asked.

'Everybody else belongs here,' Smith responded in a hushed voice. 'We're the only odd ones out.'

They sat down, waiting in silence as they listened to the muffled sounds of the police officers spreading out through the building. There were a lot of them.

'Somebody's betrayed us,' Smith whispered. 'Sol leaves, and suddenly we're getting turned over by the police.'

'It wasn't Sol!' Cleo hissed. 'It could have been anybody! He would never—'

The engineer held up his hand to silence her. Somebody was on the other side of the bookcase. On the screen, they could see the cops examining the shelves, but there was no sign that they were looking for the door. Clumsy hands rifled through the books. The door could not be opened from the outside, once it had been locked from the inside, but Cleo still watched with dread for the first crack of light from the doorway.

Eventually, the noise of the search passed. They waited another two hours after the last sound, and then carefully emerged from their hideout. The whole building was empty of people.

'They've taken everyone in for questioning,' Smith said finally. 'We're not safe here any more, but there's a chance they could be watching the exits.'

'So what do we do?' Cleo asked.

'I don't know. We're in a bit of pickle here.'

'It wasn't Sol—'

'I know – if it was, they'd have known about the safe room. A daylighter maybe – it doesn't matter. We can't trust anybody now.'

Cleo sank to the floor, putting her face in her hands.

'Jesus, is this ever going to end?'

The door to the staircase burst open, and Solomon staggered in, supporting Maslow. The Clockworker collapsed to the floor, barely conscious, blood soaking through his trousers and jacket around his hip. Sol dropped onto his hands and knees, exhausted. He slid a heavy burlap roll off his shoulder and looked up at Smith and Cleo.

'What's new?' he asked.

'The police raided the place,' Cleo replied. 'We have to get out of here. And they might still be watching the building.'

'Don't think there's anybody downstairs.' Sol heaved in big breaths. 'But I'm not going down those faggin' steps again until I've had a rest.'

While Sol and Maslow rested, they all talked. An idea had been forming in Cleo's head, one she had tried to discuss with Sol before he took off. To her surprise, he asked her what she had been trying to tell him, and discovered he had been thinking along the same lines. Like her, he could see there was no future in running. But before they could put their plan into action, they had to get out of this building in case the police came back.

It took them half an hour to do what they needed to do, and leave. Maslow could no longer walk, so they fashioned a stretcher out of a bed frame and a blanket, and painstakingly eased him down the stairs. Cleo led the way outside, scouting ahead.

They had nowhere to go. Sol was intent on heading back to the deserted sewage works, but it soon became clear that they couldn't sneak through the sub-levels carrying the stretcher – there was too much climbing involved. Instead, they stopped in the shadow of a wide footbridge, hidden behind two of its massive shock absorbers. It was still dark, but morning was fast approaching.

'This is as far as I go,' Maslow said to them in a strained voice. 'You need to go; you've got what you need from me. Get on with the job.' He paused to draw a shuddering breath. 'If you start thinking too much, you might chicken out . . . and the longer you're hanging around, the more likely you are to get caught before you can get it done.'

'We'll be fine,' Smith agreed, taking charge. 'There isn't much security – this kind of attack just hasn't been anticipated. We'll be done before the police even start rolling.'

'It's not the police you need to worry about.' Maslow shook his head. 'Not the normal ones, anyway. They'll just arrest you. Schaeffer will want you rubbed out, or taken and interrogated in private. Years ago, we put plans in place for assaulting the Hub, in case we needed to take control of the media . . . Once the alarm is raised, the first move will be to seal it off – there aren't many exits – and cut off all means of communication with the outside, including the police lines. My guys – the . . . the Clockworkers – will want to handle this their own way – quietly. You don't want to get caught by them.'

'So we want the cops to get there, but not too early,' Cleo concluded.

'And the right cops,' Sol added. 'Not the Clockwork ones.'

'Right.' Maslow winced, and tried to shift his hip to a more comfortable position. 'After that . . . well, I don't know what's goin' to happen after that.'

They all crouched in a morose silence, daunted by the task ahead of them. Each secretly nursed some hope that everything would work itself out before they had to act. A stupid, naive and deluding wish that things would change for the better all on their own.

Maslow finally gasped in exasperation.

'Get off your asses and get on with it!'

And so they did.

Inspector Mercier was completing a report on the shoot-out at the Third Quadrant Hospital. There were a lot of unanswered questions, not least the possible connection to the riot at the Schaeffer building. And the possible connection with Solomon Wheat. And the man who was running with him, who seemed to be nothing less than a rogue Clockworker. And then there was the tragedy of what had happened to Wheat's teacher, Ana Kiroa.

His screen chimed, interrupting his thoughts.

'Call for you, Inspector,' the police operator's bored voice informed him.

'Thank you.'

The call was patched through; a girl's face appeared onscreen.

'Inspector Mercier? My name's Cleo Matsumura, I'm in Sol Wheat's class?'

'Yes, I remember you, Miss Matsumura. What can I do for you?'

'Well' – she paused, looking somewhat embarrassed – 'I don't feel right doing this, y'know, but—'

'Please, carry on.'

'Well, I know you're looking for Sol, and I just got a call from him.' Her eyes wouldn't look straight at the camera. Classic guilt complex. 'And . . . and he asked me to bring him some money. Said he was really stuck.'

Mercier was half out of his seat, leaning towards the screen.

'And where did he say he was, Miss Matsumura?'

'He said he'd meet me under the big screen, outside the Communications Hub. Is he in a lot of trouble, Inspector?'

'Not any more, dear.' Mercier was grabbing his coat. 'You told him you'd meet him, yes?'

'Well, yeah . . . I'm on my way there now – I just stopped to make this call.'

'Good girl . . . good girl. There'll be no need to show up, I'll see he's all right. Thank you very much. We'll be in touch.'

He switched off the screen, and strode out through the door, rushing past the desks of detectives.

'Baiev!' he shouted.

'Sir?' The big sergeant raised his head from his screen.

'With me.'

'Sir.'

As they hurried towards the car pool, Inspector Ponderosa emerged from the toilets ahead of them, only to be barged aside by Baiev.

'Watch where you're going!' he snapped. 'Where you off to in such a hurry, Mercier? You misfile a report or something?'

317

Mercier shot him a hostile glance, but kept walking. Ponderosa gazed after them, chewing the inside of his lip. He watched them until they disappeared round the corner, and then pulled out his radio.

Section 22/24: Propaganda

Despite its name, the Communications Hub was located by the city wall, in an area known as Silicon Village. A twelve-storey tower with spiralling windows in blue and silver, its top half bristled with antennae and solar arrays. Its upper floors could be reached by walkways from the wall itself. All the media companies had their headquarters there, but the feed to all the webscreens was still controlled by the city council itself.

The area around the Hub was where most of the city's technology was manufactured. When it came to providing the computers, screens, smartsuits and the scores of other technological devices essential for life in the city, there was real money to be made for high-tech suppliers, and it was reflected in the standard of the buildings of Silicon Village, and the security measures that protected them. Most of the buildings had dedicated guards, and cameras and bright lights lined the streets. With the dome completely covered by a new blanket of ice and snow, Silicon Village remained one of the brightest places in Ash Harbour.

The city's main control centre took up the top three floors of the Hub. Whenever Smith's group of campaigners planted a virus in the system – the viruses that forced every public webscreen to display irritating questions about the way the city was run – the entire system could be shut down, scanned and cleared by the men and women in the control centre. None of these displays lasted more than a minute and a half.

Cleo, Sol and Smith had a slightly longer broadcast in mind. And to make sure the city got to hear the message, it was essential that nobody in the control centre interrupted it.

Smith knew his way around the tower: he had worked there as an electrician in one of his many careers. They entered from the wall, at the third balcony level. This put them only three floors below the control centre. It was just before six, still too early for most of the work crowd. The glass-walled reception on this floor was manned by a single overweight female security guard, who also watched over the screens for all the cameras on this floor. There was no one else in sight. Sol and Smith were both carrying the larger guns beneath their jackets, and bags on their backs; Cleo took the lead, walking straight up to the desk with a beatific smile on her face, her hand reaching for the palm-pad to log herself in.

'Hi,' she chirped. 'We're visiting the twelfth floor. Don't get up.'

With one hand on the desk, she vaulted over, her feet catching the security guard full in the chest, knocking her backwards out of her chair. By the time the guard was up on her feet, she found herself looking down the barrels of a shotgun and a sub-machine gun, while Cleo sprayed industrial glue over the alarm button under the desk.

They tied up the woman and gagged her, depositing her in a nearby janitor's cupboard. She would be discovered before long, but they only needed a few minutes' head start.

The guard's key-chip gave them access to the secure elevator and allowed them to open the doors on any floor they wanted. They punched the button for the twelfth. Solomon and Smith tucked their guns back under their jackets.

The elevator reached the top floor and chimed cheerfully. They stepped out past two middle-aged men who were waiting to descend, and Smith led his young accomplices to the anteroom that opened into the open-plan office area, with its digitally printed clay brick walls. Beyond that they could see the double doors to the control room. This door was made from the same denceramic as the walls – it was kept locked. Their newly acquired key-chip could not open this door. It was so early and yet there were already four people at their desks. They looked up at the visitors.

New faces were a curiosity here. Smith, Sol and Cleo sat down on couches in the anteroom as if they were waiting for somebody.

At six o'clock, two men in their thirties, dressed in casual clothes, came out of the elevator and strolled through the anteroom towards the control-room door. This was the shift change, here to take over from those on night duty. As they reached the door, the three intruders rose to their feet and walked nonchalantly into the office area. One of the men at the door turned and raised his eyebrows expectantly as they approached. The door was already reading their key-chips, and the lock clicked open.

'Can we help you?' he asked as his partner stepped into the control room.

Sol pulled the shotgun from his jacket and fired a shot into the floor at the man's feet, charging forward as he did so. The gunshot caused the man to stagger back, and he fell, blocking his partner from closing the door. Sol ran right over him, slamming his fist into the second man's sternum, knocking the wind out of him, and then crashing through the door. Inside, another man and a woman were looking up from the instrument panels in shock. Sol fired another shot into the ceiling over their heads, making them jump, and then levelled his weapon at them, trying to hide the tremble in his hands.

'Don't even faggin' twitch!' he roared, his voice shrill with tension.

Go in hard and loud, Maslow had told them. Go for maximum shock. Sound like you're out of your mind, he'd said. That bit would be easy, at least.

Cleo was in the door, holding it open, a powerful revolver in one hand, while Smith kicked and shoved the two day controllers back outside. Once they were out, Cleo slammed the door, letting the lock click back into place. Smith slung the bag off his back and took out a tube of denceramic resin. He squirted some all the way around the edges of the door; within two minutes it would be sealed tight. It would take an industrial laser to open it. With Cleo keeping her gun on the controllers, Sol crossed the windowless room to the only other way out – the double doors out to the roof, where all the antennae were mounted. He opened it and peered out. If anybody was going to force their way in, it would most likely be through here.

A winding ramp balcony led from the door up to the roof above. Keeping below the lip of the balcony, he scurried up the curve of the ramp until he could see both the door of the control room and the floor of the roof. Most of the control room's transmissions went out over the antennae array. If it was attacked, the broadcast could be stopped. It was his job to protect it for as long as he could.

He hunkered down, pulled his bag off his shoulder and unzipped it. It was still dark, with a weak glow filtering through from the snow-covered dome. He took a set of goggles from the bag and put them on, pressing a switch on the side. They powered up, and he could see the world clearly, the light enhanced by the goggles' lowlight scope. They were Maslow's; the Clockworkers would have the same gear. It was cold up here – he could see his breath steam in the chilly air. He pulled up his hood, leaned back into the shadow of a solar panel and waited.

Smith walked up to the two controllers. He held out a data chip.

'Put this in, download it to every screen,' he told them. 'Loop it and let it run. Don't try and fake it – I know the system. Don't reach for any alarms. We don't need you alive.'

Cleo cocked the hammer on her pistol to punctuate the threat. She fervently hoped they would do as they were told – there was no way she would be able to shoot anybody. But the controller obeyed; faced with crazy people with guns, he was less concerned with calling their bluff and more worried about holding onto the contents of his bladder. He slotted the data chip into the panel in front of him and touched some buttons.

The woman was more defiant. She tried to out-stare Cleo.

'Anything you do, we'll undo later. You know that?' she said sourly.

Cleo smirked.

'Then you're going to have your hands full.'

★　　★　　★

324

Throughout the city people were setting out for work, their movement pumping power into the Machine. The full day shift of trams began their clockwise and anti-clockwise routes around the streets, their weight and the weight of the crowds on the daily commute pushing down on pumps, pistons and shock-absorbers, turning flywheels that spun generators that converted the kinetic energy to electricity. Transformers in sub-stations transferred the various power feeds into the central circuit that powered the Heart Engine. And the Heart Engine, its generators suspended in friction-free electromagnetic fields, fed all that power back out to the city's most vital industries: water supplies, food processing, sewage treatment and ventilation. The Machine drew on this power, awakening to the new day.

All through the city, webscreens started to flicker. And then they went white. A whining buzz announced the speakers were being turned right up, something that only happened for emergency announcements. Everywhere, people conditioned to soak up whatever information the media threw at them turned to watch the screens. A man's face appeared, his once-dark skin pale from some unspecified pain, and from a life spent beyond the dome's daylight. His face was lined and his eyes hard – he had the look of a weakened and weary predator.

'My name is Sergeant Elijah Osman Maslow, of the Fifth Unit of the Covert Operations Group – a group most of you know as the Clockworkers. On the orders of my commanders I have murdered fifty-six people, and have killed many more in acts of sabotage designed to look like accidents. All of these operations were ordered by Vincent Schaeffer, of the Schaeffer Corporation, and by men and women like him. Their sole purpose was to maintain absolute control of the Machine, even if it meant risking the lives of every person in it.'

While Maslow's recording played, all the information that Smith had collected over the years on the accidents he had investigated was downloaded to individual hard-drives across the city. But this was something for later, to nurture the seeds of rage that were being planted as he spoke.

As Maslow began to relate the details of operations he had carried out, more and more people stopped to listen. They stopped walking, stopped climbing stairs, using elevators and escalators; they stopped moving. The drivers of the trams rolled to a halt near the huge adscreens to hear what was being said. People in the pedal stations stopped cycling; those in the foot stations stopped pumping on the stair-climbers. Standing motionless in the dark streets and half-lit buildings, the city's inhabitants ceased feeding power to the Heart Engine.

Solomon, who could not see the control room's monitors, watched the city instead. He had never seen it so still. A noise reached his ears over the quiet murmur from below. A mechanical whirring creaking. He looked up to see one of the gantry cranes sliding along the grid of stout girders that hung beneath the dome. He shouted a warning to Cleo and Smith. The Clockworkers were coming.

'Look at them,' Smith said softly, staring at the monitors, which showed various streets in the city centre. 'They're finally listening. We've woken them up.'

Sol kept himself hidden beneath the solar panel. A rope dropped down from the crane as it glided overhead. First one, followed by a second, then a third man started to slide down the rope. They were all wearing body armour. He took aim with the shotgun. His hands were shaking even worse now. Once he started shooting, they would zero in on him. Maslow had said to expect snipers in the cranes.

'This is it,' Smith was saying. 'We're finally going to turn this thing around.'

Sol steadied the gun, sighted on the first man as he descended towards the roof. He was only ten metres away – silhouetted against the dome. Sol pulled the trigger.

His shot caught the man in the hip, taking a chunk out of the Clockworker's harness, knocking the rope loose. But the man managed to hold on with his hands and feet. Even as the report from the gunshot was fading from Sol's ears, bullets started to impact around him. He kept his nerve, aimed and fired at

327

the second man on the rope. The blast caught his target square in the chest. His armour saved him, but his hands released their grip on the rope and he crashed down onto the man below him. They both plummeted down to the roof and landed with a double crunch. Sol fired two more shots up at the crane itself, to try to deter the sniper, and then made a run for the control-room door.

Cleo was standing, firing her pistol up at the crane, when Sol came pounding down the ramp. He was almost at the door, when a sudden blast of heat and debris hit her from behind, throwing her forward. She screamed as she saw Sol lifted off his feet and pitched over the balcony wall towards the ground far below.

Her ears hurt from the blast, and the control room was full of dust and smoke. The door Smith had sealed was a ragged hole in the wall; Smith himself was lying in the middle of the floor, blood leaking from his ears. The two controllers were also unconscious. Cleo crawled towards Smith, lifting her gun as figures in grey fatigues and body armour rushed into the room. One of them kicked the weapon out of her hand and stamped her head down against the floor, her cheek slamming against the tiles.

'Make sure of the other one,' a voice commanded. 'I don't want any loose ends. Christ, did you have to do so much damage? The place is a wreck!'

Cleo coughed in the dust, tears streaming down her face. They should have had more time. A man had his knee on her back, pulling her arms behind her and cuffing her wrists.

'It's going to be hard to get them out past the police,' he said. 'Are you sure you want to keep them alive?'

'Just make sure the boy's dead first.'

Cleo craned her neck to watch as one of the men walked across to the balcony doorway and peered over the wall. He leaned further over, looking right and left.

'He's gone! He must have fallen. Don't see the body, though.'

'Find it.'

Sol lay stunned for a moment, wondering why he wasn't falling to his death. He opened his eyes and found himself looking straight up the outside of the Communications Hub. One of the lenses in the goggles was cracked, but they were still working. He was lying on a gold-coloured solar panel, which was just level enough to prevent him sliding off into empty space. But only just. The shotgun was lying by his side, but when he tried to grab it, it slipped away from his hand and dropped off the edge. He didn't hear it land.

The panel was two metres square, and trembled when he moved. The flimsy construction was one of an array that stood out on thin arms from the wall of the building. They descended the wall in a spiral that complimented the architecture's helical structure. The arm holding this panel creaked ominously.

He could hear men's voices from the control room

above him. It would not take them long to check over the balcony wall and find him. His first instinct was to help Cleo and Smith, but he would be no good to them against a team of Clockworkers – their best chance was for him to escape, to survive. How did the Clockworkers get here before Mercier? He had to get away and find some honest cops. The gantry crane was just out of sight beyond the roof. He had to move now.

As he shifted his weight, the panel tilted further and he only just grabbed the edge of it in time as he flailed with his legs for purchase. Gasping desperately, he stretched out and his feet found the arm of the panel alongside, and he reached out for the aluminium frame from which the arms jutted, and pulled himself under it. One glance down told him he should keep his eyes to the wall, his stomach attempting to hide up between his lungs.

'He's gone! He must have fallen,' he heard someone shout. 'Don't see the body, though.'

Dangling precariously, he started to work his way along like an ape, swinging from one arm to the other, following the sloping curve of the frame around the building, struggling under each panel arm that blocked his way. Minutes later he was round the other side of the building, his arms feeling as if somebody was trying to pull them out of his shoulders.

He was perplexed to find a rope dangling out in front of him. Looking up, he realized it was the very same one that the Clockworkers had come down on. The shooters in the crane could still not see him beneath the solar panels. Two floors down, and less than three metres over, was a walkway connecting the building to the crater wall.

'Ah, nuts!' he grunted. Letting go with one hand, he stretched out, grabbed the rope and pulled it towards him. Bracing his feet against the wall, he shoved himself out, but as soon as he released his other hand from the frame he started to slide, and the rope started to burn his hands. He tried to squeeze harder, but the plastic rope was thin – impossible to grip. A scream erupted from his mouth as he forced his hands to clench tight, feeling the rope tear through his skin. He fell too fast, but his push had sent him out over the walkway, and he landed hard on its floor, his backside taking most of the impact. The automatic in his jacket pocket fell out and skittered towards the door. He lunged after it, but just as he did so, he saw a man and woman through the glass door, running across the foyer towards him.

Sol staggered to his feet, wincing as he pushed off the ground with his burned hands. His bottom felt as if he might have broken something, but he willed himself on, breaking into a run. The door slid open behind him, and he barely made it to the end of the walkway and round its support pillars as silenced gunshots sent bullets buzzing past him.

And so he found himself running again, his hands

pressed to his sides to try to ease the intense pain in his palms and fingers. Down the empty promenade balcony he sprinted, darting past shocked individuals staring at the now-empty screens. Finding an entrance to a stairwell, he pushed through the door and scrambled up the steps. Behind him, from beyond the doorway, a taunting voice called out to him.

'Where are you going, Sol? There's nowhere left to run!'

He was halfway up the flight when the lights went out, and he was enveloped in darkness.

Section 23/24: End

The man hit Cleo hard across the face with the back of his hand, splitting her lip. She fell against the dead instrument panels, hurting her ribs. Getting to her feet again, she spat blood and glared defiantly at the Clockworker.

'How many others are involved?' he asked again.

'It was just us,' she rasped. 'That was all it took.'

'Where's the boy gone?'

'I don't know.'

He slapped her again, snapping her head to the side. She sniffed as she felt blood drip down her left nostril. She wiped the drop away, determined not cry.

'Where were you going to go, after you got away?'

'We didn't expect to get away,' she said, with a tight throat.

'Where's Maslow?'

'He's dead. He died of gunshot wounds after he made the recording.'

Off to one side, Vincent Schaeffer was standing in

front of the blank monitors. His plump face with its long white sideburns was burning with suppressed fury.

'Can't you get anything?' he snapped.

The man sitting at the desk was one of the day controllers that Smith had forced out of the door before he'd sealed it. He was trying to restore any kind of function to the banks of equipment, so that they could counteract some of the damage done by Maslow's broadcast.

'The explosion knocked out a lot of the electronics; I'm doing my best,' he retorted. 'What was all that about anyway, sir? That guy made some serious charges.'

'Shut up! Just do your goddamned job and get us back online.'

The controller had one of the panels open, trying to close some of the fuses. There were a few clicks, and then some of monitors fizzed into life. They were displaying the feed from the cameras on the streets in the city centre, showing people milling around, shouting and arguing.

'Christ, they're still there,' Schaeffer growled. 'This is turning into a goddamned mess.'

As the power from the city's movement dwindled and died, the Heart Engine's movement started to stutter and become erratic. Without external power from the Machine, the Heart Engine was slowing down. The city's lights dimmed and flickered. Still, the crowds did not move. They waited in front of the screens, waiting for more, wanting answers. This sudden stall was more than the damaged, abused Machine could withstand. Its batteries holding onto the scantest electrical charge, the Machine's Heart Engine ground to a halt. Every electric light in the city went out. Every electrical device went dead. With the dome covered, there was no sunlight for the solar panels to supplement the power. No electricity to open the valves allowing water to flow through the hydroelectric generators. Even the majority of the gas lamps fizzled out, their pumps dead. Here and there, battery-powered emergency generators hummed into life, but their temporary existence barely registered in the dark, quiet city.

In the control room of the Communications Hub, everybody was working their jaws, putting their hands to their ears, puzzled by a strange new sensation. Cleo felt it like a yawning emptiness. For the first time in her life, there was complete and utter, aching silence. The ever-present rumble that underscored their lives – the sound of the city – was gone.

'Good God.' Schaeffer stood on the balcony, gaping out at the black landscape before him. 'The . . . the fools. The goddamned fools! They've let the Heart Engine die.'

He looked at the four Clockworkers who stood around him, then at the controller staring impotently at the blank screens.

'For God's sake, we need to talk to them! There'll be panic . . . chaos! Get us online before they go berserk. We have to . . . we have to get it started again . . . We can't . . . There'll be riots.' He faltered, looking from one face to the next.

'There's nothing we can do.' The controller sighed resignedly. 'We have no power.'

Glaring over at Cleo, Schaeffer snarled like an animal.

'You stupid, stupid bitch! You've . . . Do you know what you've done? We're about to be made *extinct* because of your goddamn mindless . . . stupid stunt. We're all going to freeze!'

Cleo ignored him, gazing dispassionately at the men around her. None of them seemed to know what to do. Brushing past the one who had been interrogating her, she walked out to the balcony. Schaeffer was crumbling.

'Some of us can survive. Maybe a few years . . . maybe,' he babbled to himself. 'We have the weapons, we can fight off anybody who tries to stop us. Seal off a small section, stockpile the last of the food. There has to be something we can use as fuel . . . things to burn. If we can find enough things to burn . . .'

All his power and influence came from his control of the Machine. That had changed now. Cleo stood beside him and looked out over the city. She felt unnaturally calm, as if she were waiting for something she knew would happen, but she had no idea what or when. There was nothing for her to do but wait. Beside her, Schaeffer began to hyperventilate.

★   ★   ★

The goggles needed some kind of light to pick up and enhance, but in the stairwell there was almost none. Probing with outstretched hands through the darkness, Sol found the door at the top of the stairs and pushed it open, wincing as his shredded hands left blood on the handle. For a moment he was silhouetted against the faint light outside, and a bullet smacked off the door frame by his head. He ducked through, hearing footsteps hurrying up the stairs after him. He closed the door behind him, hoping that the darkness would slow down his pursuers, and ran on.

Sprinting headlong through the gloom, he looked around, disorientated. Out over the rail to his left, the city was cloaked in black, as if covered in shadows, and it took him a minute or two to realize what had happened. Everything had stopped moving. Ash Harbour was dying.

'God Almighty,' he panted, his stride faltering. 'This can't be happening . . .'

They'd never considered that the Machine might already be so weak. Without realizing it, they had dealt the final blow to the dying city.

'Sol,' the voice shouted from back in the gloom. 'There's nowhere to go! Make this easy on yourself. Give it up, kid, and we'll get it over nice and quick.'

They weren't shooting. They couldn't get a decent shot at him in the murky shadows. Slowing down, he trod softly, making no sound, trying to keep the pillars in the centre of the wide balcony between himself and his hunters. Reflective signs on the wall told him where he was. The top floor, little more than half a kilometre from the daylighters' depot. They would help him get to the police.

'Come on, kid.' A woman's voice this time. 'We've sealed the place off, you're not getting out of here. We'll find you eventually.'

They're mad, he thought. The Machine was lying still below them, and they were still worried about catching him. As if he mattered any more. He wanted to yell at them, telling them how insane they were, but any sound would help them to find him. Was the air getting colder already, or was it just his imagination? How long would it take for the whole city to freeze over?

He saw movement ahead of him and heard the electronic voice of a radio. Darting into an alcove, he peered out. Another three figures, carrying torches, swept the shadows ahead of him. Another hundred metres and they'd be on top of him. Sol looked back. He could hear footsteps closing on him from behind. He had seconds left.

Further ahead, the wall curved round and he could see a number of doors. He recognized one of them. It led to the maintenance depot, where he and Maslow had gone out on the dome. It was a way out, but only as far as the Arctic temperatures outside. Maybe he could make it to the daylighters' depot that way. But they would anticipate that; the Clockworkers would wait for him at the other entrances. It was too late for the police now. He would run towards the daylighters because it was the only option left to him. But the maintenance depot was the only way out. Sol swore – he'd have to charge right at the Clockworkers to reach the door . . .

Don't think. Run. His trainers squeaked on the floor as he took off. They spotted him almost immediately, raising their weapons. He was twenty metres from the door.

'Don't shoot!' he cried. 'I give up. I can take you to Maslow – just don't kill me!'

'Slow down, kid,' one of them called. 'It's over. No more running.'

Sol turned and shoulder-charged the door. It crashed open, and he slammed it shut after him, even as the shots punched through it. There was a bolt on it, and he pushed it home, then bounded down the corridor to the door at the other end. It was locked, and he already had his lock-pick out, fumbling it into the keyhole. Two gunshots blasted away the bolt in the far door. He felt the lock click, and shoved the door open, kicking it closed as he slipped in. There was a heavy steel cupboard beside the door, and he pushed it over, barricading himself in.

There were eight safesuits hanging on the rack. As shoulders started hitting the door, he pulled one down and sat on the floor, gritting his teeth as his sore backside made itself felt. He hurriedly kicked his shoes off and slid his legs into the trousers, and then the boots. Shrugging his shoulders into the sleeves, he did up the triple seal and pulled up the hood. He switched on the power unit, saw it was only half-charged – it would have to do – and pulled on the mask.

He grabbed an ice-axe, threw the other suits onto the ground and smashed the power unit on each one with the axe. Then he pulled on his gloves, took up a second axe and strode over to the airlock.

'Faggin' hell.'

There was no power. He would have to open and close it manually. The door behind him was starting to give way, the cupboard shifting on the floor. Breathing hard behind the mask, he cranked the wheel on the wall that opened the airlock door, until it was just wide enough to admit him, and then he squeezed inside. The inner door had to be closed before the outer door would open. It was a safety feature. He cranked the door closed again and strode to the other end. He was turning the wheel for the outer door when someone knocked on the glass of the door behind him. He glanced round, but kept spinning the wheel.

A man's face stared through the glass. The man drew his finger across his throat.

Sol got the outer door open far enough, then slipped through, leaving it open. They would have to crank it closed again before they could get out. It was a clear, crisp morning outside. A heavy fall of snow covered the dome, and the bright sun on the snow would have blinded him had it not been for the protective tint in the mask's smart-lenses. He should have used one of the ice-axes to block the outer door, so that it couldn't close, preventing them from using that door. But he didn't. He should have started running for the daylighters' depot, less than half a kilometre away. Instead, he dug the axes into the hardened snow and started climbing the dome. He climbed as far as he could before the first of the Clockworkers came through the airlock door. Then he turned round and looked down the slope, waiting for them.

If he was going to die up here, running away would not be his final act.

Cleo didn't know how long she stood there. It could have been a few minutes, or an hour or more. Schaeffer was hunched over the balcony, trembling. The Clockworkers were standing pensively, waiting for orders, nervous that the police would be on their way. The whole place had an expectant air. Cleo's eyes swept back and forth over the darkness. A few remaining gas lamps dotted the streets, offering the only light.

Then, from above, a shaft of sunlight shone down. Still faint, but there nonetheless. Others broke through from different sections of the dome. A watery morning sun reached through the snow-blanketed glass and touched the darkness. The daylighters had started their shifts – either they were unaware that the city was dying beneath them, or they knew and had gone to work anyway. But it made a difference; suddenly there was a break in the gloom overhanging Ash Harbour.

And then Cleo thought she saw a new light ignite in the shadows. And then another. Like dying embers being rekindled, the lights began to come back on. An electrical hum started up from inside the control room, and she heard the controller gasp.

Inside, some of the monitors had activated; lights blinked all over the instrument panels.

'The power's back,' the controller said in disbelief.

On the screens, people were moving. The streets were filled with men, women and children, walking the routes they had walked all their lives. People had put their shoulders to the trams, and were pushing them along their tracks. Across the cityscape, in pedal and foot stations, dynamos began to turn; everywhere, power was being pumped through the system once more. Painfully slowly, the Machine was resuscitated. Cleo smiled slightly as hundreds of thousands of individual efforts breathed life back into their home.

'You see,' she said quietly to Schaeffer. 'They knew what to do. They've *always* known. And they didn't need *you.*'

Schaeffer had the expression of a man who had just learned he was no longer terminally ill. His new-found relief hardened to anger as he took in the room around him. There was still a rebellion to crush.

'Call the mayor in,' he barked. 'As soon as the public screens are back online, I want her to stamp on this conspiracy before it grows legs. And find that kid! We have to contain this situation. If he disappears again—'

'*Contain* the situation?' Cleo exclaimed incredulously. 'The whole damn city just came to a standstill! Can't you tell when you've lost?'

'And somebody gag this bi—'

'Nobody move,' somebody shouted from behind them.

Smith stood near the ruined doorway, sub-machine gun in hand. Distracted by the events in the city, nobody had noticed him regain consciousness. The four Clockworkers tightened their grips on their weapons, but he fired a burst over their heads, making them freeze. Cleo walked round to him, scarcely able to believe their luck. They were going to make it.

'The police will be coming,' she said to him. 'We only have to hold them until then.'

'I can't hear you,' he said loudly, gesturing with his free hand to his bleeding ears.

'I said—'

But Mercier was already here. His trenchcoat flapping around him, he strode through the doorway, nodded to Cleo and put a gun to Smith's head.

'No—!' she had time to gasp.

He pulled the trigger. Cleo screamed, falling backwards with blood on her face as Smith toppled forward onto the floor.

'Two schoolkids and a washed-out engineer,' Mercier spat at the Clockworkers, 'and you cock it up! Where's the boy?'

'He got away – pure blind luck,' one of them replied. 'But Janus and Rhymes are on 'im.'

'Imagine my relief,' Mercier snorted. 'This has become an absolute fiasco. Get her out of here; I'll tie things up for the cops. Mr Schaeffer, you shouldn't be here.'

'I was just leaving. Make sure that boy is caught and killed, Inspector. You've let too many things slip lately.'

The four Clockworkers led the way, two of them dragging Cleo with them. She stumbled after them, the shock of what had happened taking her breath away. Mercier was a Clockworker. He was giving *orders* to the Clockworkers. She struggled feebly, her fear overwhelming her. She had been counting on him to get them out of here and they had played right into his hands. Now the Clockworkers had come for her, and she was all on her own.

The motley group made it as far as the office area. Facing them were a dozen heavily armed ISS troopers, their guns aimed and ready. Mercier's sergeant, Baiev, was lying handcuffed, face down on the floor. The Clockworkers considered putting up a fight, and then thought better of it. Their weapons clattered on the tiles.

'Mr Schaeffer, Inspector Mercier,' Ponderosa greeted them with barely contained smugness. 'You're under arrest for . . . well, where should I start?'

Sol watched his five hunters struggle up the hill. A glance at the readout on his smart-lens told him the temperature outside his suit was -67°C. He no longer

345

felt the pain in his hands, or his backside. Savouring the weight of the ice-axes, he waited patiently for the Clockworkers to reach him. They were not finding the climb easy. Without the power units on their suits, their masks were not heating up the air they were breathing; the freezing air would be burning their windpipes and chilling their blood – and they would be breathing too hard because of their hurried climb. Long exposure would cause haemorrhage in their lungs. The smart-lenses of their masks would not work either; without the tinting, the glare of the sun off the snow would be blinding them.

Their guns too were of no use to them. The fingerless mittens prevented them from pulling any triggers, and nobody who wanted to keep their fingers took their gloves off in these temperatures.

The first Clockworker stumbled up the shallower part of the slope towards him, holding a hand up to shade his eyes against the dazzling light. His chest was heaving in short, shallow gasps. Not having to look in their faces would make this easier; he couldn't even tell if they were men or women. Sol stepped towards the man and swung the axe in his left hand at the Clockworker's head. The man blocked it, leaving himself open to the right, and Sol caught him square across the side of the face. The ice-axe smashed the edge of the mask free of the suit. The shock stunned the man, and Sol kicked him hard in the chest, pitching him over. He had time for one more blow before the next Clockworker was upon him.

He managed to deflect the first strike with his right arm, but the axe was knocked from his hand. The masked figure brought his own ice-axe down hard, twice, three times, each time Sol just barely blocking the blows, almost kneeling under the force of the impacts. A third Clockworker was staggering towards them. Sol kicked out at his opponent's knee, taking the leg out from under him. As the man fell, Sol punched him with his free hand, then swiped him across the shoulder with his axe. The third charged him before he could finish off the second. Solomon fell back, got his feet against the second man's chest and shoved him into the path of the new assailant.

They fell together, in a tangle of limbs. Sol was up like a shot, screaming venom through his mask, lunging at them, the first man taking the full force of the axe against the top of the head. The other two had caught up now, and he stumbled back as he found himself facing three of them. They edged round him, encircling him. He was breathing hard, but they were too, and every breath was damaging their lungs. One of them was already unsteady on his feet, panting like an exhausted dog.

With another roar, Sol hurled himself at the weak one, and the others lumbered forward to tackle him, moving clumsily in their constricting suits. As the full force of his weight collided with the Clockworker, they hit the ground hard, and something gave way beneath them. The snowdrift, nearly two metres deep, collapsed inwards, and they tumbled into a hollow in the snow, landing awkwardly on the concraglass of the dome beneath them. Sol's body came down solidly on top of the Clockworker, and the man gave a stifled shriek. Sol was already struggling to his feet; there was a creaking, crunching sound seeping from the drift around him. Scrambling up the bank of freshly broken snow, he frantically hauled himself over the top and started running up the slope. He knew that sound: Gregor had once played him a recording of it.

The two remaining Clockworkers hesitated for a moment and then gave chase. They were too slow, and too late. A massive crack appeared from the point where Sol and his opponent had fallen through the drift. Ponderously at first, and then with irresistible force, the drift of snow started to slide down the dome. A stretch fifty metres wide cracked, tore from its anchors and tumbled in a thunderous avalanche towards the edge of the mountaintop. The snow fell away behind Sol's feet and he dived forward, jamming his axe into the ground in front of him. But it disintegrated under him, carrying him backwards, rolling him over and enveloping him in a crushing, frozen white grip.

It took him a minute to realize where he was. He

must have been knocked unconscious. He could move one arm, but that was all. It was dark grey beyond the mask, and he was finding it difficult to breathe. Shovelling snow away from his face, he found daylight, and after some more digging he was able to get his shoulders up out of the snow. There was no sign of the Clockworkers below him, just the remains of the avalanche piled up near the edge. Five complete strangers who had tried to kill him. He was glad they were dead.

Above him, there was a cleared stretch of glass. From off to one side, he could see a team of daylighters hurrying towards him, carrying shovels, pickaxes and heat-hoses. At least, he hoped they were daylighters.

Digging his legs free, he crawled up to the cleared glass and cupped his hands around his face to block out the glare of the sunlight as he lowered his mask to the surface. There were lights in the darkness below. He could see movement on the streets; the trams were running, people were working the Machine once more. He had been wrong, the city wasn't dead. He broke into shaky, exhausted, hysterical laughter. It wasn't over. Life went on.

Cleo sat out on the fire escape of the condemned warehouse building that was being used to temporarily house all of the people made homeless by the fire in her apartment block. Wrapped up in a blanket, she was savouring a well-earned smoke as she gazed up at the pink evening light cascading down in wispy shafts from the dome above. Putting her fingers to her cheek, she found tears there. Here was her grief, making its presence felt at last.

Ana Kiroa was dead. The woman posing as a doctor had killed her with an injection of morphine as she lay helpless in her hospital bed, while Sol and Cleo stood there – right there in the doorway. In truth, Cleo had known it even as they had fled from the hospital. But she hadn't wanted to face it – *couldn't* face it – until now. The police were holding an investigation, but Cleo doubted Ana's killer would ever be found. It was what the Clockworkers did, after all: murder and then disappear without a trace.

It was the first recycling ceremony that Cleo had ever stuck with through to the end. Sitting between Solomon and Ana's boyfriend, Julio, she had watched the body being given back to the city, and she had felt nothing but an aching numbness. Sol had not said a word, avoiding eye contact by keeping his hood up. Julio had cried like a little kid.

Cleo shivered miserably, wiping the tears from her face, and pulled the blanket up to her chin, drawing on the pungent joint. A rustle of fabric made her look off to one side in time to see Sol dropping down from the walkway above her. He landed lightly, wincing as he flexed his bandaged hands. She smiled slightly and then went back to staring up at the dome.

'Hey,' she said.

'Hey,' he replied.

He sat down beside her and they huddled up to share warmth; Cleo threw her blanket over his legs.

'Don't get the wrong idea,' she muttered.

'I know, I'm not your type.'

They said nothing for a while. Cleo knew that Sol had taken his father's death hard. He had no family at all; he'd lost everyone he loved. He'd had a crush on Ana – their whole class had known that – and he'd lost her too. Now he had taken to spending days out, wandering the city alone. He seemed to be getting money from somewhere, and she suspected he was spending time with the daylighters, and maybe even the Dark-Day Fatalists. That was something, at least. All this being alone couldn't be good for him, though. He needed to be among friends. She sniffed. He needed to *make* some friends.

'When you going to come back to school?' she asked.

He shrugged.

'Still don't feel right,' he said.

'You never will,' Cleo told him. 'Not after all this. But you've still got to live. I mean, what are you going to do when you finish school? I was always putting off thinking about it, but now . . . now I feel like I should be *doing* something, y'know?'

Solomon nodded.

'Have you noticed the city's colder lately?' he asked her.

'With Schaeffer gone, they have to fix up a lot of stuff,' she said, speaking around the joint in her mouth. 'Julio said they've shut down some of the ventilation heaters so they can rebuild them. There's a lot of that happening now. They have to pull things apart to put them back together properly. He said it'll take time.'

There was a quiet pause again.

'I've been thinking of joining the police,' Sol said abruptly. 'Maybe even try to get into the ISS.'

'Jesus! Really?' Cleo coughed out some smoke. 'You serious?'

'Yeah. I want to help sort things out. And I want to learn more about the engineering too, get my head around how the whole system works, y'know? The guys in the DDF think we've got to come up with more ways to survive outside the dome – stop relying so much on the Machine. They've loads of ideas for adapting to the whole deal; they say the Neanderthals survived the Ice Age, so we should be able to go one better. But I figure the Machine's all we've got for the moment. Things're going to go a bit mad for a while, and I think we need to get on with doing something practical.'

She nodded reluctantly.

It did not matter that Maslow had lied about having proof of Schaeffer's control of the Clockworkers. Once the word was out, dozens of people had come forward with stories. It turned out that Inspector Ponderosa had been trying to nail Schaeffer and his kind for years, but could never get enough evidence. Now he was on a witch-hunt, purging the cabal of industrialists involved in the sabotage and assassinations. They would be trying the cases for years. There were rumours that Ponderosa would be running for mayor, now that Haddad was destined for prison.

Cleo was planning to use her new-found fame to get gigs for her band in some of the city's best venues. They'd got the end-of-year gig after all – with Julio's help – but she found it wasn't nearly as important to her now. Sol had preferred to keep out of the public eye. Maslow had completely disappeared after becoming the most famous man in Ash Harbour. Looking sidelong at Sol, Cleo guessed what he was thinking.

'You'll probably never see him again, huh?'

'Don't want to,' he murmured. 'Not after what he did. I'm done with him. That's the end of it.'

Cleo took a breath of smoke and gazed up at the light.

'Wonder if we can change enough,' she mused. 'Hard to think that there might be no one left, a few hundred years from now.'

'Dunno,' he sniffed. 'Make for some good song lyrics, though.'

'Damn right.' She blew a twisting smoke ring. 'Music to become extinct to. The Gig at the End of

353

the World — now *that* would be a party. I wanna be there for that one.'

Sol grinned.

'You've got to have something to live for,' he said.

About the Author

Born in Dublin in 1973, Oisín McGann spent his childhood there and in Drogheda, County Louth. Art college ruined any chance he had of getting a real job, so when he left in 1992, he set himself up as a freelance illustrator. In 1998 he moved to London, and through no fault of his own he ended up working in advertising as an art director and copy writer. After three and a half years he began to fear for his immortal soul. He returned to Ireland in the summer of 2002 much as he had left it – with no job, no home and some meagre savings.

Ever the optimist, he now works once more as an illustrator and mercenary artist by day and escapist writer by night.

www.oisinmcgann.com

ANCIENT APPETITES

by

OISÍN McGANN

In an alternative Victorian world where highly advanced machines roam wild and are tamed like animals, the rich and powerful Wildenstern family have a tradition of ascendancy by assassination. The richer you are, the harder you are to kill, and this is reinforced when some ancient ancestors are found during an attempted robbery and turn out to be not quite dead . . .

Another epic blockbuster from the outstanding mind of Oisín McGann.

www.oisinmcgann.com

DOUBLEDAY
978 0 385 61086 5

THE BLACK TATTOO

by
SAM ENTHOVEN

Esme's hard brown hands lifted fractionally from her sides.
Her amber eyes glittered as she faced her enemy.
'No tricks,' said Esme. 'No more lies. You and me are going
to fight this out to the finish. Right now.'

Jack doesn't know what he's got himself into. One minute
he and his best friend, Charlie, were in Chinatown having
crispy duck with Charlie's dad, then suddenly they were in
a mysterious room above a theatre, with some of the
strangest characters they'd ever encountered.
And they were about to take The Test . . .

The Test transformed Charlie – leaving him with the
distinctive markings of the Black Tattoo. The boys' meeting
with Esme – a young girl with the most impressive martial
arts skills this side of Bruce Lee – her huge and hairy father,
Raymond, and the mysterious Nick, seemed to have swept
Charlie and Jack into a world they had no idea existed.
And it was only going to get weirder . . .

978 0 385 60965 4
DOUBLEDAY

The BARTIMAEUS trilogy

by

JONATHAN STROUD

A roller-coaster ride of magic, adventure and political
skulduggery, set in a London where spells and demons are
part of everyday life. Young magician Nathaniel, fast rising
through the government ranks, must summon up the
troublesome, enigmatic and quick-witted djinni,
Bartimaeus, if he is to hang on to his job.
Or his life . . .

'A hilarious read with a stroppy young wizard
whose demon, Bartimaeus, is funny, cynical and
totally out for himself' Observer

Book I: the Amulet of Samarkand
978 0 552 55029 1

Book II: The Golem's Eye
978 0 552 55027 7

Book III: Ptolemy's Gate
978 0 552 55028 4

by
BALI RAI

the whisper

The Crew didn't think things could ever get that bad again.
They were dead wrong. Someone's grassing up the dealers and the
whisper on the street says it's Nanny and the Crew – they need
to act fast before the situation explodes . . .

'Exhilarating sequel to *The Crew* . . . unflinching
and authentic' *Publishing News*

978 0 552 54891 5
CORGI

the crew

When you live in the concrete heart of a major UK city and
someone leaves a bag full of cash in the alley behind your house
you had best leave it alone. It's got to be bad news – after all,
what kind of people leave fifteen grand lying around?

'A jewel of a book' *Independent*

978 0 552 54739 0
CORGI